# Looking To Belong

My steps faltered when I sensed that two of the pursuing wolves had sped forward on a larger circuit to intercept me. I launched toward a tree and used my feet to ricochet off the trunk at a ninety-degree angle without slowing down.

The wolf right behind me had been too close to change direction with such short notice, but his companion was able to correct his path. His footsteps pounded against the leaf litter behind me as he put on a burst of speed.

I looked around wildly as I started to panic. There were no larger bramble bushes in this area for me to hide under, nor did there seem to be any other sort of shelter. As if noticing my lack of options, the wolves began closing in.

I saw a black hole under a small bramble bush and desperately raced towards the rabbit burrow. I darted under the edge of the bramble bush and into the hole.

My relief was short-lived—the rabbit that had dug this burrow had obviously not survived long enough to finish it.

# Looking To Belong

**Crystal Scherer**

*This is a work of fiction. All characters and events in this book are fictitious. Any resemblance to real people or incidents is purely coincidental.*

*All rights reserved. No part of this book may be used or reproduced in any manner whatsoever without written permission of the publisher except for the use of brief quotations in a book review.*

LOOKING TO BELONG

Copyright © 2017 by Crystal Scherer

First Print Edition: October 2022

Second Print Edition: August 2024

ISBN: 978-1-9990117-2-7

Cover design by: Getpremades.com

The text of this book is set to: Spectral. Font 11. Spacing 1.2

10 9 8 7 6 5 4 3 2 1

### *Dedication*

*As always, I'm grateful for my dedicated editors and their herculean efforts, particularly Niels Collyns, Jane Barnaby, Cathy Scholz, Dianne Goble, Amber Andrews, and Erika Lin.*
*Without all of you, this wouldn't have been possible.*

# Chapter 1

I yawned and shook my head, which caused bits of dirt to fall into my fur as my ears brushed against the top of the den. I uncurled and tried to stretch in the limited room of the old rabbit burrow. My muscles were stiff from sleeping in the cramped space, but such places were safer for someone as small as me.

The rabbits around here grew almost twice as big as their cousins on the other side of the mountains, but that still wasn't enough space for a proper morning stretch. With another yawn, I crawled through the tunnel toward the surface as my belly fur occasionally brushed against the dirt.

As I approached the entrance, I paused and slowly inhaled, carefully testing the scents in the air. Even though I was a runt, there was nothing wrong with my nose. The normal scents of coniferous trees and grasses were strong. I could tell that at least four rabbits had passed through this area since I had gone inside. There were no hints of larger predators.

Cautiously, I poked my head out of the burrow and glanced around. After making sure the coast was clear, I exited the burrow and shook my light gray fur to get rid of the lingering bits of dirt. I also took the chance to properly stretch and twist as I limbered up for the day.

My view was limited to the underside of a large, sprawling bramble bush. It was one of many in this part of the forest, and one of the biggest reasons I took shelter here. I could easily get underneath the branches, but anything larger than me would get a face full of large, sharp thorns. Those same thorns were why I took care not to raise my head too high. I had ended up with scratches on my ears more often than I would care to admit.

A cream color to the side caught my attention. I trotted over to inspect the small mushroom poking through the leaf litter. This type was edible. It must have sprouted after the rain last night. My tail wagged in anticipation; where one had appeared, more would be nearby, and fresh mushrooms were always easy to trade.

Using my paw, I pushed it over and broke the stem, then gently picked it up in my jaws. If I bruised them, people wouldn't pay as much for them. I quickly carried it to the edge of the bramble bush and set it on the ground.

I peeked out from under the leaves and pricked my ears up to catch any sounds. No alarm calls or predator alerts interrupted the morning birdsong, nor did I smell anything strange.

I eased out from under the bramble bush and scanned the area before shifting. Seconds later, I was standing in my some-what-tattered jeans and t-shirt, with my backpack on my back.

Taking a deep breath of the cool morning air, I relaxed somewhat. I was more at ease in my human form because my wolf shape was so small. Most werewolves were large enough to almost look a human in the face. I, on the other hand, could barely lift my head high enough to reach someone's knees. A runt. I had seen some house cats bigger than me.

At that size, quite a few creatures considered me a possible menu option. Bears, coyotes, or even a big eagle was a poten-tially lethal threat while I was in wolf form. Cougars were my personal nightmare; if they were hungry, they wouldn't care which form I was in. One had almost caught me when I was young. Thankfully, my parents had been nearby and driven it off.

A butterfly fluttered past me. I kind of wished I could shift into my wolf form and chase after it, but that longing would have to go unheeded. It was simply too dangerous for me to drop my guard out here, even for a bit of innocent play.

Shaking my head, I refocused on the task at hand. I bent down and carefully extracted the mushroom from under the edge of the bramble bush, then went to a nearby lean-to to get a small willow basket.

I wandered around as I picked various types of mushrooms that were growing after the recent rain. Occasionally, I shifted into wolf form to retrieve them from underneath the bramble bushes. When my basket was almost full, I began heading east. There was a pack not far away, and they often traded with rogues like me.

True, some rogues were bloodthirsty killers or lawless troublemakers who caused endless problems, but most weren't. Some had been kicked out of their packs for things like theft or disobedience. A few left simply because they were unable to tolerate the authority that Alphas could wield. Others could be a bit anti-social and had a hard time living with a pack, since they usually had several hundred members.

I had even met a rogue who had been exiled because he dated a lady who later discovered she was the Alpha's mate. He had no interest in dating someone who had found their mate, but Alphas could be extraordinarily jealous and paranoid.

I was still a rogue because most packs didn't want to let a runt join their group. They usually accepted a runt if they were born into the pack, but most drew the line at letting one join—even if it was a twelve-year-old child. I had gotten accepted once when I was younger, but it hadn't turned out to be a long-term solution.

My heart grew heavier as I thought about how many years I'd spent trying to find another pack to accept me, only to be turned away. Their rejections had become more blunt as I aged into the twenty-one-year-old I was now. People simply didn't want a runt in their pack, not even other rogues.

Rogues traveled in small groups and lived in the large expanses of no man's land between various packs, rarely staying in one spot for long. Their large, powerful wolf forms were easily capable of bringing down a deer, whereas I was limited to snares, archery, and small game like rabbits.

Most rogue groups didn't mind my presence, but they wouldn't wait for me during their travels. There was no way for my human form to keep up, let alone my cat-sized wolf form. It was as if I didn't belong anywhere.

I sighed and looked skyward. No answers hovered up there, although gaps in the leafy canopy revealed a few clouds that looked dark enough for rain, so I'd have to keep an eye on them. I hadn't brought my tattered raincoat with me, and like most runts, my fur had never grown guard hairs. I only sported my soft undercoat. Rain would cut right through my fur and leave me chilled.

I continued walking down a deer path leading to the pack's territory. This particular pack allowed me to cross their border and visit the marketplace without being escorted. Even though people were wary of rogues wandering around their land, they rarely considered runts to be dangerous.

Ahead of me, the worn-down trail in the leaf litter marked the pack border where the outermost patrols ran. Normally, a visitor howled to let the pack know of their presence, although the Alpha had told me not to bother during my visits since such a howl could interrupt patrols. They preferred it if I walked in without such a disruption, especially since my trips to the market had been made in exchange for the promise I wouldn't cause any trouble and would give a howl if I saw something dangerous heading toward their borders.

I hid my bow and arrows under a nearby bush, just so I wouldn't be walking through their territory with a ranged weapon. My belt knife was visible, although it had never gotten more than one or two looks.

As I crossed the dirt trail, my heart pounded in my chest—it always did when I entered a pack's territory. As a rogue, I had no protection from the guards or fighters if someone decided to attack me. It had never happened in this pack, but it had in a few other places I'd visited. Sometimes it was a case of mistaken identity, but sometimes it had been deliberate.

My battered shoes crunched in the dry leaves under my feet—I made no attempt at silence since that could send the wrong signal if any guards were watching from afar. I had lived near this pack's border for several years, so luckily, most knew me on sight.

Eventually, I made it to the edge of the village where the marketplace was located. Most of the pack members ignored me as if I were a clump of dirt.

Flashes of my old pack flickered through my mind. Warm, smiling faces that stood as a stark contrast to the people in front of me, who barely even glanced my way. A speck of grief floated through my heart as I longed for the days of my youth, before a pack of ferals had wiped out everything I'd known, somehow overlooking the pup hidden in a rabbit burrow.

Without pausing to gaze at the delicacies and various goods in most of the booths, I headed directly toward a table with an elderly lady. She looked up and smiled when she saw me approaching.

"Ah, Jade," she greeted me. "Nice to see you this lovely morning. I hope the western border is quiet."

I smiled at the elderly lady who had always traded fairly with me. "Good morning, Mrs. Elderan. It's good to see you looking so well. Things have been pretty quiet, although I've seen a black bear on and off throughout the week." I kept my voice quiet and demure to seem like less of a threat. It usually prevented troublemakers from taking my words amiss or trying to pick a fight with me.

As she put down her knitting needles, she said, "I'll let the others know to keep an eye on the younger children, just in case the bear decides to wander in this direction. What do you have for me today?"

I removed the cloth covering the basket and held it out to her.

"Will the usual trade work?" she asked as she examined the mushrooms.

"That would be great."

She put several loaves of bread on the table in front of her. They were the dense grainy kind that filled you up fast and kept you full for a long time. She had only checked the mushrooms briefly and hadn't questioned if they were edible. When I had first started trading with this pack, they had inspected everything, but after a year, they no longer bothered since every scrutinized object turned out to be edible.

I had spent almost half of my life as a rogue and had been partially raised by one, as well as meeting quite a few others during that time. Some had felt guilty when I wasn't able to keep up, so they had done their best to make sure I wouldn't starve.

Some had taught me archery and snares, although most focused on plants, mushrooms, and similar edibles. They had been *very* thorough in their training, and I probably knew almost every edible thing in the forest.

The elderly woman placed the bread in a paper bag and passed it to me. We chatted until someone else approached her booth, and I bid her farewell as I turned to walk back through the busy market.

Nearby, two people sat on a bench kissing, clearly mates. Seeing them paired up didn't surprise me; they had somewhat gravitated toward one another, even before they were old enough for their mate bond to manifest.

I subtly scanned the crowd but didn't see the Alpha or Beta. The two men were probably out meeting other Alphas, working out trades, and dealing with the endless world of politics.

On the far side of the market, their mates were helping several elderly women with their tables. The Alpha and Beta usually dealt with policy and relationships with other packs while their mates—the Luna and Beta female—usually concentrated on smaller details and events within the pack.

A heavily-built man crossed my path and keep going. He was one of the pack's Enforcers and was probably on his way to break up a growing argument at one of the booths.

The Alpha and Beta relied on the Enforcers to keep the peace in their absence. They were skilled fighters and could usually equal an Alpha's speed and strength if a fight broke out. A pack usually had one or two Enforcers at any given time, and they almost never went outside the pack's borders. Like Alphas and Betas, they were born with their powers in their blood. One could not simply choose to become an Enforcer.

I nodded politely to one of the pack's Omegas. He nodded back and kept going, obviously on a task of some sort. Unlike during the dark ages in the distant past, packs rarely abused Omegas since it caused the pack to become unbalanced. Omegas might be the lowest ranking members in a pack, but their presence helped the other pack members relax.

People could get uneasy with so many higher ranking and powerful pack members constantly around. If an Omega was relaxed, it meant everything was calm, which reassured the others. Omegas practically had a second sense for trouble and could pull a disappearing act in seconds, particularly if the Alpha was irritated. If an Omega looked nervous and left the area swiftly, it was a wise idea to make yourself scarce as well.

Even though the Alpha and Beta traits were almost always hereditary, the Enforcer, Omega, and runt genes were only inherited by their children about half of the time. The other half of the time, they randomly appeared in normal families. No one in my family had been a runt.

Even though I hadn't been born an Omega, I had joined a pack about seven years ago and had been assigned that role. It was uncommon for someone to be officially assigned the Omega role, but not unheard of when the person in question was a rogue the pack didn't particularly want.

My time with that pack had come to an end a year later when the old Alpha had died without an heir. Even though I had left when neighboring packs started closing in, that stint as an Omega had given me an impressive set of skills that helped me detect and avoid bad situations. Luckily, the skills had remained even after the designated rank had disappeared.

I was almost out of the market when whispering reached my ears.

"I still don't know why that runt is allowed in here. She should have to stay out like the rest of the rogues."

One of the other teenage girls snorted faintly. "So? She's a runt. She might chew on your slippers, but she's incapable of doing any other damage."

I took a slow breath and kept a straight face, refusing to rise to their bait. Anything I said would only make things worse and possibly attract attention. In an argument between a pack member and a rogue, the pack member would always come out on top, regardless of who was at fault.

Any argument or fight would be noticed by an Enforcer, the Beta female, or the Luna. And if any of them got involved, it would be brought to the attention of the Alpha, and anything that caused him additional work was trouble for me.

The five teens obviously lacked something constructive to do with their time since they did this whenever they saw me.

They made sure their voices were loud enough for me to hear, yet out of range of any adults who might reprimand them.

I failed to see why they always tried to antagonize me. Admittedly, as a runt, my wolf form was next to useless in a fight and my human form was weaker than the average werewolf in human shape, but I had been a rogue for quite a few years, and that meant I had a *lot* of tricks at my disposal.

If we had been in no man's land, they would have been at a severe disadvantage, but we were in a market on their pack lands—and that changed everything.

"It isn't like she will ever find a mate, so I don't know why she keeps coming here to trade. Why doesn't she go to some other pack and bother them."

"Maybe she is seeing if someone who lost their mate will take her in."

"Like *that* will ever happen . . ."

I gritted my teeth at their obvious attempts to goad me into retaliation. I knew runts rarely ever found their mate, but they didn't have to rub it in. I bet they never said such things around the Enforcers even though that rank had a low chance of ever locating their partner. And no one ever looked down on them for it!

It was terrible to watch couples happily in love when you knew you'd likely never have that chance. Besides, those who lost their mates rarely ever got over their loss to the point where they could consider marrying another, unless the mate bond granted them a second chance mate.

I took a deep breath but picked up nothing besides the usual smells of the marketplace. No trace of an unusually alluring scent lingered in the air, which would have been the first sign if I had a potential mate in the area.

I finally reached the edge of the forest. At this point, all I wanted to do was enjoy the quiet of the forest away from people who enjoyed seeing another person in pain.

I checked my snares, two of which had rabbits. I hadn't seen any wildlife on the way back and my stocks were low, so I was glad for the meat.

Carrying the rabbits, I detoured to the south where I had built a small and well-hidden smokehouse to smoke excess meat. If I ate my fill in one form, I was full in both. With my wolf form being so small, I almost always ate as a wolf since it made my food supplies stretch further.

I cut up the rabbit and put the thin slices of meat in the smoker. I could eat raw rabbit in my wolf form, but I preferred it cooked. After that, I started fletching some new arrows. I was decent with a bow, which was a good thing considering any type of melee combat was completely out of the question for me.

As I leaned to the side to pull a bucket closer, my brown braid swung forward, almost touching the water inside. I flipped it over my shoulder and regarded my greenish eyes in the water's reflection, the same jade color I had been named after.

A sudden uneasy feeling made me look around warily, although I didn't know what had me on edge. Leaving the feathers on the ground, I grabbed my bow and swiftly climbed the tree I had been leaning against.

Once I was halfway up, I peered out of the branches. My instincts were sharp, and I preferred not to doubt them, even if I didn't know what was wrong.

I heard a faint noise and turned my head in that direction. I squinted through the thick leaves and finally spotted eight wolves stalking through the forest. No, there were twelve. Several had been hanging further back. I didn't recognize the patterns on their fur, and the way they were moving had me on edge.

I stilled when I noticed their red eyes. Ferals. Bloodthirsty creatures that killed even when they weren't hungry. They were as close to madness as a werewolf could get, and they weren't able to shift. Some of their human craftiness and ability to reason remained, although the human mind was nowhere to be found. They were just animals, albeit rather dangerous ones that often attacked without provocation, almost as if they were rabid.

They entered the clearing below and circled around. The remains of the rabbit carcass was the first thing to disappear. One tentatively pawed at the smoker and backed up when wisps of smoke emerged.

I remained motionless among the branches, hoping they wouldn't look up. Finding nothing else edible and not wanting to tangle with fire, they eventually headed southeast.

I waited for some time before climbing higher into the tree. I walked out along a branch and held onto smaller ones as I skipped over to a branch on another tree. In another spot, I had to swing like a monkey to get across the gap.

Rogues called it the forest highway, although they rarely used it since traveling along the tree branches was much slower than running. Since my wolf form wasn't an asset, I used it quite frequently. I had also discovered that very few people actually looked up into the trees. Another perk was that it was nearly impossible for someone on the ground to track scents left among the upper branches.

I paused and took a quick sniff of my clothing to see if I still smelled like this part of the forest. Like many rogues, I had a habit of occasionally rubbing a mixture of local plants on my clothing and shoes to conceal my scent. We smelled like the forest we lived in, and thus, were very difficult to track—and I didn't want those ferals to be able to find me.

When I was quite some distance from the smoker and my camp, I shifted into my wolf form while carefully perching on a thick branch. I threw my head back and howled a warning call into the evening sky. The pack patrols would hear it and would be on high alert in case potential trouble appeared.

With the warning given, I swiftly shifted back to my human form and used the forest highway to put distance between me and where I had howled. There was a good chance the ferals would try to track down the wolf that had just given away their location.

I was very thankful they were unable to shift or climb, although it would be even better if they never found me. I really didn't want tenacious and aggressive wolves stalking my movements.

I darted along the tree branches as I made my escape. The only creatures that noticed my passage were the birds and squirrels.

As I sat high in a spruce tree, I kept an eye on the ground. Luck must have been with me since I hadn't seen or scented the ferals all afternoon or evening, nor had I heard any noise from the border, so the ferals hadn't attacked the pack yet. Perhaps they had gone a different way or were waiting for the cover of darkness.

I remained upwind of the smoker while waiting for the rabbit meat to finish cooking. The smoke was also helping cover up my scent. My gaze roamed across the ground, constantly on watch for the ferals in case they returned.

The ground didn't feel safe right now, and I wasn't about to rely on my usual rabbit burrow or its two escape tunnels to keep me safe from a pack this size. Ferals were persistent enough to tear the branches off bramble bushes and dig up a burrow. It may take them most of the day, but rationality didn't apply to them.

The sun was starting to set and I didn't want to be out after dark tonight, so I used the forest highway to head toward a certain tree. From the ground, the small structure looked like an old hawk nest, but it had a hole in one side and it was hollow. The inside was slightly bigger than the rabbit den, and it was quite roomy for my wolf form.

It had been a few weeks since I last checked on my treetop hideout, so I made sure the roof was undamaged. Once I was satisfied I wouldn't get wet if it rained, I dug through my backpack and put some smoked meat inside for my breakfast.

I pulled the winter scarf out and shook any debris off it. After tucking it inside and rearranging it, I pulled some dried leaves out of my backpack and crumpled the pieces onto the scarf to help keep my scent balanced while I slept.

After I scanned the ground for potential trouble, I sat on the big branch in front of the opening and carefully shifted. With one last glance down, I went through the opening, grateful that my small wolf form allowed me to shift without falling out of a tree, a feat no regular-sized wolf could manage.

I curled up in the middle of my comfy nest and rested my head in the opening to watch the sunset. The spectacular pinks and oranges had almost completely faded when I noticed movement in the forest below. I peered through the branches and watched a handful of wolves trotting eastward. I had already warned the pack, and ferals were infamous for attacking at night, so I pulled my head inside my shelter and drifted off to sleep.

Hours later, howls in the distance disturbed my sleep. The ferals must have finally decided to attack the pack. Unfortunately for the ferals, I recognized the howl of the Enforcer along with dozens of other fighters, who had obviously been waiting for them.

As I drifted back to sleep, I wondered if any of the ferals had escaped.

# Chapter 2

I yawned as the birds started serenading the new day. In theory, it sounded like a lovely way to wake up, but they started singing at an appallingly early hour. The sun hadn't even risen yet.

This was why I preferred the rabbit burrow. Down there, I could at least sleep past daybreak if I wanted. I yawned as I sleepily blinked in the grayish pre-dawn light. While waiting for the sun to rise, I nibbled on a piece of smoked rabbit meat.

Eventually, I climbed out of my comfy nest and onto the branch. I didn't see any movement below, but I couldn't really trust scents this high in the trees due to the light breeze whisking them away before they had a chance to drift up here. I shifted into my human form and stretched a bit more.

I never walked on the ground beneath my tree penthouse in case the scent attracted attention, so I used the forest highway to return to the smoker. After carefully scanning the ground, I climbed down. Some smoke was still trickling out of the chimney pipe, but the rabbit would be done by now.

I absentmindedly grabbed a handful of leaves off a bramble bush and lightly rubbed them on my arms and clothing. A sniff told me that I'd have to find several grasses to balance out my scent. If I smelled too strongly of one plant, it would stand out, so I had to use a variety of leaves and grasses. Most werewolves wouldn't notice the slight difference, but rogues would. And so would those ferals.

I opened the smoker and checked the rabbit meat, which was done. Using a set of tongs, I moved the meat to a cooling tray on a stump. The quiet snapping of a twig made me glance over my shoulder. There was nothing except for trees and shrubs. The faint sound could have easily been a rabbit or some other harmless creature, but I wasn't about to take any chances.

Just to be on the safe side, I ducked down and shifted before scooting underneath a small bramble bush. I perked my ears and swiveled them back and forth, trying to pick up any additional sounds. I didn't hear anything, but that in itself worried me. The small songbirds had gone silent. They ignored my human presence and runty wolf form, so another predator was nearby.

I sat and peered out from under the shrub as the minutes ticked by. The wind wasn't blowing from the direction the sound had come from, so I couldn't pick up any scents. No rustling of grass or crackling of dry leaves disturbed the silence.

Eventually, the birds resumed their songs, so the predator had likely left the area. The smoked meat would be cold by now, so I could quickly grab it and return to the forest highway. I really should visit the nearby pack and check if any of the ferals had escaped.

After one last look around, I crept out from under the shrub and trotted toward the meat. A glimpse of tan in the corner of my eye made me freeze in my tracks. My head whipped around, but it had disappeared. The only movement was that of the leaves on the bushes fluttering in the gentle breeze.

My heart started beating faster—that color had been the right shade for a cougar. I took a hard look at the shrubs as I realized how high up that flash of tan had been. Either this was a monster of a cougar or something else...

I tilted my head in concentration; it had been a long time since my short stint as an Omega, but the rather limited abilities still remained. It had been months since I last used them to check if werewolves were in the vicinity.

My senses spread out, confirming there were four werewolves arranged in a half circle facing me. I wasn't able to sense ferals with my Omega abilities, so this was another group of werewolves.

Considering I couldn't see them, I didn't think they could see me, although the tan one had almost certainly spotted me and alerted the others through their mindlink.

The wind swirled around briefly, and I finally caught their scent. My eyes widened in nervousness. It was a pack scent—and not a pack I had scented before. In no man's land, pack rules didn't really apply, and some packs were well known to attack rogues for fighting practice, even if the rogues had done nothing wrong.

My Omega senses informed me that they were focused on me, which only made my heart beat faster. I took a few slow steps back as I realized I wasn't close to any trees big enough to climb. The nearby bramble bushes would have stopped a cougar, but not a werewolf.

If I made a break for it, they'd hear me and possibly give chase. So now the question remained, did they mean me harm? They had remained hidden for at least half an hour while they waited for me to come out, so that wasn't a good sign. Most friendly rogues or pack members would shift into their human form and call out.

Only trouble stalked and waited in ambush.

All four were male, and my Omega senses suggested they were strong fighters, which was another worrying sign. My eyes darted to the side as a dark brown shape skulked through the long grass. The wolf was crouching so low his belly would be skimming the ground in his effort to keep out of sight.

His eyes met mine and widened when he realized he'd been spotted.

I whirled around and raced in the other direction as fast as my small feet could carry me. My heart sank as I heard four sets of footsteps follow in hot pursuit.

Like many small animals, my immediate tactic was to go where larger creatures were unable to follow. I darted under a bramble bush and kept going out the far side. A yelp came from behind as one tried to follow and belatedly realized the thorns were capable of piercing even a full-grown werewolf's fur.

Using his lesson to my advantage, I kept ducking beneath bramble bushes and fallen logs, forcing them to detour around the obstacles. I was spurred on by my fear, and even though it was enough to keep out of their reach, I wasn't able to hide from their sight long enough to climb into the trees and escape.

Thankfully, the rabbits had beaten many paths into the ground around here, and I raced down the trails with my heart flying even faster than my feet. The larger wolves kept up with relative ease as my breathing became heavier.

My steps faltered when I sensed that two of them had sped forward on a larger circuit to intercept me. I launched toward a tree and used my feet to ricochet off the trunk at a ninety-degree angle without slowing down.

The wolf right behind me had been too close to change direction with such short notice, but his companion had been farther behind and was easily able to correct his path. His footsteps pounded against the leaf litter behind me as he put on a burst of speed.

I looked around wildly as I started to panic. There were no larger bramble bushes in this area for me to hide under, nor did there seem to be any other sort of shelter. As if noticing my lack of options, the wolves began closing in.

I saw a black hole under a small bramble bush and desperately raced towards the rabbit burrow. I darted under the edge of the bramble bush, and the tan wolf went around, expecting me to come out the other side like I had before. It gave me the precious seconds I needed to squeeze down the tunnel. If he had remained on my heels, he would have caught me.

My relief was short-lived—the rabbit that had dug this burrow had obviously not survived long enough to finish it. There were no escape tunnels, and the den itself was far too close to the surface. I turned around with immense difficulty in the cramped den.

The tunnel was twice as long as a human arm and almost completely straight. I could clearly see the bramble bush above the tunnel opening. I tried to quiet my panting and sent a silent prayer in hopes the bramble bush was enough of a deterrent to keep them from realizing just how shallow this burrow was.

I strained my ears as I waited anxiously. My Omega senses were rusty from disuse since I rarely encountered werewolves in no man's land. But like stiff muscles, they just needed to be limbered up, and boy, were they getting an impromptu workout now.

My senses tracked all four as they gathered around the small bush and inspected the obstacle. The bramble bush wasn't much larger than the average wolf, so I wasn't sure how much of a deterrent it might be for them. They knew I was here, and they were still focused on me.

One of the wolves shifted into his human form, and not long after, I saw a rope pass over the burrow entrance. I didn't realize the implications until the bramble bush began shaking. I inhaled sharply when I realized they had looped it around the base of the plant.

A man grunted as he and one of the wolves hauled on the rope. Another wolf joined in, and with a rustle of leaves and loose dirt, the bramble bush was uprooted from the thin, rocky soil.

Moments later, blue sky shone above the entrance. The view was blocked as a black wolf peered into the tunnel. His sharp brown eyes locked onto my frightened ones as he gauged the distance between us.

He backed up a step and started digging at the tunnel entrance. The dark brown wolf joined him, and their powerful legs made short work of the loose dirt and pebbles as they widened the tunnel.

I squirmed against the wall behind me and looked around desperately, but I was definitely at the end of the burrow, and there were no half-hidden escape tunnels. As they got closer, I started shaking. Soon, there wasn't enough room for two of them, and the black wolf backed up to let the brown one take over the digging operation.

I whined in fear as his claws scrabbled through the dirt just beyond my reach. He sat back on his haunches and examined the remains of the tunnel. I flinched when he shifted, although I didn't have time to think about sneaking past him before he leaned forward. I pushed myself back against the dirt wall behind me and growled at him.

He stuck his large hand into the tunnel as he muttered, "Come on out . . ."

I snapped my teeth at his fingers in a warning, but both of us knew my jaws weren't capable of inflicting serious damage. With my back still against the wall, I lashed out with my paws, digging my nails into his fingers while trying to keep him from grabbing my legs.

He reached further into the burrow as if I had merely flicked him with a feather. I snarled a terrified warning and snapped my teeth again, although I was reluctant to clamp down on his fingers since he might be able to grab my jaw and pull me out.

His arm blocked all the light, and when his fingers brushed against my shoulder, I swung my head around to bite his hand. My teeth clamped down on his warm skin. He grunted in surprise, and his hand jerked upward in an automatic reflex.

The sudden movement banged my head against the top of the tunnel. Stunned by the impact, I let go and shook my head, trying to clear it.

He quickly took advantage of my dazed condition and skillfully grabbed the scruff of my neck. I yelped in fear but wasn't able to land a second bite due to the way he was holding me. My claws scrabbled against his wrist and forearm in panic as he dragged me out of the tunnel. I writhed in his grip, trying to get loose.

There wasn't enough room to shift, and even if I could, it probably wouldn't help against a trained fighter. He quickly pinned me to his chest with both arms, which was a known tactic to prevent runts or young pups from shifting back to their larger human shape. I struggled in his grip to no avail.

He backed out of the hole he had dug before turning around to face his three friends, who were standing behind him in human form. The men, who looked like they were in their mid-twenties, grinned at their accomplishment of digging me up.

The guy holding me chuckled. "Sure has sharp claws. I was beginning to wonder if I had grabbed a cat."

The man who'd been the tan-colored wolf stepped forward, and I redoubled my efforts to get loose. The guy holding me kept me firmly pinned in his arms, not fazed by my struggles.

The approaching man blinked at my fearful attempts before speaking as if to a scared wild animal, "Easy. Calm down."

I practically froze in disbelief as he started to softly pet my fur, although not much of it was visible the way the man had me pinned. I stared at him in shock. They had waited in ambush for half an hour, chased me halfway through no man's land, dug me out of the ground, pinned me, and then one of them told me to calm down? What the hell was wrong with these guys?

He blinked in surprise. "Wow. This kid sure has soft fur."

The guy holding me snorted. "Those teeth and claws aren't so soft."

The third man came closer and tilted his head as he examined me in growing confusion. "Uh, guys. I don't think that's a pup."

The other two looked at him like he was crazy before turning their gazes back to me. They thought I was a pup? They obviously needed their heads checked. Pups resembled puppies with oversized paws and ears. My body proportions were normal for a grown wolf—I was just much smaller. To give them credit, I was close to the size of an eight-month-old child if they were in wolf form.

At this point, their faces all reflected varying expressions of disbelief and confusion.

The one guy sniffed the air. "Well, he doesn't have any scent."

Pups didn't really gain a scent until they hit adolescence, but they were missing the obvious fact that I smelled like the forest instead of having no scent at all. That was a huge difference for those who paid attention to what was going on around them.

I tried twisting loose, but this guy was obviously much stronger than me. The fourth man who'd been hanging back finally came closer.

He quietly said, "Some rogues are able to camouflage their scent. Look at his ears—they aren't oversized like a pup's would be. Come to think of it, a pup wouldn't have been able to evade us like that. He had far too much coordination and pulled way too many evasion tricks for a pup."

The guy holding me looked down in surprise and growing doubt. "But a runt wouldn't be able to survive as a rogue . . ."

As the man came closer, the two others parted to let him through. I stilled in fear as my Omega senses picked up his Beta blood. He wasn't an actual Beta, but he was likely the brother to one. If nothing else, he definitely had Beta parents as well as the added strength and speed the bloodline gave him.

He leaned his face close to mine, and I bared my teeth in a silent, terrified warning.

He glanced up at the guy holding me. "And you thought those were baby teeth?" He shook his head as one of the others started chuckling. He lowered his gaze back to me. "If we put you down, can you shift so we can properly apologize for our actions? Preferably without you inflicting damage on us?"

I blinked slowly, although it wasn't as if I had much choice in the matter when I was surrounded by four fighters. I was kind of surprised they wanted me to shift so the apology could be given face to face. It was a more respectful gesture than if they had apologized while I was in my undersized wolf form.

The one who pinned me had already loosened his grip with an embarrassed expression. When I nodded warily, he knelt down to set me on my feet before standing up and taking a few steps back to give me some room.

Had they seriously thought I was a pup or was this a trick? They obviously had the advantage over my wolf form. They also recognized me as a rogue at this point, and rogues often had weapons and tricks hidden up their sleeves in case they got cornered in human form, so asking me to shift was a bit of a risk for them. I glanced at the four surrounding me before shifting.

A mere second later, I stood on two feet. I warily eyed up the four around me as I shifted my weight and weighed my possible escape options. The guy who had pinned me was turning bright red, and all of them glanced at each other in shock. I glanced down at myself, but I was wearing my usual clothing.

My belt knife was visible, as was my bow and arrows on my backpack. They wouldn't have been able to see the handful of slim blades hidden in various sections of my clothing.

There were several trees not too far away. One on one, I had half a chance of escaping into a tree. With all four surrounding me, I wasn't going anywhere unless they let me. Where was a feral when you needed one?

"You're a girl," one stated, his jaw dropping.

I blinked slowly at his shocked greeting. They must have assumed I was male like most rogues. Under my silent, wary gaze, he turned bright red at his slip of tongue. He looked to be in his early twenties and was a bit slimmer than the other three.

He shuffled his feet as he mumbled, "Uh, sorry about that. It just took me by surprise . . ."

I nodded slowly in acceptance of his apology. The fourth man—the one with the Beta bloodline—stepped forward, and I shifted my weight uneasily.

He cleared his throat and said, "Please accept my apologies for what happened. We thought you were an orphaned pup. None of us has seen a runt before and the possibility didn't cross our minds. We truly didn't intend to harm you."

I relaxed slightly as my senses reassured me that he spoke the truth. My curiosity finally outweighed my caution, and I asked, "Why did you think a young pup in no man's land would be an orphan?"

He gestured to the east. "Last night, we heard a bunch of howling and arrived just in time to help a pack fight off a dozen ferals. We caught a whiff of smoke from the west and went to see if the ferals had found or injured someone. We came across a camp, although we couldn't find anyone in the area.

"On the way back, we caught a glimpse of you and thought you were a pup. We waited to see if you were calling your parents or group in. When no one showed up after so long, we thought they might have been caught by the ferals. Our original plan was to take you to the pack just to the east in case your caretakers were still around."

The guy who pinned me shrugged and added, "It didn't seem right to leave a pup all alone in no man's land. We just didn't realize you weren't a pup. Sorry about pinning you like that, but I have to say that you have very sharp claws."

I regarded the dozens of scratches on his wrist and forearm. They would heal by the end of the day, but it did look like he had grabbed a wild barn cat by the tail. I wasn't about to mention I recently sharpened my claws so it was easier to walk along tree branches.

"You could have tried talking while you waited or before you started digging," I told them. "It would have saved you a lot of trouble."

It would have been much easier on me as well. They were obviously *not* used to dealing with rogues.

They nodded, and the one with Beta blood replied, "I'll keep that in mind for next time."

His friends walked over to stand by him so they were no longer surrounding me. I appreciated it. As a runt and a rogue, I was more cautious than most. Being surrounded made me uneasy, even if they claimed they meant me no harm.

One of the others inquired, "What are you doing all the way out here anyway?"

I shrugged and said, "Most packs won't adopt a runt because it makes them look weak."

He looked surprised. "I never thought of that. How do you manage to survive out here?"

"Mostly by hunting and gathering. I occasionally trade for things I can't make on my own."

The one with Beta blood looked intrigued. "What do you trade?"

"Usually edibles, such as berries or mushrooms. Sometimes I bring in hides, precious stones, or other things I find."

"Hmmm . . ." He got a faraway look in his eyes that meant he was having an intense discussion with someone via the mindlink. His eyes refocused on me. "I just spoke with the Luna. She's surprised you've done so well out here, and she wishes to invite you to join the pack." A corner of his lip lifted in a smile. "She also has a soft spot for mushrooms."

I stilled with surprise, although it quickly turned to suspicion. People didn't wander around and approach rogues with offers to let them join the pack, *especially* runts. It just didn't happen. That had been hammered home each time I was turned away by the dozens of packs I'd asked over the years. I carefully gauged his expression, trying to figure out what I might be missing.

Taking a chance, I said, "There's something you aren't telling me."

He blinked in surprise, then sighed in defeat. "Our Luna . . . She's unable to have kids. Even though she knows you aren't a pup, your small wolf form is still kicking her Luna instincts into action. The Alpha has no problems with you joining, and if you're good at foraging, you could be an asset to the pack."

I listened carefully, relying on my Omega abilities in case he was lying. It was the complete truth though, and their invitation now made sense. Lunas had a tendency to protect any in their pack, particularly the children. Even though I was an adult, my tiny wolf form made that fact a moot point to her instincts.

It wasn't unusual for most wolves to treat runts in their pack somewhat like pups. I often used a few puppy-like behaviors when in wolf form since it tended to keep others more laid-back and tolerant. Even when I had visited other packs, it was just a small number of prejudiced or biased individuals who caused difficulties. The average person didn't have a problem with my presence. They just didn't want me in their pack.

There was another wolf rank that had the small size of a pup, called a Comforter, but they never lost their puppy features. They were only found in about a third of the wolf packs, so they were almost as uncommon as runts. They were usually kept away from outsiders, although I had spoken with one once.

He had told me that he considered his most important task to be that of comforting others. His tiny size and puppy features made the pack members want to cuddle with him. My small size gave me some leeway, but I looked like an adult, just in miniature. I also lacked the powerful calming abilities the Comforters had, so I couldn't rely on that approach.

For a runt, life as a rogue was always dangerous and often short. I kind of missed being part of a pack, although I wasn't sure how well I could adapt to pack life after so many years as an independent rogue.

The men waited for me to decide.

I finally said, "I think I would like to try. Which pack is this?"

"Nightwind Pack."

I tilted my head. "I've never heard of it, so I suspect it isn't nearby. I'm not exactly able to keep up with other wolves . . ." I trailed off, waiting to see how they would respond.

The Beta looked deep in thought. "It's about a week's journey to the west. Hmmm . . . If we can get a picnic basket, would you allow yourself to be carried in it?"

I didn't see any problem with the solution he was offering. At least he hadn't suggested carrying me by the scruff of my neck like a pup. Riding on their back might have been another option, but that was usually only done with mates, family, or close friends.

"That would work," I said. "I'd also like to let the pack to the east know I'm leaving."

He grinned. "That's easily accomplished. Another member of our pack will be stopping there in a few days." His eyes got a faraway look, and a few moments later, he refocused on me. "Done. He'll relay the message. Now, all we have to do is find a basket."

Considering we were in the middle of no man's land, that task was easier said than done. I glanced around; my wild run hadn't covered too much distance, so I knew exactly where I was. I did a quick inventory of where I had hidden various baskets and bags.

"If someone is willing to run back to where you found me," I said, "there was a big basket in the raspberry patch beside the smoker."

One guy said, "I'm on it." He promptly turned around and started to run back. He jumped over a log and shifted mid-leap into the tan wolf I'd first seen. I blinked as he disappeared from sight and glanced at the one with Beta blood.

He shrugged. "Andy will be Andy." He held out his hand to me, saying, "In case you didn't catch it, I'm Bruce."

I shook his hand. "I'm Jade."

He nodded and gestured to the others. "The one to the left is Phil, and the other one is Terry."

I shook their hands, still a bit uneasy in the presence of these strangers as we waited for Andy to return with the basket. I wasn't too sure what I was getting myself into, but the chance of getting accepted into a pack was too tempting to pass up. I could always leave if I had to.

# Chapter 3

I watched the forest go by as Andy took a turn carrying the basket in his jaws. The ride was a bit bumpy but not as bad as I had feared. They traveled farther in a day than I could in a week.

It was a silent run, at least for me. They were probably mindlinking one another and others in their pack, but I wouldn't be part of the pack link until the Alpha bound me to it in an acceptance ceremony.

Our group stopped every couple of hours for a break, usually by a river or creek. At night, I slept in the basket while they curled around it. It was hard for me to sleep in such an exposed location, but I trusted them to keep any predators at bay. Most wildlife wouldn't tangle with a full-grown werewolf.

I learned more about my four companions during our evening talks around a campfire. Overall, they were a laid-back and easy-going bunch, so I had high hopes for this pack. They were also endlessly curious about life as a rogue, although they didn't seem to understand most of my explanations. They just couldn't wrap their heads around such a different lifestyle.

I took a deep breath as the lingering traces of spruce trees grew and faded, even though no such trees were nearby. It was a rogue's trail, although it was quite faded. None of the others flared their nostrils or seemed to take note of it. This wasn't the first trail we had crossed, but when I had mentioned it one evening, they'd been confused and told me they hadn't noticed anything.

Then again, no one in this group could even pick my scent apart from the scents of the surrounding forest despite more than a few attempts. Perhaps I had been a rogue for too long. Perhaps they needed their noses checked.

I lifted my head and confirmed the pack scent ahead matched the undertones on my companions. We were finally close to Nightwind's territory. It wouldn't be long until we arrived.

About ten minutes later, we crossed the boundary. The scents of several sentries were present, along with the patrols that had passed through mere minutes ago.

I gazed into a tree to the side and saw a human sitting in a game blind among the branches. The sentry blinked in surprise, possibly taken aback by how quickly and easily I had spotted him. Andy started chuckling even though the basket was securely held between his teeth. The other three glanced at me with somewhat impressed looks, so I assumed the sentry had mindlinked them.

I wasn't sure why my observation skills surprised the sentry. His game blind didn't blend in that well, and his scent was entrenched in the area. A rogue lived in the forest, and we were used to the forest's natural rhythms. Anything slightly different or amiss caught our attention like a bonfire in the middle of the desert at midnight. I didn't even need my Omega senses to inform me of his presence.

I had been using those abilities frequently during our trip, trying to get back into the habit of relying on them. It had been years since they'd been of any assistance, so I hadn't used them. If I was joining a pack, they would come in handy once again.

Without slowing down, they continued trotting down the trail. I didn't see any other sentries or patrols, although I sensed a few others when we passed them.

About an hour later, the trees finally thinned, and we could see the town ahead. There were about thirty or forty shops and other buildings lining several central streets. A number of small cottages were visible among the trees on the other side of town.

No tree could possibly hide the huge packhouse that stood among the oaks like an earthy jewel on display. Its brown brick walls were softened by dozens of vines that climbed up all five stories on trellises. The sprawling building had several newer-looking wings, evidence of expansions over the years. I had no idea how far back it went into the forest, but it could probably house the entire pack if needed.

The manicured trees in town were similar to the ones in the surrounding forest, but their scent was slightly different. It was enough to make my own scent stand out slightly, regardless of which plants I found.

I gave myself a mental shake; once I was accepted into the pack, there was little point in covering up my scent. The thought had been a rogue's automatic thinking, not something a pack member would likely ever think about.

Andy stopped and put the basket down before shifting. He looked down at my wolf form and said, "We figured you might want to enter the town on your own feet."

I jumped out of the basket and shifted. The other three had shifted seconds after Andy did, so they were human by the time I stood on two feet. They walked with me across the grass separating the town from the forest. The main part of town was fairly busy with people coming and going.

"How many members are in this pack?" I asked.

Bruce shrugged. "About three hundred."

That was about average for most packs. Fewer than a hundred were visible in the town, but I knew the members would be scattered about on various tasks. Some were fighters and scouts, while others would be cooks, storekeepers, or any other job that was required.

Our path led toward the packhouse.

"Are we going to see the Alpha or Luna?" I asked.

"The Alpha is visiting another pack at the moment, so we will introduce you to the Luna," Bruce replied. "She's looking forward to meeting you."

I nodded, although I was still surprised they'd accept a runt so willingly. I had been turned down by at least a hundred packs over the years, and I still couldn't wrap my mind around their offer to let me join.

Even if a rogue had excellent fighting skills, it was extremely rare for packs to approach one with an invitation to join them. For a runt, such a thing was unheard of, although it was extraordinarily rare to find a runt living as a rogue, so it was hard to say for certain.

We walked past several pack members who were also using the path. Quite a few glanced at me in curiosity, although gossip vines in a pack spread information like wildfire in dry grass, so they undoubtedly knew I was the new member who happened to be a runt.

It had been years since I had used my Omega senses in a pack situation like this, and after practicing on our trip here, I was pleased to discover my abilities hadn't weakened from the lack of use. I was also relieved I couldn't sense any hostility. It was mostly just curiosity.

We got closer to the huge building, and I extended my Omega senses with some difficulty. I could sense a bright, soft aura in the packhouse which would be the Luna. The packhouse was pretty empty since it was mid-afternoon, but there were about twenty sparks in the same spot the Luna was. The shimmery one would be the Beta female. Two were Omegas.

I had no idea what the last one was—it was like a red-hot coal at the heart of a fire. It had an odd feeling to it, like it was slumbering and just waiting for something to fan it to life.

The rest of the sparks were normal pack members, although I suspected there was an Enforcer in the room from the ringing quality. He wasn't using his abilities right now, so I wasn't able to pinpoint which spark was his.

As we walked down the street, I admired the gardens on either side of the main walkway. It was like the forest had pulled back to form a clearing just for the packhouse. The place was clean and well kept, and I couldn't spot anything that looked like it needed maintenance.

It wasn't super fancy, but it tied together with earthy tones that fit in beautifully with the trees around it. The whole town had a similar look; well-kept and tidy with plenty of ties to the surrounding forest.

We left the street and walked up the path to the packhouse. The big double doors looked inviting, although that didn't help my nerves. I wiped my sweaty palms on my pants, trying to tell myself that meeting the Luna wouldn't be that bad.

It was hard to lie to myself though. I was a rogue—and a runt to boot. I was worried about being turned away, and this time, I would be in an unfamiliar area with no stockpile of resources or supplies like I had built up at my previous location.

The breeze brought the scents of lilac trees and jasmine to my nose, along with a strange undertone. I took a deeper breath trying to identify it. I had never smelled anything like it before. It reminded me of the rich smell of the deepest parts of the forest on cool nights. The scent practically demanded attention.

A runt I may be, but slow of wit I was not. Scents of the forest could not demand the attention of a rogue. I stopped dead in my tracks and stared at the door in complete disbelief, which swiftly turned into unease and worry as I realized I wasn't mistaken. Being turned away from the pack was now the least of my concerns.

When I stopped dead in my tracks, the four walking with me turned around. Andy took one look at my expression and asked. "Jade, is something wrong?"

My oldest and strongest fears rose to the front of my mind. It was said that runts rarely, if ever, got mates. And of those who did, most were rejected since regular werewolves rarely accepted a runt as their mate. Wolves were often prideful creatures, and to be paired with a weak runt was a huge blow to both their personal and family pride, which many wouldn't tolerate. My biggest fear was to find my mate only to have him reject me.

I didn't remove my eyes from the closed doors as my mind whirled around the lingering shock. My voice was quiet and shook slightly as I admitted my fears. "That smell—I can smell my mate. I'm scared he'll reject me."

Rejection was a terrible fate. I had met a few who'd been rejected, and it had left them with a shattered heart and scars on their soul that forever changed them, even years or decades after the event. It wasn't an exaggeration or something you could just shake off. The pain of rejection was excruciating, often destroying their heart or reducing them to ferals. I had no desire to even contemplate going through such pain.

My four companions stared at me, completely stunned by this news. They had probably never imagined my mate might be in their pack. I was highly tempted to run for the hills instead of risking such pain, but the temptation of finding my soul's other half kept my feet from moving. That tiny bubble of hope kept me here, at least for the moment.

The scent was mesmerizing and drew me in, making me want to follow it. Caution and worry held me back. Until I actually looked my mate in the eyes, it was possible for me to turn around and leave.

I glanced at the four around me, checking their reactions. Their eyes were unfocused, indicating an intense mindlink discussion was happening. I sensed movement inside the house as three people exited out the back door while the rest gathered not far from the main entrance.

Bruce turned to me, meeting my eyes as he said, "I mindlinked those inside. There are several who don't have a mate yet. I told them that you're a runt and are currently a rogue. Anyone who might have rejected you left through a different exit. The rest are waiting eagerly."

I examined his expression carefully. He was telling the truth and had likely questioned each eligible wolf inside. My senses detected his irritation with those who had left. I slowly nodded and looked at the doors with trepidation.

That doorway was a crossroad; if I passed the threshold and met my mate, there were two possibilities. One path led to a mate bond filled with love and happiness, and the other path was rejection that would leave me crippled.

Rejection was rare but not unheard of. It mostly occurred to those who were rogues, Omegas, or runts. The average werewolf would have flown through that door to find their other half once they caught the scent. As a runt and a former rogue, I had a huge chance of getting rejected.

Bruce's intervention was the only reason I took a slow and cautious step toward the front door. The formation of the mate bond required eye contact, so I was going to be watching my feet until I was sure I wouldn't be rejected.

Terry opened the door for me, and I dropped my eyes to the ground as I went inside. My hands shook slightly, and I was sure they noticed. The alluring scent was stronger in here and made it hard to concentrate. I hesitantly followed Terry and Andy down the hallway. Bruce and Phil took up the rear, possibly to keep me from bolting in fear. I shook my head to try and clear it, but it didn't work.

My Omega senses weren't working properly, and it made me even more uneasy. All I could sense was that coal. It had started glowing once I entered the house, and it was overwhelming any other information my senses might have given me.

The now-smoldering coal must be my mate; our proximity was rousing the potential mate bond from dormancy. He was just around the corner. Whispering came from ahead, although none of the voices belonged to my mate—they lacked the pull his voice would hold.

"Hey, Eric. Do you smell anything yet?"

"No, just the guys and a foresty smell. Nothing overpowering."

"Yeah, me neither. We'll have to ask her how she cloaked her scent like that later. That is so cool."

As difficult as it was, I kept my eyes down as I trailed behind Terry and Andy. My rogue instincts made me want to look around to evaluate the situation and identify all possible escape routes. The smell was driving me crazy. I wondered what someone would look like with that kind of scent. Nothing could ever beat it. I loved that smell . . .

Silence reigned as I nervously followed them into a room. I felt the coal glow brighter, like a fanned ember. A few moments later, a set of heavy footsteps began to approach me. A couple of the others inhaled in shock.

One of the earlier voices murmured, "You've got to be kidding me . . ."

I stopped where I was and shifted my weight uneasily at that comment. My presence hadn't surprised them—they were shocked by the identity of whoever was walking toward me. It made me very nervous, to say the least.

My worry and caution urged me to look up to see why they were so astonished, but I knew I'd almost certainly make eye contact, and the risk of rejection wasn't easily dispelled. Trembling with nerves, I focused my gaze on my shoes as my mate drew closer.

My reading ability was unable to detect anything. The glow of the coal in my mind was far too strong. It flickered with tiny flares of fire, completely overwhelming everything else in my senses.

A pair of heavy boots entered my view as he stood right in front of me. They looked like they had seen hard use.

A deep voice spoke softly. "Will you raise your eyes?"

The voice gave me goosebumps. He was definitely my mate, but my long-held fears kept me from looking up.

My voice shook as I quietly replied, "Are you sure you won't reject me? If you aren't sure, I can leave to give you more time . . ." I trailed off. I didn't want to leave. I would miss that intoxicating scent, and his voice would haunt my dreams despite only hearing it once.

A large hand slowly entered my view. The callouses showed he was no stranger to hard work. Two of his fingers gently touched the bottom of my chin, resulting in an explosion of invisible sparks that raced along my nerves like an addictive chemical. He lifted my face until my green eyes met his amber ones, and time stood still.

My senses were flattened as the flickering coal burst into an intense flame. A powerful, blinding wave of energy cascaded through my senses and body as the mate bond took root in my heart and mind. Sensations and feelings I couldn't even name flooded my mind before settling.

Sparks flared up again as he gently brushed his thumb across my cheek. His eyes held nothing but love.

He gazed down at me with a soft smile. "I will never reject you."

Both the forming mate bond and my slowly recovering Omega senses reassured me that he told the truth. My fear of rejection finally dissipated like morning mist under the rising sun.

# Chapter 4

I slowly sipped my tea as I stole another glance at my mate, who was sitting beside me at the table. He was adding cream to his coffee, but I could tell he was keeping most of his attention on me despite watching the cream pour into his cup.

The others at the table were still recovering from their shock. My Omega senses had mostly recovered from the battering of the mate bond, but it would take some time before they reached their former level of ability.

His amber eyes trailed over to me as they had countless times during the last five minutes. With a smile, he said, "By the way, my name is William, although everyone calls me Will."

His presence and scent had me relaxed in a way I wouldn't have thought possible.

I grinned at him, completely at ease in his presence. "I'm Jade, although you probably know that already."

His silent grin showed it wasn't news to him.

The Luna, Emily, smiled and said, "It never even crossed my mind that your mate could have been Will."

She had suggested that we have a cup of tea or coffee while we got over our surprise. Will was an Enforcer, and the chances of an Enforcer finding their mate were almost as low as a runt's odds of finding theirs.

Will put an arm around my shoulders and gently pulled me across the bench until I leaned against his side. The sparks were gentle and welcome. The burning coal in my senses was no longer overpowering my Omega abilities, although it was still the strongest presence in my senses. I was slowly learning to tune it out, although I wasn't using my senses much since they were still recovering.

"I know what you mean, Emily," Will said. His arm was still around my shoulders, and he showed no signs of letting me go anytime soon. "I didn't expect it either; I was so stunned that it took me a few moments to go to her."

I glanced up at my mate, who dwarfed me, even in human form. I was slender and barely stood over five feet tall while he was well over six feet and heavily built. In that fashion, he was a typical Enforcer, which were usually larger and stronger than most werewolves. I simply couldn't figure out how an elite fighter got paired with a runt. It defied all possible logic.

I had the strangest urge to run my hand through his short, dark brown hair. The mate bond was already playing havoc with my usual thought processes, and I was beginning to understand why newly-found mates acted so infatuated.

Emily watched us with amusement twinkling in her eyes. "Well, you might as well give her a tour of the place once she finishes her tea. Roland will be back tomorrow, and he can perform the acceptance ritual then."

One of the guys who I hadn't been introduced to joined the conversation. "Can I ask why you don't have any scent?"

I tilted my head as I examined the teenager. "It isn't that I don't have a scent. I just rub various plants on my clothing to mask it."

Phil snorted in good humor. "Yeah, that's what she keeps telling us, but we couldn't differentiate her scent from the trees when we were traveling. I can smell it inside since it stands out, but until now, I haven't been able to pick up any scent to indicate she's even standing there."

Will looked at me in curiosity. "Bruce mentioned you picked up the scent trails of other rogues even though he couldn't smell anything."

I thought for a moment before saying, "Their scents were slightly different from the surrounding forest. Rogues use a mixture of plants to keep one from being overly strong and noticeable; so, for example, the hint of a willow tree when none are in sight is a dead giveaway. My current scent still has a tang of cedar even though I haven't seen a cedar tree for two days. I've seen lots of oaks around here, but I haven't brushed against them, so my scent is unbalanced compared to the local forest."

Phil shook his head. "I wouldn't have thought of that."

I looked at him in confusion. "How else would you know if a rogue is around? It isn't uncommon for ferals to roll in leaves and also have a forest-like scent."

Andy glanced at Phil with a somewhat concerned expression and said, "She's right, you know. She almost entered the room before anyone even picked up her scent, and that forest smell obviously didn't belong in the house. If a feral did this in the forest where someone was running a patrol . . ." He trailed off, leaving the obvious outcome unspoken.

Phil frowned. "Perhaps Jade can help us learn to identify such camouflaged scents once she settles in."

I was still stumped by their inability to notice the differences in such scents. They were wolves, and even though I'd been a teenager when I entered the life of a rogue, I had managed it within mere weeks. I thought it was a common ability and assumed my four escorts had been humoring me. I slowly finished my tea and listened to them talk about how such an ability would come in handy.

"Why don't you and Will go for a run in wolf form? He can show you around the nearby forest, and if you find anything amiss, you can let us know," Emily suggested.

Will looked at me in growing excitement. "Do you want to go for a run? I know we won't be able to mindlink yet, but I'd love to see your wolf form."

Smiling shyly, I said, "Sure, as long as you don't mind going slowly. I'm not exactly the fastest thing around."

He grinned. "I have no problem traveling slowly. It'll give me more time to stare at you."

My cheeks heated in a blush. No one had ever flirted with me before, so I wasn't sure how to react.

Andy chuckled. "Don't irritate her, or she might chew on your ankles. I hear her teeth are quite sharp."

Phil elbowed Andy in a clear attempt to make him stop talking. Will raised an eyebrow in askance. He must not have heard how they had met me, although it might be best if he didn't learn about it at this second.

It wasn't wise to antagonize Enforcers, and Will might not react well if he discovered they had chased me through a forest and pinned me. A new mate bond was known to cause both wolves to react somewhat unpredictably, and I wasn't sure I wanted to know how unpredictable an Enforcer might become.

I shook my head and retorted in a teasing tone, "Why would I chew on his ankles when toes are a much more sensitive target?" I rose to my feet and smiled at Will. "I wouldn't mind stretching my legs and having a look around."

The distraction worked, and he stood up. He was taller than anyone else in the room, but he towered over me. I didn't even come close to his collarbone. I stepped to the side to let him take the lead, but he took my hand and guided me out of the kitchen.

As we exited the packhouse through a different door, I looked around. This side of the packhouse faced the forest, and there was a large expanse of neatly cut lawn and a playground. Will let go of my hand, and I stretched my arms before shifting.

I shook out my fur and glanced up at Will. If I thought he was big before, he was absolutely massive compared to my tiny wolf shape. With an enchanted look on his face, he knelt down on the grass and gazed at me with soft eyes.

I walked over and put my front paws on his knees. He leaned forward, and I reached up to give his chin a small lick, the equivalent of a quick, shy kiss. He smiled as he gently ran his hand along my back, causing sparks to cascade along my spine.

"Your fur is so soft . . ." he murmured.

Before I realized what he was doing, he scooped me up in his arms and cuddled me against his chest. It took me a second to recover, then I rubbed the top of my head against the underside of his chin as an odd purring sound rumbled in my chest. He buried his face in my fur. It felt like I was surrounded by gentle sparks. I listened to the sound of his heartbeat contentedly.

After some time like that, I heard his muffled voice as his warm breath spread through my fur. "I'm not sure I can put you down after this. I could stay like this all day."

With a wolf chuckle, I leaned over to nibble on his fingers. It took more than a few nibbles before he raised his head with a smile. He lowered me back to the ground and stood up. When he took a step back to shift, I watched intently, eager to see his wolf form.

For a split second, it looked like he was concealed by a heat haze before a dark gray wolf stood in front of me. I blinked in surprise as I gazed up and up. He was nearly as big as an Alpha, although the large size was common among Enforcers. It was rare for me to see an Enforcer in wolf form, and I'd never seen one up-close while I was also in wolf form. This was a first for me.

I wouldn't say it out loud yet, but he was definitely handsome. The shading on his coat was subtle, being slightly darker on top and lighter on his stomach. I trotted closer as his amber eyes watched me.

I wove a figure eight between his two front paws, leaning lightly against his legs as I enjoyed the warmth of the sparks. To my amusement, I didn't even come halfway up his legs. I grinned up at him and wagged my tail before darting toward the trees. He immediately followed me.

Darting under a jungle gym, I glanced back and gave a laughing bark as he was forced to detour around the obstacle. Even if he tried, I wasn't entirely sure he could wiggle his way into the middle of this piece of playground equipment in his wolf form. He was simply too large for something designed for kids.

While I might have been running at a good speed for my size, he was only doing a fast trot to keep up. I slowed down as we neared the trees, and Will took the lead.

I followed him up and down various trails as I studied the forest around us. His fast walk had me trotting beside him. He kept checking on me, as if ensuring I wasn't having any trouble keeping up. The one time he had slowed down, I trotted ahead, forcing him to speed back up.

We entered a small meadow, and I perked my ears at the bushes on the other side, although I wasn't worried since I could both scent and sense the approaching sentry. With a rustle, a dappled gray wolf emerged. Will didn't look surprised to see him and went forward to greet him.

I wasn't able to hear their discussion since they were in wolf form. Whatever it was, it must have been important since they gazed at each other intently.

After a couple of minutes, I felt kind of awkward and decided to get a drink from the small creek at the edge of the clearing. The clear water was cool and refreshing.

I started to meander back to Will and the sentry, who still hadn't moved. Out of habit, I rubbed my side along a nearby shrub. I could sense another pack member approaching and continued trotting toward Will.

A brown wolf came out of the bushes and paused as he caught sight of me. His eyes flickered in surprise before he pinned his ears back with a snarl. I froze, stunned at his unexpected reaction. His approach hadn't been quiet. Surely he knew all three of us had heard him coming? It wasn't as if I had been trying to hide.

Neither of us had time to do anything before a thundering snarl came from the side. A charcoal gray wolf charged forward, sliding into a protective stance in front of me. It was the sentry's turn to freeze in fright.

My previously laid-back and cuddly mate had just turned into an enraged beast that crouched as if to pounce. His back legs were in front of me, and his loud snarls made the air vibrate in their intensity. His hackles were standing straight up, making him look twice as big.

As an Enforcer, he was normally a force to be reckoned with. The fact that he was protecting his mate only added to his power. Considering he was focused on a member of the pack, this was a bad situation.

I took a few careful steps forward. When I reached his back leg, I leaned against it, hoping the contact would calm him down, or at the very least, make him reluctant to pull away in order to attack the brown wolf.

Will's posture shifted slightly, taking on a more defensive stance instead of an offensive one. I could sense his reluctance to charge forward and leave me exposed in the middle of the clearing, but I could also feel the anger and protective feelings rolling off him.

The brown wolf saw the change and bolted back into the shrubs behind him. I leaned harder against Will's leg; if he left, I would end up rolling in the dirt. I sighed in relief when Will didn't take off after him. The first sentry also relaxed as the tension eased, although he didn't move from where he was standing.

I studied Will's tense form; I didn't think he would leave me to chase a wolf through the forest, but I really needed a better distraction. With that thought in mind, I leaned over and gently nipped the top of one of his toes. Will turned his head to look at me incredulously, as if he couldn't believe I had actually dared to chew on an Enforcer's toes.

His hackles were slowly flattening now that the immediate danger was over. I yipped at him and trotted forward as I stretched my neck up. He lowered his head, and we bumped noses.

Sparks tingled through my nose in a bizarre sensation, and I sneezed before plopping my rear end on the ground. I perked my ears and tilted my head innocently, gazing up at him with a puppy-like expression.

Will heaved a huge sigh and visibly relaxed now that his control was no longer strained. I was somewhat surprised when he shifted to his human form. He scooped me up and buried his face in my fur. I felt the last of the tension slowly leave him as he used my scent to calm down. I reached up to give his neck and the side of his chin a few small licks as reassurance.

He lifted his head so he could see me better. "Sorry about that. I kind of lost it when he snarled at you. To think I once thought other males overreacted when it came to their mate's safety . . ." He shook his head. "I wasn't aware the drive to protect one's mate was so intense. It's much stronger than anything I've ever felt, even as an Enforcer."

I looked up at him and perked my ears attentively. I kind of wished we could mindlink each other, but that wasn't possible at this moment. I would either have to be part of his pack to access the pack link or be fully mated to him to use the mate bond.

He gazed at my face, as if committing it to memory. "I did apologize to him via the mindlink, so he knows he can stop running. He says he's sorry for snarling at you."

I wagged my tail, although with the way I was held, it beat rapidly between his arm and his chest. He chuckled. "If you're trying to be cute and distracting, it's working."

I wolf-grinned in triumph. That hadn't been quite what I was aiming for, but if it worked, who was I to complain? Bonus points for me!

The sentry off to the side spoke up, having shifted to human at some point. "The Luna made a formal announcement telling people that a gray runt will be joining our pack, so we shouldn't have any more misunderstandings. She didn't say anything about Will being your newfound mate because she's hoping you two can enjoy some time alone before being inundated with well-wishers."

I yipped a thank-you at him, and he nodded in response.

Will looked down at me. "How about we finish our run and do a quick tour of the town?"

My tail beat faster as I gave a quiet yip. He set me down and shifted, taking the lead as he guided me down more trails. I tried to commit them to memory. Wolf packs had more trails close to their packhouse than any rabbit warren, although I was pretty sure it would only take me a week to memorize the ones close to town.

# Chapter 5

I sniffed the air more deeply and slowed down. Will noticed my change of speed and also slowed, alternating his attention between me and the surrounding forest. I sniffed a few more times and followed my nose as I tracked the familiar scent.

I circled the nearby area and sniffed the ground carefully as Will watched me in confusion. It took me a few moments to locate it, then I started digging at the base of a tree. As I got deeper, the smell got stronger, and I went more carefully. Will padded closer to see what I was doing, still confused and perplexed.

Less than a minute later, I had dug a ring around the black jewel in the middle. I carefully undermined the valuable object until it gently rolled off its pedestal. I shifted and kneeled down to pick up the baseball-sized object. With a triumphant grin, I turned to show Will, who was still watching in his massive wolf shape.

In response to his blank gaze, I said, "It's a black truffle. If the pack has a chef, they'll be absolutely thrilled. Whenever I brought one to a pack to trade, the pack members practically broke into fights over who got it."

Will looked at the lumpy black object dubiously. I grinned at his expression and dug around in my backpack for the small collapsible box I carried for this sort of delicate treasure. I quickly put the box together and set the truffle inside before tucking it into my backpack.

After filling in the hole, I shifted back to my wolf form. My backpack and all of its contents disappeared, keeping them from being harmed or bounced until I shifted back to my human form. I trotted ahead, and Will shook his head in disbelief as he trailed after me.

We paused at a stream to get a drink. Nearby, a big tree stretched across the creek, one end resting on the other side. Since the far bank was higher, the tree trunk angled up. I glanced at Will, who was still drinking, and I quickly scrambled on top of the log.

He raised his head and gazed at me in curiosity. I was now at the same height as his face, which was a first. He remained standing beside the log and watched me with soft eyes.

My lips pulled back in a playful grin. I knew I would never win a wrestling match against any wolf, let alone an Enforcer, but that didn't stop me from launching myself off the log and onto his back.

I wasn't sure if he even felt the impact of my fifteen-pound body as I landed on his shoulders. My toenails dug into his fur for traction, although I knew they wouldn't be able to reach through his thick pelt, let alone scratch him.

I grabbed a mouthful of his fur and tugged it side to side playfully. His back vibrated with his chuckling laugh as he flopped to his stomach. He hit the ground with enough force to dislodge me, and I went tumbling into the grass beside him.

Twisting around to face him, I dipped into a play bow with a wildly wagging tail before launching myself at his neck. His amusement rolled off him in waves. I could only imagine what someone would have thought of our wildly unequal game. A charcoal gray wolf the size of a small horse being playfully attacked by a cat-sized wolf. His head alone was almost as big as I was.

Will rolled onto his side as he gently mouthed my neck. I halfway climbed on top of his head to grab his ear. He twisted his head to the side and sent me rolling into the grass once more. As he rolled back onto his stomach, I charged forward again and tried to wrap my forepaws around his muzzle. I couldn't reach his ears, so I grabbed a mouthful of loose fur on his cheek and tugged on it.

He raised a paw larger than my head and gently pinned me to the ground with a mischievous grin, thinking I wouldn't be able to get loose. Unfortunately for him, a rogue had once taught me how to get out of this particular position. The move only worked for someone as small as a runt, so he probably didn't know about it.

I twisted my body in that special contortion and slid out behind the back of his paw before renewing my assault on his neck. I could feel Will's surprise before his amusement and love overpowered the emotion.

With a chuckle, he dropped his head on top of me, effectively pinning me upside down. I wiggled a bit to the side, pushing against his neck with my feet until I slid out enough for my head to rest on his forearm. I lay on my back, panting in silent laughter.

Will lifted his head to examine me as I used his leg as a pillow. He leaned down and gently licked the underside of my chin. I wasn't that dirty from rolling around, but he proceeded to wash most of my fur anyways.

It tickled, and I squirmed and tried to make a break for it, but he used his paw to catch me and drag me back so he could wash my back. I could sense his amusement as he foiled my various escape attempts. He eventually let me go as his tongue rolled out the side of his mouth in silent laughter. I stood up and shook my damp fur, trying to straighten it back out.

I may have smelled like the forest before, but now all I smelled like was Will. Even my nose couldn't pick up any trace of greenery in my scent. If he had planned to keep my mate status low on the radar for the next day or so, that had been blown right out of the water.

Anyone who came within scenting distance of me would smell it with ease, although I shouldn't have been surprised. Most new mates wanted to ensure no one would flirt with their partner, and a higher-ranking wolf, such as an Enforcer, would probably prefer any potential rivals to keep their distance.

I narrowed my eyes mischievously at him and skipped back a few steps. When my feet splashed into the creek, I swiped hard at the water, spraying some water droplets into Will's face. He jerked back in surprise, and I took that as my chance to jump over the tiny creek and race away.

I forgot to take his speed as an Enforcer into account. Mere seconds later, Will loomed over me and gently grabbed the scruff of my neck, lifting me off the ground mid-stride. He was being gentle, so his hold didn't hurt. He proceeded to show off his speed as the forest blurred past us.

He launched over logs and obstacles with ease; those huge jumps made my heart race in a way that the tree highway never had. I had never traveled this fast before, and I could tell he wasn't going at his top speed either. It had taken us over an hour to get out to where we had met the sentry, and we covered the same amount of distance in less than fifteen minutes. He slowed as he reached the edge of the forest and put me down.

My fur was dry after our run, although his scent had also dried into it. Simply rubbing against a few plants wasn't going to do anything to mute it. I shifted forms and stretched before draping an arm over Will's furry neck. It wasn't the easiest since his shoulders were still higher than mine, even in wolf form.

He leaned lightly against my side, and I ran a hand through his fur absently as we gazed at the town we'd returned to. After a while, he shifted to his human form and took my hand in his as he guided me toward the buildings.

I got a lot of looks as we walked past people. When they noticed Will was holding my hand, many started whispering excitedly to those nearby. When I used my senses, I picked up surprise, happiness, and anticipation. A couple were envious, and I did sense one or two flickers of disapproval, but overall, most were positive emotions.

Will walked with me as we went up and down each street so I could see the forty-some buildings. As we went by each store, he explained what they sold or what they did. My eyes were drawn to the small library. I didn't read very well or very fast, but I liked trying. I didn't get many chances living as a rogue. It always amazed me how much information was hidden in books.

Will noticed how my gaze lingered on the books we could see through the windows and he asked, "Do you want to go in?"

"If we have time, I'd like to. It's been years since I got a chance to go into a library."

Realization crossed his face as he remembered I had lived as a rogue for who knows how long.

"Yes, we have plenty of time," he said as he held the door open for me.

A young lady behind a desk smiled at us as we entered. "Hello, I'm Cassie. Can I help you find something?"

I returned the smile. "I'm Jade. I just popped in to take a look around for a moment, but you'll be seeing more of me later."

She tilted her head and glanced between me and Will. Her expression brightened. "Oh!" she exclaimed. "You're the newest member in the pack! Welcome! You'll enjoy it here, and I speak from experience since I arrived last week. Everyone is so welcoming in this pack."

Her enthusiasm was contagious, and my smile grew bigger. "Thank you. I'm glad to hear that."

"I'm sure we'll get to know one another later since I spend most of my time here, but in the meantime, don't let me keep you."

With a chuckle, Will said, "Oh, I don't mind. I'd rather have my mate show interest in visiting a library as opposed to the bar."

I sent a mischievous glance over my shoulder at Will, and humor laced through my voice. "Not much fear of that, although if I catch you at the bar watching strippers, we'll be having words."

He grinned at my teasing tone, more amused by my potential jealousy than the fact that a runt was trying to threaten an Enforcer. Cassie pursed her lips, trying not to laugh.

Will promptly replied, "Such pursuits didn't interest me in the past, and at this point, I only have eyes for you."

Well. He apparently knew how to score brownie points. My heart melted. I stepped back so I could reach him and wrapped an arm around him in a hug. Both of his arms encircled me as he placed a small kiss on my forehead.

I had never been one for public displays of affection, so these sudden changes took me by surprise, although part of me wasn't at all bothered by it. I knew I could blame the mate bond for that.

We parted and gazed into each other's eyes for a long moment. Will took my hand and guided me back outside, giving Cassie a goodbye wave as we left.

We continued walking down the street as Will gave me a tour of the town. When I stared one second too long at a small sign that advertised soft ice cream, Will dragged me inside and bought us both a small ice cream cone. He blocked me when I tried to pay, much to the amusement of the old lady at the cash register.

We sat on a bench outside to enjoy the creamy treat. I hummed in delight as I savored mine.

Will watched me with a soft smile. "I assume you're enjoying it?"

"Immensely."

In a tentative voice, he asked, "When was the last time you had ice cream?"

I could feel his curiosity warring with his caution, worried this might be a sensitive topic. It took me a few seconds to skim my memories for the answer. "I think about six or seven years ago when I joined a pack for a short time."

He blinked slowly, stunned. "Wow. If you don't mind me asking, why did you leave that pack?"

I made a face. "It was the Black River pack when old Doug passed away."

He winced at the mention of the well-known event. The Alpha, Doug, had passed away with no children and without naming an heir. The neighboring packs had fought over his land in a procession of bloody battles. It was the biggest example in recent history about why Alphas had to have an heir lined up at all times.

"Sorry to hear that."

I shrugged. "I had only been in that pack for about a year, so there wasn't much tying me there. I knew what was going to happen, so I left as soon as the funeral was over. The neighboring packs didn't have the best ethics, and they weren't the type to let a runt join them. I made sure to get out of the area before the first fight broke out."

Curiosity danced in the back of Will's eyes. "I don't want to intrude, but could you tell me about your life? It feels like I found a handful of puzzle pieces, and I really want to see the whole picture. You can ignore the question if it makes you uncomfortable."

Quite a few rogues had tragic pasts, and he likely didn't want to open old wounds if that had been the case with me.

I licked my ice cream as I contemplated his question. I eventually said, "My life wasn't as eventful as most rogues. My family and original pack were wiped out by ferals when I was twelve. Some rogues found me shortly afterward, and I traveled with them for a while. They got adopted into a pack, but the pack didn't want a runt, so I kept traveling. I met a lot of rogues over the years; most didn't mind sharing tips and tricks to help me survive in no man's land."

I nibbled on the ice cream cone before continuing, "About seven years ago, I joined the Black River pack since they needed help keeping the packhouse clean and tidy. I was given an Omega position. They were fair to their Omegas, but as a runt, I was the elephant in the room. Apart from the Alpha and Luna, everyone preferred it when I kept out of sight."

"And after Alpha Doug passed away?"

"I slowly traveled north and west as the years went by and eventually settled in the area where Bruce and the others found me. The Alpha and Luna in a nearby pack didn't mind me trading in the marketplace, and they even let me walk in unescorted. Then I came here. Pretty boring story compared to most rogues." I looked up at him. "What about you?"

Will slowly blinked, possibly still absorbing my short explanation. "I was born into this pack as an Enforcer. That was a bit of a surprise since there had never been an Enforcer in our family before. I had an easy childhood and went into training fairly early. Most Enforcers rarely ever go past the pack borders, and I've never set foot over it. We haven't had any big fights. Ferals show up occasionally, but otherwise, things are quiet. Your story sounds more exciting than mine."

"I bet you got into plenty of mischief growing up."

He flashed a grin at me. "I'm not admitting to those events."

I chuckled, knowing I'd likely hear some stories as I got to know his family. I nudged my backpack with my toe. "Do you happen to know a cook who likes to make fancier dishes?"

"Yes, there's a good one down the street."

Once we finished the ice cream, we wandered down the street until Will stopped in front of another store that had baked treats displayed in the windows. When he opened the door, we were greeted by the creamy smell of chocolate and the sharper tang of caramel, along with the heady scent of freshly baked bread.

A lady in her mid-thirties glanced up as we entered. "Ah, Will. It's nice to see you again. Who's your friend?"

With a grin, Will put an arm around my shoulders and pulled me closer. "This is Jade."

The lady blinked in shock at his actions, then realized the significance. She sent a genuine smile in my direction. "Congratulations! I'm so glad Will managed to find his mate!"

Since it was a rare occurrence, it was normally a big deal if an Enforcer found their mate. I smiled at her and gently poked Will in the side. His arm snaked down to hold my hand instead of hugging me close.

I grinned up at him while I told the lady, "I'm pretty glad I found him too."

Will sent a heartwarming smile down at me, and I could feel his relief and pride that I was accepting him so easily. Rogues often had difficulty settling down with a newfound mate. Going from a free rogue to being part of the complex pack life was a huge adjustment.

Gently pulling my hand free from Will's, I took my backpack off and brought out the box. As I held it out to her, I said, "Here, this is for you."

She frowned slightly in confusion as she took the box and opened it. Her excited eyes darted to me. "How much do you want for this? This is a beautiful truffle and out of season too."

I shook my head. "Nothing. It's yours."

Her jaw dropped. "Are you sure? This thing is worth a lot."

A big truffle out of season was very uncommon and expensive. Apparently, she knew it too. Truffles like this were the reason I had money in my backpack.

"Well, if you ever happen to be cooking at the packhouse, I would love a refresher course on some of the appliances." I laughed lightly. "I looked at the stove in there, but I haven't used one in years, and I have no idea which one of the fifty buttons on that thing actually turns the oven on."

Both of them laughed with me, and Will said, "Don't ask me. I wouldn't have the faintest clue where to start with that thing. They kicked me out of the kitchen years ago."

"That was because you kept trying to eat the desserts as soon as they came out of the oven," the cook replied, her eyes twinkling in amusement.

Will shrugged but looked unrepentant.

The woman shook her head and told me, "Well, I'll be more than happy to show you anything you want in the kitchen. I have a morning shift there three times a week, so feel free to join me. I'm Sylvia."

"Thank you for the offer, Sylvia. I'll be sure to stop by."

She lifted the truffle out of the box to examine it more closely. "Where did you find this lovely thing?"

"To the west, not far from where the creek splits." I glanced sideways at Will as another grin tugged at my lips. "Although you should have seen Will's face when I started digging it up."

Will gave the lumpy object another confused glance. "I fail to see how anything that looks like that can possibly be edible."

Sylvia and I grinned at each other in amusement, not bothering to enlighten my mate. After visiting for a while longer, Will and I left her store to finish my tour.

Once I'd seen every building in town, we headed back to the packhouse. From the sheer number of people I could sense inside, mostly in the dining area, I guessed this was roughly when dinner was usually served.

I followed closely behind Will as we entered the crowded hallway. His large bulk cleared a path through the thronging masses as he guided me into one of the smaller living rooms just off the main hall. There were a handful of people talking in the far corner, although they didn't seem to notice us.

This room was a welcome reprieve from the crowded hallway. Will must have realized I would be uneasy in huge crowds after spending so much time alone. I breathed a sigh of relief and realized Will was oddly silent. When I glanced up, his eyes had a far-away look.

The ringing of his Enforcer aura appeared in my senses and strengthened. He blinked and looked down at me in concern. "I have to go break up an overly rowdy group of teenagers. Will you be okay in here?"

I really didn't want to be left alone in a house full of strangers, but I knew he had responsibilities. "I'll be fine. I think the main bulk of the people are heading for the dining area, so I'll wait for you here. Most probably don't even know I'm in the house. I'll give a shout if I need you."

He ducked down to plant a kiss on my cheek before disappearing out the door. I slowly blinked as the warmth of his presence faded from the room. I had been beside him most of the day, and his sudden absence was as if the sun had hidden behind the clouds. He had only been gone a few seconds, and I couldn't believe how much I missed him already.

I glanced around the room again. When we had come through the house, I had been following so closely behind Will that most people likely hadn't seen me. And since I smelled like Will, I doubted anyone had picked up my scent.

The four people in the room still hadn't turned around or noticed my presence. My Omega senses told me that they were truly unaware of me and not simply ignoring me.

I walked silently to the side to examine the various pictures on the wall. I recognized the Luna in one and began checking if Will was in any of them. My senses shifted when the other four realized they weren't alone in the room. I turned around as the girl and three guys came closer with curiosity coloring their minds.

One guy held out his hand. "Hi, I'm Tim. I don't believe we've met. I just returned from visiting Brandon's pack."

I shook his hand. "I'm Jade. I actually arrived today with Bruce and his group."

His face lit up as he asked, "Are you planning on staying long?" I was somewhat shocked at his hopeful look. How did he not pick up Will's scent on me? Or was he assuming that Will had passed by and brushed against my clothing?

The girl beside him was clearly more observant and snorted. "Tim, use your nose before Will chucks you out the window."

Tim gave her a blank look before taking a deep breath. His eyes went wide as he realized his oversight. "Uh, sorry about that. I didn't realize you had a mate."

"No worries. No harm done," I said.

The girl shook her head at his denseness. "I'm Samantha, but you can call me Sam. And this is John and Mark."

John shook my hand. "Nice to meet you. Sam happens to be my mate."

I nodded and asked Mark, "And your mate is Cassie from the library, right? I met her earlier today. She seems nice."

Mark shook his head. "No, I haven't met my mate yet."

I quickly apologized. "Sorry about that. My mistake." I ducked my head as my cheeks heated with embarrassment.

He seemed amused. "Don't worry about it. Tim already won the blunder award by not picking up Will's scent on you."

"I shouldn't have assumed. My apologies. What do you four normally do during the day?" I asked, trying to steer the conversation in a different direction.

They gave me a rundown of where they worked and what they did. John and Sam owned their own store, while Mark and Tim usually ran patrol and helped with oddball tasks.

When I sensed Will's approach, I glanced over my shoulder with a smile. He appeared in the doorway, and his eyes went straight to me. He wasted no time closing the distance between us. As he walked up behind me, he wrapped his arms around me in a hug. I leaned my head back against his chest to gaze up at his amber eyes.

He smiled softly at me and asked, "Do you feel like braving the dining hall? Most of the crowd has already eaten and dispersed."

"Sure."

We left the room, and the other four tagged along as well.

# Chapter 6

I laughed at John's story as he described the pranks they'd played on Will during their teenage years and how he'd gotten his revenge. I shook my head and took another sip of juice.

Dinner had been very good. It had been a long time since I last had ham, mashed potatoes, gravy, veggies, bread, and all the trimmings. My meals were usually bread and smoked meat. I hadn't been this full in a long time.

Someone leaned between John and Mark to put a plate of honey muffins on the table. Their sweet scent made my mouth water. Other than the ice cream this afternoon, the last time I had any sort of dessert was back when I'd been in the Black River Pack. And by the time I got to the table with that pack, the desserts and good stuff were almost always gone.

Will had been watching me most of the meal and instantly noticed how my eyes lingered on the plate of sticky sweet morsels just out of my reach. He reached over to snag one off the pile and held it up to my mouth.

I flushed, aware of the four people trying to hide their grins as Will held the muffin for me. Still, that didn't stop me from leaning forward to take a bite out of the treat.

The flavors exploded on my tongue, and I hummed in delight as I enjoyed my mouthful. I turned a bit red when I noticed Will was watching me with an entranced expression.

With a grin, Samantha commented, "That's the mate bond at its finest during the courting stage. Anything you show interest in, he'll try to get for you. If it's food, it's almost guaranteed that he'll try to feed it to you. All couples go through it. It'll settle down after the mate bond is completed. Oh, and don't be surprised if he gets jealous and overprotective at any given point in time."

Samantha looked pointedly at John as she finished her little speech.

He rolled his eyes. "I wasn't that bad . . ."

Mark snorted in disagreement. "No, you were much worse. You growled at anyone who so much as glanced at Sam. You wouldn't let me or Tim in the same room with her, even when you were sitting beside her."

John grumbled incoherently as he ate his own honey muffin. I mulled over Samantha's words. To complete the mate bond, I would have to be marked and mated. I wasn't ready for that yet, so the mate bond would have plenty of time to mess with Will's head or get him worked up over something.

To give him credit, he had been able to leave me in a room with three males—two of whom were unmated—so that was a definite improvement over what Samantha and John had apparently gone through.

Will juggled the rest of the muffin so a corner stuck out toward me, and I leaned in for a second bite. It was just as good as the first.

I mumbled around my mouthful, "I'm glad Will doesn't seem to go overboard in the jealousy area."

I had seen quite a few men who'd been so jealous they could barely tolerate watching their mate shake hands with another guy. Thinking back, I recalled how jealousy had stirred in my heart when a few other women had walked by during the meal. I knew the mate bond was responsible for my reaction. It might be more noticeable in males, but I clearly wasn't immune to its effects.

Will looked sheepish as he said, "I'll admit I had to bite my tongue a few times. I'm also quite grateful for all the self-control lessons Tony knocked into me during our training. They are getting a serious workout."

Strangely enough, I was secretly flattered that he would get jealous over me. He seemed relaxed at the moment even though two unmated males were at the table and talking with me. I wasn't entirely sure how I would have felt if Samantha wasn't already paired up with John.

Will popped the last bit of the muffin into his mouth, which was fine by me since I was quite full at this point. I stretched and leaned back in my chair.

"I'm stuffed," I said. "Is the food always this good?"

Mark nodded. "Yep. You rarely get the same thing two days in a row since the cooks take turns."

"I think I'll have to get some lessons from them. The food was excellent," I murmured.

My senses alerted me to the Luna's approach, and I glanced over my shoulder. Will followed my gaze, also spotting her.

"Hello, Emily. How's it going?" he asked when she got closer.

"Good. We just have to figure out where Jade will sleep tonight, then my tasks will be complete for the evening."

Will and I turned a bit red at the topic, but it was a valid question. Even if mates had just met, most were unable to sleep if they were apart. And if they succeeded in sleeping separately, the bond tended to become more volatile, making both of them touchier and more likely to overreact. Most mates took around two weeks to get to know one another and complete the mate bond, and they usually shared a room during that time.

Will turned to me, still red. "Umm . . . would you mind sleeping in my room? I won't push our relationship any faster than you're willing to go, but I know I wouldn't be able to sleep without you nearby."

I ducked my head shyly. "I usually sleep in wolf form. So as long as you don't roll on me in your sleep, I don't see any problem in it."

I also knew I wouldn't be able to sleep without Will close by. Truth be told, I couldn't even remember the last time I slept in human form. Even as an Omega, I had been so accustomed to sleeping in wolf form that I always slept on a blanket under the low bed.

Will sighed in relief. "I don't think I could possibly roll on you or harm you."

Emily nodded happily. "That makes my life easier. Enjoy your evening." She turned and left the room.

"What do you usually do in the evenings?" I asked Will.

He shrugged. "Evenings are more or less free time for everyone. I normally do some training, but I want to give the mate bond some time to settle down. I'm worried I might accidentally hurt someone today."

In a bizarre way, I was glad the mate bond wasn't only messing with my head and mood.

"Take my advice and go somewhere quiet," Samantha told us.

Will brightened at that thought. "That sounds like a good idea to me."

I nodded in agreement. I wasn't used to being around so many people, and I looked forward to finding someplace quieter.

Will guided me outside, and we wandered into the forest. The familiar smells and sounds relaxed me as we weaved between the trees. Our footsteps were slow, simply taking our time as we listened to the birds singing above while holding hands.

We hadn't gone far before we reached a small waterfall. Will and I sat on the thick grass at the base of a tree, and when I leaned against his side, he draped his arm over my shoulders. We watched the water cascade over the rocks as we enjoyed one another's company in the peaceful setting.

Close to sunset, our peace was shattered when a group of kids started yelling and shrieking in an enthusiastic game of tag. With a heavy sigh, Will stood up and held a hand out to me. I took it and let him pull me to my feet.

He commented, "It was nice while it lasted. The sun will set shortly, so we might as well head back."

We meandered down the trail, taking care to avoid the rambunctious kids. I used my free hand to cover my yawn, not willing to let go of Will's hand just yet. Between waking up at daybreak to get here and all the events that followed, it was beginning to feel like a long day.

I followed Will as he went up a couple flights of stairs and opened a door, turning sideways so I could see past him. "This is my room. Well, our room now."

I wandered in and looked around in curiosity. A small window overlooked the town. The four walls were a dark brown, and the decorations were limited to a few picture frames. It was clean and simple.

"This is nice," I said. "I was halfway scared I'd find sweaty practice clothes draped on a chair or stuffed in a closet."

He grinned at my teasing tone. "No, my practice clothing stays in the building by the training grounds where they get washed daily. I don't think I could endure the smell of them in here."

I grinned in response and hefted my backpack. "Mind if I grab a shower?"

"Go for it. There's a shower two doors down the hallway, right next to the bathroom. There are several on every floor, so don't worry about hurrying for other people." He grabbed a set of clothing from his dresser and followed me to the door. "I'll be down the hallway if you need anything."

I nodded and went in search of the bathroom, which wasn't hard to find since the door had a hand-carved sign on it. The hot water in the shower was a luxury I thoroughly enjoyed. It beat the cold water in the creek by a long shot. I dried off and brushed my shoulder-length hair.

The soap and shampoo had mostly removed Will's scent from my skin. For the first time in a long time, my own scent was detectable. I knew from discussions with other rogues that Will would have been able to pick up my scent regardless of how I masked it. It was impossible to mask someone's scent from their mate, even if they had never met.

I shook my head and meandered into the nearby bathroom to brush my teeth before heading back. When I reached Will's room, I was surprised to discover I had beat him back, which shouldn't have happened since I'd lingered in the warm shower. I put my backpack on a chair in the corner and sat on the bed before shifting into my wolf form.

As I focused on my senses, I detected his Enforcer aura downstairs. He must have gone to shoo noisy people outside so they wouldn't disturb those trying to sleep.

An Enforcer's role mostly involved minor peacekeeping events like these, which removed a potential source of irritation before anyone got overly upset. Of course, if a serious fight or attack ever occurred, they would be in the thick of it, but such things were much rarer than the usual day-to-day squabbles.

A quick sniff of the bed told me which side he normally slept on. I curled up on the opposite pillow and wiggled under the blankets for added warmth, letting my head stick out. It felt extremely strange to be settling down for the night without being in a tight spot. I had a feeling it was going to take me a long time to fall asleep.

While lying there, I tracked Will with my senses as he came up the stairs and stopped down the hall—probably visiting a bathroom—before coming closer.

He entered the room quietly. His pajama bottoms and loose top looked like they had never been worn before. He scanned the room until he spotted my gray form half-hidden in the blankets. After closing the window curtain and turning off the lights, he climbed into bed.

He rolled over to face me and whispered, "Good night."

I leaned closer and gave him a small lick as a good night kiss. He smiled and placed a gentle kiss on my forehead. I curled into a ball and snuggled into the soft blankets. To my surprise, Will's scent and presence allowed me to drift to sleep almost instantly.

# Chapter 7

It took me a while to wake up. As my mind roused from its slumber, I realized I could barely move my legs. I opened my eyes and blinked in the dim morning light peeking around the curtains.

Sometime during the night, Will must have migrated to the middle of the bed. My mate's arms were protectively caged around me, and his chest rose and fell against my back as he slept. Turning my head, I confirmed he had drawn his legs up to form another wall. Even with my small form, I probably wouldn't be able to wiggle out without waking him.

Since there was nothing pressing to do, I relaxed and listened to the soothing sound of his breathing. I unshielded my senses; other than a few people in the kitchens, and one or two elsewhere, the rest of the mindsparks were dim with sleep. A few sparks were approaching the packhouse, likely patrols whose shifts were over.

After a while, I wanted to stretch and decided to see if I could get out of Will's hold. I eased forward, moving slowly to avoid waking him. I barely even took one tiny step before he grunted in his sleep and pulled me closer to his chest. He nuzzled his face into the back of my neck, and his warm breath permeated my fur.

Well, that attempt backfired on me. His protective hold was somewhat similar to when Phil had pinned me. There was even less room to move now, and there was no chance of me shifting. I turned my head and examined my predicament as much as I could. Yeah, there was no way I was getting out of his hold on my own.

His head was much closer now, and that tantalizing hair of his immediately caught my attention. It was finally within reach, and no one was watching. I knew the mate bond was to blame, but I couldn't help myself.

Stretching up, I nuzzled my nose into his hair. It was soft and smelled exactly like I was in the middle of a forest. I loved that scent. For some bizarre reason, unknown to even me, I started to gently lick his hair as if grooming him.

Will stirred in his sleep. "Hmmm?"

He lifted his head to look at me groggily, and I started snickering at his appearance. All of the hair on this side of his head was soaked and sticking up at odd angles. He blinked sleepily at me before realizing he was on the wrong side of the bed. He pulled back, and I instantly missed his warmth.

He sat up and ran a hand through his wet hair. "What the-? What happened?" He gazed at me in sleepy confusion.

I shifted back and covered my mouth as I started laughing at his expression and out-of-control hair. "I honestly have no idea why I did that. Although in my defense, my options were rather limited."

He shook his head to clear it. "I seem to recall doing something similar to you yesterday, so I know the feeling."

I sat up and fiddled with the tattered hem of my t-shirt. "So, what are our plans for today?"

"I talked to the Alpha last night, and he's looking forward to meeting you. He should be back this afternoon, and if you're ready for it, the acceptance ceremony can be done this evening."

"That'll work. There's no sense in putting it off, and once I'm part of the pack, I'll be able to mindlink you."

He smiled at the thought of that. "In the meantime, if you feel like joining me, I usually go for a short run in the morning before grabbing some breakfast. I have to help with training today, so that will leave you with some free time."

"I'd love to go for a run. I can't run for very long, so I can come back and help the cooks with breakfast. That will give you time to have a good run without me slowing you down."

"That'll work out perfectly."

I was looking forward to our run. There was a certain freedom when running with Will or any other werewolf. I didn't have to be hyper vigilant or worry so much about predators. To run with another wolf was like a breath of fresh air after so many years of cautious, slow travel.

My thoughts were interrupted as my senses stirred. Even though he was at the very edge of my range, there was no mistaking the Alpha's powerful aura approaching the packhouse.

"It looks like the Alpha got back early," I told Will.

He paused mid-stretch with a blank look. "How do you know that?"

His comment made me realize I hadn't told him about my abilities yet. "When I was part of Doug's pack, I was designated as an Omega. Even though I hadn't been born with the rank, it let the Omega's senses slowly form over time. The designation disappeared the instant Doug passed away, but the senses remained."

Being designated as an Omega was rare since people didn't need the rank to help with the tasks the Omega's normally did. Being a runt was more of an obstacle for me, so I had agreed to the designation in order to join Doug's pack.

Not only did it take an Alpha command for the designation, but it took almost a year for the Omega abilities to form, and as handy as those abilities were, most wolves couldn't be bothered. To make it even more unappealing, a designated

Omega didn't get all of the abilities a true-born Omega had, and there was no way to tell how strong each skill would be.

Will blinked a few times with the new information. "I wasn't aware you had been designated as an Omega. Can you tell if he's in a good mood? If so, I can introduce you to him before he gets distracted with the pile of paperwork on his desk."

I checked my senses before confirming, "Yes, he's in a good mood. Hopefully, he'll have finished kissing Emily by the time we get down there."

Will chuckled and grabbed a set of clean clothes out of his dresser. He headed to one washroom while I headed to another.

After quickly making myself presentable, or at least as presentable as my good t-shirt and newish jeans could make me, I waited at the top of the stairs for Will. Just as I was starting to wonder what was taking him so long, he came out of the bathroom. I smirked when I noticed he had been forced to wash his hair to get it back into some sort of order.

As we descended the stairs, I murmured, "They moved into the small living room off the main hall. They've also stopped kissing."

Will nodded and altered his route. As I halfway expected, the Alpha was a large, heavily-built man, who happened to be gazing at Emily with adoration. When Will knocked softly on the door frame, the two sitting on the couch looked up.

Emily smiled. "Will, Jade, I wasn't expecting you quite so early. Roland, this is Jade. Jade, this is Roland."

I bowed my head. "Pleasure to meet you, Alpha."

He nodded and examined me without any hostility in his gaze. "Congratulations on finding your mate. I'm quite happy Will found his other half. Were you looking to do the acceptance ceremony tonight?"

"Yes, please."

"I can arrange that, but I have to ask the standard questions first."

I nodded and watched the couple without truly focusing my gaze on them. Since I wasn't part of his pack, staring directly at an Alpha or his mate could be taken as a challenge or an insult.

Alpha Roland stood up and walked over. I felt the shift in Will's mood as the powerful male approached, even though his expression or stance didn't change. I squeezed his hand in reassurance, and he exhaled slowly. The Alpha's eyes caught the small motion and Will's reaction.

The Alpha smiled at him. "It looks like the mate bond is hitting you just as hard as it did me. Honest, Will. I mean her no harm."

Will sighed heavily. "In theory, I know that. But in reality, rationality simply doesn't enter the equation when it comes to the mate bond."

Emily laughed merrily from the couch. "I'm sure you re-member how Roland acted when he first met me. You're han-dling it much better than he did. It's no secret that high-rank-ing wolves get hit harder by the mate bond. Your Enforcer rank evolved to defend others, and with your protective tendencies already being heightened, it'll be just as intense for you as it would for a Beta or an Alpha. I'm quite surprised you didn't growl at Roland when he approached like that."

Will winced. "You have no idea how close I came to it. The only thing that stopped me was the possibility of it scaring Jade."

With a smirk, the Alpha told Will, "If you plan on growling at me, at least do it in private like this so I don't have to uphold my status. You can chase me around the training field later if you want to get revenge."

I relaxed slightly as I picked up their close friendship. Most Alphas were as close to their Enforcers as they were to their

Betas. They trusted their Beta at their side and relied on their Enforcers to look after the pack while they were away. Such trust and friendship allowed for a fair bit of leeway in the formality department.

Roland's eyes focused on me as I felt his Alpha abilities strengthen. "These are just the standard questions I ask any rogues when they plan on joining. How long have you been a rogue?"

"Since my pack was wiped out by ferals when I was twelve, although I did join a pack for about a year some time ago."

"Why did you leave that pack?"

"It was the Black River pack, and I left when Doug passed away."

The Alpha made a face, as did his mate. With no children of their own, that pack's story hit far too close to home for this group.

"Have you ever attacked or killed anyone?"

I shook my head. "No."

Will looked amused at the question, probably recalling our wrestling match.

"Do you have any enemies who might be searching for you?"

I once more shook my head. "Not to the best of my knowledge."

He tilted his head as confusion flickered across his expression. He intently stared at me, his eyes occasionally unfocusing. After a few moments, he asked, "How are you doing that?"

I blinked in confusion. "Doing what?"

I had no clue what he was talking about. I could sense confusion from Will and Emily as well, which meant they didn't know what he was referring to either.

He took a step closer and peered into my eyes, ignoring Will's low growl. "Every time I try to focus on you closely, it's like my attention just slides off. As an Alpha, I normally have no problems concentrating on someone with single-minded intensity, and yet, those skills don't seem to be working on you."

He may have been confused, but now that he put it like that, I immediately knew what he was talking about. It was an Omega skill—one I had been unconsciously using—that amplified a passive stance. It was normally used to help an Omega avoid attention, appear like less of a threat, or get out of a room undetected by upset individuals.

With this ability, my stance was so passive that no trace of threat could be seen or sensed, and most wolves would completely ignore me like this. Apparently, it also prevented an Alpha from truly focusing his attention on me during an interrogation. It was an ability only found among the Omegas, but I no longer had the Omega rank, so he wouldn't have been able to sense it and connect the dots.

My cheeks heated up, and I stopped using the ability. "Ah, I think I know. Sorry about that. I had been designated as an Omega during my stay with the Black River pack. I didn't realize the passive stance ability would have such an effect. In truth, I didn't even realize I was using it until you mentioned it."

He examined me and relaxed now that his own ability to focus was working. "Interesting. Do you have most of the Omega abilities?"

I shook my head. "No, I just have the common ones like emotion sensing, passive stance, and checking if something is safe to eat."

Joining the conversation, Emily asked, "How good are you at using the various abilities?"

I shrugged. "My ability to sense individuals and the moods of those nearby is pretty strong. The passive stance ability is about average. My truth sensing is weak but reliable if they're close to me. When it comes to differentiating edible plants apart from poisonous ones, my ability is about average, but I've had so much practice I've really honed that skill. My ability to calm down people is nearly non-existent. It might as well not even exist in human form and is only somewhat effective in wolf form if they have no aversion to runts. I don't have any of the other abilities."

Will looked intrigued as I rattled off the long list, and I was sure he'd have questions later.

The Alpha nodded, likely committing my skills to memory, just like he would with the strengths and weaknesses of all his pack members. "In that case, I don't have any concerns. Welcome to Nightwind Pack. I'll see you after dinner for the Acceptance Ceremony."

I bowed my head slightly. "Thank you."

Roland went back to sit by Emily, so Will and I took our leave and headed out for our morning run.

# Chapter 8

I chuckled as I darted under a huge rose bush and kept running. Due to his sheer size, Will had to go around the thorny shrub. I eagerly scanned the area for other large bushes, finding it amusing to pick a path that required him to detour the farthest. At least he was getting more exercise than if he had been just running beside me.

Our lazy run had turned into a game of "catch me if you can," and Will hadn't been able to get close to me for almost five solid minutes even though I hadn't stopped to hide. It was a pretty impressive feat considering I had never been in this part of the forest before.

He could see me, but he couldn't get to me, and this had the mate bond goading him into greater speed and more determined attempts to reach me. Since Will was still enjoying himself, I kept going. I wasn't sure how he'd react if someone came between us, so I relied on my senses to make sure no other pack members were anywhere near our trajectory.

There hadn't been much time for us to get used to the mate bond and how it made us react, so it was best to err on the side of caution. His control had been quite good so far, but it wasn't something you wanted to test with unsuspecting pack members.

With a wolf grin at Will, whom I could barely see through the leaves, I darted in a different direction, aiming for another large bramble bush. Such sprawling plants were getting fewer and fewer as we went along, and they were the real reason Will hadn't caught me yet.

A faint huff of frustration came from Will as the plants forced him to keep his distance. I kept changing direction as I zigzagged between the sheltering plants. If nothing else, it kept him on his toes as he tried to anticipate which way I'd go next.

I was running out of options though. There were only a few trees around here; nothing he wouldn't be able to squeeze between or go around easily. The various bushes and shrubs were rapidly becoming sparse, and the spaces between them were getting larger.

I raced across the distance between two such plants. Will charged forward, but I managed to dart under one just before he got to me. Without slowing my headlong run, I pinpointed the next shrub, which was even farther away.

Will put on a burst of speed I didn't know was even possible and blasted in my direction. I tried to weave to the side, but he used his forelegs to block my escape as he skidded across the leaf litter. He trapped me between his forepaws and dropped down, gently pinning me under his neck.

I wiggled a bit before simply lying there and panting while my tail attempted to wag. That run had been fun, and I had definitely gotten my exercise. Then I noticed Will was breathing somewhat heavily as well. That was odd since such a run shouldn't have tired any normal wolf, let alone an Enforcer. I tried to squirm out, to no avail. He was simply too big, and he wasn't giving me any chance to sneak away.

Sparks rolled across my skin wherever his fur touched mine, but I stilled when I picked up an undercurrent of powerful emotions in Will's mind. I didn't like prying, so I had only been keeping tabs on his surface emotions.

I carefully extended my senses into Will's mind and was stunned by the swirl of emotions that were starting to overpower him. How he had been enjoying himself mere seconds ago was beyond my comprehension. Nor did I know how he had suppressed it so well or even how he was still mostly in control.

Our little game had the mate bond in severe overdrive, and it had somehow tapped into his Enforcer rank's desire to protect. At the moment, his control hung on by a thread—and that thread was because he was in direct contact with me.

My brush with his mind had me pulling my senses back, slightly overwhelmed by the powerful emotions generated by the mate bond. It was a good thing it had only been plants keeping him from me. He would have destroyed anything else. The waves of protectiveness that rolled off him were practically visible at this point.

I could feel the mate bond's drive for him to mark and claim me as his. He was fighting it, but the mate bond was solely focused on the fact that we had been separated and my shoulder didn't have his mark. A mark warned off other males—a declaration that I was his—and he was having some control issues without its presence.

I remained motionless, hoping the mate bond would ease up now that we were together. I was fervently glad no one was near us. At this moment, he would probably snap if anyone or a larger predator approached. I decided my best course of action was to wait until he regained control.

Several minutes later, I nudged Will with my muzzle and whined lightly. He hadn't moved yet, and I was still pinned. The protectiveness in his mind began to swirl with concern.

With no warning, he suddenly shifted into human form and crushed me against his chest in a bear hug as he sat in the grass. I nuzzled the side of his neck in reassurance since I still felt him fighting for control. Thankfully, the mate bond was easing up, and he was rapidly gaining the upper hand.

His voice was gruff with strain. "Give me a moment. I almost lost control back there."

I rubbed my head along the front of his shirt as I tried to comfort him. Eventually, he sighed and loosened his grip, letting me slide into his lap.

I looked up at him in concern, but his eyes were closed as he continued to focus on settling the mate bond. It had been bad enough when I simply brushed against his emotions, but he had experienced their true force firsthand.

A few moments later, he opened his eyes. "Sorry. I had no idea the mate bond would have that effect on me."

I tilted my head before shifting as well, which left me sitting sideways in his lap. In an unsuccessful attempt to hug him, I wrapped an arm as far as it would go behind his back.

"It's partially my fault. I knew the mate bond was starting to act up, but I kept going since I could sense your happiness. The next time the mate bond starts to give you problems, it might be best to let me know so I can stop doing whatever is setting it off."

I wasn't entirely sure if he heard my words since he simply stared at me, momentarily stunned by the fact that I was now sitting on his lap. He blinked and promptly wrapped both arms around me. His face dropped into the crook of my neck as he inhaled my scent, and his muscles almost immediately relaxed.

His voice was muffled, and the heat from his breath sent goosebumps down my back. "I'll have to remember that, but I hope it never gets to that point again. At first, it wasn't too bad, but then it just skyrocketed without warning."

Apparently he *had* heard me. But it was now my turn to struggle for control since his breath, scent, and voice all made dirty thoughts appear in my head against my will. That conniving mate bond was starting to try different tactics . . . I could sense Will was almost back to normal now. It was just me who had to get my head on straight.

He chuckled and lifted his head. "I think we better get going. If your arousal gets any more noticeable, we won't be leaving this forest for quite some time."

I flushed beet red before shifting into my wolf shape and hopping off his lap. I was thankful it wasn't possible to tell if a wolf was blushing, although my body language would still betray my embarrassment.

He grinned before shifting as well. He padded forward to give my ear a few licks that sent more goosebumps down my back. I reached up and gave him a small lick under his chin, then turned and trotted down the trail before the mate bond found another opportunity to mess with my head and body.

I kept to the main trail, and Will walked beside me. I could sense his amusement at my reaction as well as a few firmly suppressed flickers of desire. Thankfully, his flickers were disappearing as my arousal faded.

We set a lazy pace on our way back since we both wanted the side effects of our run to completely fade. If Will could pick up any trace of arousal on me, I knew he wouldn't let me step foot in the town until it faded.

We shifted at the edge of the town and walked toward the packhouse while holding hands. Other people trickled in the same direction. Those who lived in their own homes often made their own breakfast, so it was just those who lived in the packhouse who were looking for food.

The dining room had numerous large tables and chairs spread out like an oversized cafeteria. We were too late to help cook, so we grabbed a plate and picked food from the buffet tables before heading over to a table.

Occasionally, I sensed people looking at me in curiosity while I ate. Samantha and John joined us, sitting on the other side of the table. I watched in amusement as Will was somehow managing to eat everything he had loaded onto his plate. I simply couldn't figure out where he was putting it all.

I turned my head in faint alarm when I felt a flare of powerful emotions from someone focusing intently on me. Shock, excitement, and ambition were prominent in her mind as she began crossing the room.

Will noticed my sudden distraction and glanced across the room with narrowed eyes. When he saw her, he groaned and dropped his face into his hand as she swiftly made her way toward us. Her low heels clicked against the tile floor as her skirt gently swirled with the speed of her walk. Her eyes were locked onto me.

I quickly dug a bit deeper into her mind to see what I was dealing with, and my senses informed me that she was Will's sister. From the mix of excitement and disbelief radiating from her, I suspected Will hadn't told his family about finding his mate, and she wasn't impressed about it.

She came to a stop beside me and took a deep breath. Her excitement flared as she confirmed her suspicions. She cast an accusing frown upon her brother. "How could you have found your mate and not told us?"

Will raised an eyebrow, not at all intimidated by his sister. "Mom, Dad, and Brad all know. If you hadn't blocked off your mindlink yesterday, you'd have also known."

She dropped down on the seat beside me with an exasperated sigh before turning to me. "Brothers. They withhold critical, need-to-know information at the worst possible time. Please tell me that you didn't have to put up with brothers when you were growing up."

I felt Will stiffen beside me, but I smiled at her. "No, I never had any siblings."

She sighed in relief. "You are so lucky." I could feel the tension rolling off of Will, Samantha, and John at her unwitting words. They had carefully avoided any topic that might touch on my past in case it contained sad or painful memories.

Will's sister somehow remained oblivious to the other three at the table as she replied, "I'm Tiffany, Will's sister. What's your name? When did you get here?"

"I'm Jade. I arrived yesterday, early afternoon I think."

She mumbled something incoherent before looking back at me. "Which pack did you come from?"

Will's low growl made all of us glance at him as he eyed up his sister, who blinked at him in shock.

I rubbed Will's arm, trying to get him to relax, while replying, "I was a rogue living not far from the Delby pack. Sorry about Will's reaction. The mate bond took us for a ride earlier today, and our control isn't exactly at its best."

Tiffany blinked, shock and remorse echoing through her mind, now realizing just how inappropriate her earlier comments had been.

Samantha broke the silence before it became uncomfortable. "I was wondering how the mate bond would affect Will. From what I heard, Enforcers get hit by the mate bond almost as hard as an Alpha since their protective tendencies are amplified."

John shook his head. "From what you two said at supper, I didn't think you were having any issues. I assume the mate bond is strengthening?"

Will made a wry face. "I'll say. If it doesn't slow down, I'll be behaving worse than you did when you first met Samantha."

Tiffany shuddered and shook her head as she swiftly said, "No, let's not even contemplate that. That was a terrible two weeks."

While John grumbled something about how he hadn't been that bad, Tiffany refocused on me and said, "Those clothes look like they have seen some rough terrain. We'll have to expand your wardrobe. Will is on the training roster today, so I can take you shopping."

I blinked at the swift topic change. I had only traded for essentials with nearby packs, so I'd never actually gone shopping before. After a quick mental tally of the money in my backpack, I nodded. "I wouldn't mind another outfit, and I'm almost out of toothpaste."

Tiffany chuckled and rubbed her hands together gleefully. I hoped her tastes in clothing weren't too expensive. I only had so much money, and I hadn't been here long enough to look for a job.

Will pulled out his wallet and handed a shiny plastic card to Tiffany. "Here, make sure you don't let her pay for anything. There is a limit of five hundred dollars on it, so don't go too crazy. That card is for her purchases, although I will let you spend a hundred of it as long as you keep any guys at a distance."

Tiffany quickly pocketed the card and grinned at me. "I'm liking this already. He's never given me money for shopping before."

I shook my head. "That isn't necessary. I have my own money."

Tiffany quickly overruled me. "Then save it for a rainy day, and don't look a gift horse in the mouth. Honest, you'll agree with me one day." She grinned at Will. "For your generosity, I will make sure she buys at least one pair of lacy undergarments."

Will's eyes darkened as he slowly inhaled. He looked fairly calm, but I felt him quickly suppress an intense emotion before it got strong enough for me to identify. I didn't extend my senses to determine what was lurking beneath the surface either.

I looked down at my plate to try and hide my blush. I had never owned any sort of fancy clothing since I became a rogue.

Other than undergarments, I hadn't ever had any *new* clothing. It had all been second-hand or used. And I had *certainly* never owned lacy undergarments.

John chuckled at Will's reaction and said, "That was probably the last image he needed in his head."

Tiffany grinned triumphantly. "This is my way of helping everyone. Will gets to exercise his imagination, you might get an easier training session if he is distracted, and Jade gets new clothing."

She was interrupted as Mark—who looked rather flustered and excited—slid into the last empty spot at the table. His eyes were bright, and he was radiating quite a few strong positive emotions.

"You were right!" he told me. "It was her! Thank you!"

The others looked baffled, although I quickly connected his emotional state and his words and said, "Congratulations!"

Tiffany gave him a blank look. "Uh, what rogue dragged you backward through the bramble bush, and what are you talking about?"

Mark turned to her, still excited beyond belief. "When I met Jade yesterday, she asked if the woman at the library was my mate. Anyway, on my way here I decided to pop into the library since the name Jade gave me didn't ring a bell. And it was her! Cassie is my mate!"

Jaws around the table dropped before they all started congratulating him. He grabbed a plate of food and joined us. John teased him about not catching her scent earlier, but Mark had recently returned from visiting his cousins in a different pack and usually detoured around the town.

Once we finished eating, Tiffany stood up and nudged me with her toe. "Come on, let's go shopping before too many people see the new stuff the shopkeepers might have put on the shelves this morning."

Samantha and John grinned at each other in a fashion that made me ask, "How scared should I be when it comes to shopping with her?"

John looked at me solemnly. "Be afraid. Be very afraid . . ."

Tiffany rolled her eyes and dismissed him. Will gave me a one-armed hug, and I rested my head against the side of his chest as I murmured, "Your sister doesn't have any grudges against you, right?"

Quiet laughter rumbled through his chest as he replied, "Not that I know of."

Tiffany grabbed my hand and dragged me to my feet as she grumbled, "Okay, enough of that lovey-dovey stuff. We're going shopping."

As his sister pulled me out of the room by, I could feel Will's reluctance to let me leave without him. The feeling was mutual.

# Chapter 9

Tiffany held up a skimpy black piece of fabric for me to see. I looked at her in disbelief. "For stores that are supposedly family rated, how do you keep finding those things?"

She grinned at me. "This is exactly why they are called family stores. These lovely little objects help people increase the size of their family."

I snorted faintly and said, "I'll never be able to look at half of these stores the same way again . . ."

"If you want fancier styles, I know several places with a special display in the back."

I shuddered lightly. I was beginning to think her mind traveled into the gutter more than mine did—and she hadn't even found her mate yet!

Faced with my silence, Tiffany shrugged and said, "Well, I forced you to get one set, so I won't bother again. Let's see what else we can find."

So far, I had accumulated three small bags, one of which was tucked into the bottom of a larger one. It held the silvery pieces of clothing I hadn't objected to the instant I saw them. I had been three seconds too slow, and Tiffany had ignored my protests as she deposited the lingerie in her basket.

I was also the happy owner of two pairs of jeans and a light jacket, which Tiffany had whisked out of my hands and used Will's credit card to pay for. His sister was taking her job seriously, and I didn't have a chance of sneaking to the till to pay for them.

I glanced at the contents in the half-hidden basket that Tiffany had spotted with ease. I shook my head as I muttered, "The less material they have, the higher the price tag. That is just unbelievable."

Tiffany laughed as she kept leafing through the racks of clothing. She was the kind of girl who loved shopping and was somewhat put out by my lack of interest. I managed to get Tiffany out of this store without either of us buying anything.

We walked down the street, and I paused to look at a seafoam green shirt in the window. Tiffany was quick to grab my hand and drag me into the store as she muttered, "Finally, a proper reaction while shopping . . ."

I laughed since her low grumbling was at complete odds with the excitement radiating off her as I finally took interest in a piece of clothing. A quick walk around the store revealed the shopkeeper had several other shirts and pants that interested me. I picked out another shirt, but made a mental note to come back with my own money another day.

We left the store and kept walking since Tiffany refused to give in until I had at least three new shirts. When she paused to look in a window with dresses on display, I gazed around in boredom, having no interest in dresses.

My attention was drawn to two men walking down the street. I pulled up my passive stance ability and hoped they would keep going. To avoid looking at them, I turned to the window and pretended to be interested in the dresses. The men's foresty scent drifted over as they got closer. They clearly didn't belong to this pack.

My attempts to avoid notice were in vain since they stopped behind us.

The taller guy spoke first. "I bet that dress would look good on you."

Tiffany looked over her shoulder and gave a low growl when she realized the comment had been directed at me. Her mindset shifted to unflattering emotions as she bristled.

The other guy grinned at her reaction. "No need to get jealous. I can buy you a dress as well." Their flirting comments were halfway idle, hoping for interest without being too pushy.

Tiffany narrowed her eyes, unimpressed with the offer. "I advise you two to continue on your way before I tell my brother that you're flirting with his mate."

The first guy looked faintly amused. "Simply talking to two pretty ladies isn't a crime."

Tiffany smirked, which appeared to throw the men off balance. "Oh? You aren't worried about irritating an Enforcer?"

Their eyes widened as their posture changed from light flirting to caution, mirrored by the shift in their mood. They had zero interest in tangling with an Enforcer, and at this point, they simply wanted to put distance between us.

"Uh, sorry about the misunderstanding. We'll be on our way. Have a good day."

They beat a swift retreat, and I asked Tiffany, "Can we please delay telling Will about this until later? Preferably when there isn't anything breakable nearby?"

"He's training some advanced fighters now, and those rogues left, so I guess it can wait. I told the other Enforcer, Evan, and he is going to keep a subtle eye on our guests. Supposedly, they only came here to buy supplies, and they'll be on their way in an hour."

Sighing in relief, I replied, "That's good to know."

"You make it sound like he'd go on a rampage or something."

I shrugged as I scuffed my worn sneaker against the packed dirt. "He almost lost control this morning, and his antagonist was only a bramble bush."

Tiffany burst out laughing. "How did a bramble bush irritate him?"

"I ran under it while he was trying to catch me, and he couldn't reach me. By the time we realized what was happening, the mate bond had gone way overboard, and he almost lost control."

Tiffany nodded slowly as her expression became serious. "I can imagine that. If someone can't get to their mate, it can push them right to the edge. It's a well-known fact with Alphas, and it probably applies just as much to a Beta or Enforcer." She tilted her head in sudden confusion before asking, "How did you get under a bramble bush without getting all scratched up?"

I shifted my weight uneasily. "I'm a runt, so I simply ran underneath it. I barely even needed to duck."

She blinked in shock, then grinned. "You're just full of surprises, aren't you? You might be just the thing Will needed to keep him on his toes."

I was relieved she wasn't bothered by my diminutive wolf form and returned her grin. "Oh, you should have seen our wrestling match in wolf form yesterday."

"That would have been hilarious. I'd love to see you shift one day."

"Remind me when we get back to the packhouse."

"Sure."

An hour later, Tiffany finally said. "You haven't looked at anything in the last two stores, so I'm getting the feeling that you're done shopping."

"I have enough for now. Besides, if I counted correctly, you spent the money Will allotted for your personal shopping."

She sighed dejectedly as she gave in. "I really hope he'll let me take you shopping like this again in a few weeks."

I laughed and shook my head at the exuberant shopper. We headed back to the packhouse. Once we put our clothing in our rooms, Tiffany led me out of the packhouse and into the forest. Her slender frame shone with excitement in my senses, and I followed in curiosity.

"Where are we going?" I finally asked as she ducked onto seldom-used trails.

"We're going to spy on the training area."

I furrowed my eyebrows. "Spy? Is it off limits?"

"No, but it'll let you see Will while he's training others."

That definitely caught my interest. "That'll be interesting. Although it won't take long before they pick up our scents."

"Drat. I forgot about that. We'll just have to be sneaky and stay back from the edge. Do you have any tricks to make us less noticeable?"

A smile touched my lips. "Let's make a quick detour."

It didn't take long for me to find a variety of leaves and grasses.

"What are you doing with those?" Tiffany asked, staring at the wad of greenery in my hands.

"Cloaking our scent so they won't smell us as easily."

Tiffany continued to regard the leaves dubiously. "Are you sure this is going to work?"

"It worked for me for nine years. It won't hide my scent from Will, but from what I've seen, no one else is observant enough to pick up a rogue's scent if it's masked this way." I handed her a fistful of leaves.

"I can't believe I'm doing this..." she muttered as she took the leaves and copied me as I rubbed them across my clothing and skin.

After a quick application, I took a deep breath. My normally faint scent had disappeared under the odor of the plants. Will's scent had slowly been wearing off throughout the day, so it was easily masked. Only the faintest scent of Tiffany's perfume lingered in the air.

The balance of plants wasn't quite right, but it wasn't as if we were sneaking around no man's land. We were just going to watch some fighters while they were training, and I was sure our scents were covered sufficiently for that.

"This should be good enough," I told her.

She promptly dropped the leaves and grabbed my hand, pulling me through the forest. "Come on! I'll show you the best spot to spy on them."

Before long, we sat on two large tree branches to watch the proceedings in the clearing. It had taken some reasoning with Tiffany to finally persuade her to climb into the tree.

It was interesting to watch the men and women sparring, although my eyes kept drifting to one particular shirtless figure who was supervising them.

"If you stare much harder, you're going to start drooling . . ."

My gaze snapped over to Tiffany, who was watching me with amusement. I stuck my tongue out at her and retorted, "Just wait until you get your own mate."

"Oh, I'll probably drive that poor guy completely crazy. I have an entire drawer of lacy clothing just waiting for him to show up."

I halfway choked. "Way too much information!"

She pulled a piece of bark out from under her rump and flicked it to the ground. "Can we get out of these trees? We can see them just as well from the ground."

"Probably, although we'll be easier to spot. It's up to you. I doubt they'd object if we watched from the sidelines, and we'd have a much better view from the benches."

"Their actions are more natural this way," she said. "They act a bit differently when there are people watching or if they know their mate is around. They have a tendency to show off. This lets you see how Will normally trains people. I just wasn't aware I was going to get impromptu lessons in skulking around like a rogue while helping you spy on him. I still can't pick up either of our scents. Would another rogue be able to scent us?"

I nodded absently as I watched Will. "If they were experienced, quite easily. Your perfume isn't quite covered, and the ferns in my scent are too strong. Both of our scents would stand out noticeably for a rogue, but if the fighters down there have noses like Bruce and his friends, they won't notice us."

Tiffany readjusted her grip on the branch, still not at ease on her perch. "I noticed you liked the scent of those ferns. Attempting to balance out scents sounds way too complicated, so I guess the life of a rogue is out for me. By the way, what is your plan for explaining our scent when we get back?"

I grinned at her. "Isn't it obvious? We went for a run and had a game of tag. You tried to pull me out from under several shrubs, and I ran through a lot of long grass."

"Hmmm… That excuse might work."

My gaze turned back to the field. Will was a natural at what he was doing. This was a side of him I hadn't seen yet. Occasionally, he just watched the others and called out advice, although he spent a fair bit of time wrestling in both human and wolf form while helping others learn various fighting styles. Watching Will from the trees could become a new hobby for me.

Eventually, Tiffany grew bored, and we headed back to the packhouse. She led me into the kitchen, and I gazed around eagerly as I asked, "Can you possibly show me how this stove works? I haven't been able to bake since I became a rogue, and that's one of the things I missed the most."

She helped me locate ingredients as I measured and mixed everything together. Before long, we sat on tall stools by the counter while the cakes were baking. I turned to the doorway with a grin as Will entered. He promptly came over for a hug and buried his face in my neck. He lifted his head to look at me with curious eyes.

"Why do you smell like the forest again?"

Behind him, John exclaimed, "Second question, why does Tiffany have leaves in her hair?"

I glanced over to see John and Samantha looking shocked as the normally impeccably-groomed Tiffany ran a hand through her hair, dislodging a couple of leaves and a piece of fern.

Tiffany regarded them in mock horror and turned to stare at me. "You didn't tell me I had stuff in my hair!"

I suspected what she really wanted to ask was how and when I had managed to tuck those leaves into her hair. I shrugged innocently, replying, "After our run in the forest, I'm amazed you only have a few leaves in your hair after running through some of those bushes."

Will relaxed when he noticed his sister's lack of scent and easily accepted our story. I was amazed at how easily he accepted the explanation since it made no sense to me. Their patrols and sentries didn't come home smelling like the forest. To completely cover one's scent was a deliberate action.

The oven dinged, and Tiffany quickly checked the cakes and pulled out the ones that were done, leaving several in for a while longer.

John scratched his head, looking utterly lost as he asked, "Since when do you cook?"

"I don't," Tiffany said with a shrug. "Jade did most of it. I'm just here to work the oven and do simple tasks."

John greedily eyed up the cakes Tiffany was covering to properly cool. "What kind of cake is that?"

Tiffany raised an eyebrow at me, and I replied, "I'm not sure of the name, but it has chocolate, peanut butter, and caramel in it."

Intrigued, Will said, "I'll definitely have to try a piece at supper. How many did you make?"

I glanced at Tiffany as she did a quick mental count.

"We still have five ovens going," she said, "so I think we filled twenty pans."

"Not everyone is a fan of cake," John said, "and there will be other desserts as well, so there should be enough for those who want to try it."

"This is good," Will said as he tasted the cake.

"Thanks," I murmured, secretly pleased it had turned out so well after my first baking attempt in several years. Nor was it just flattery on his part since John was already grabbing a second slice.

Once they finished their dessert, we headed out to the backyard where several people were getting prepared for my acceptance ceremony. Sam and John went to chat with Tiffany, giving Will and me some quiet before the event.

The Beta walked onto a small raised platform, and as he put a razor-sharp knife on a small table, I noticed Will's eyes were locked onto the weapon.

Nudging his arm, I said, "Please promise me that you won't turn my acceptance ceremony into a bloodbath. I've done this before, and truth be told, I've gotten worse scratches from rose bushes. Most Alphas barely break the skin, and I'm sure Roland won't do anything that would hurt me."

Will sighed as he looked away from the small blade. "I know. I've seen it done dozens of times, but the mate bond is convinced that any injury is a serious matter."

Perhaps distraction was in order... "Well, look at it this way. You let your close friend give me a tiny scratch and you'll be able to hear me through the pack link. Is that sufficient motivation?"

A hint of a grin touched his lips. "That just might get me through this."

We waited as a few more people showed up. Usually, only those close to the one being accepted attended the ceremony. John and Sam had followed us out here, Will's family was present, Bruce and his group put in an appearance, and even Mark and Cassie showed up. They formed a semi-circle around Will, and I hoped their supportive presence would help him remain calm.

Roland and Emily arrived last. Emily went to stand with the others, while the Alpha walked up the two stairs onto the platform. He took his place and motioned me to come over. I went up and stood in front of him.

He addressed me. "Do you swear that you mean no harm to this pack, and that you will support it as long as the pack follows what is right and true?"

I looked him in the eye. "I, Jade, previously rogue of the forest, swear to this."

He held up his hand and lightly cut his palm. I held out my hand, and he lightly cut it as well. It was so shallow the blood barely beaded to the surface. He clasped my hand in a handshake, and as the blood mixed, I felt the pack link merge with my mind.

Roland's voice echoed both in the mindlink and my ears as he spoke aloud, "Welcome to Nightwind Pack, Jade."

I responded likewise. "Thank you."

He nodded, and we left the platform. It was over. Short and simple, bound by blood into a new pack. I began walking toward Will, who was already coming over. I'd felt him struggle with his control when he watched Roland bring the knife down on my hand.

Using the mindlink to speak with him alone, I said, *"I'm fine. It barely even bled enough for the ceremony. It will heal in a few hours."*

His eyes widened when he heard my voice in his mind for the first time. A relieved grin appeared as he picked me up in a hug and spun us around in a circle. Once he set me down, he introduced me to his parents and brother.

"Why don't we go into one of the living rooms to visit?" Tiffany suggested.

Everyone was in favor of the idea, and we went inside. Will and I entered the room last.

With an impish smirk, Tiffany informed us, "There's only one chair left. I guess you two will have to share."

The others watched in amusement as Will's face went red. I knew he didn't want to push things too fast, but there was an easy solution for this situation.

I idly commented to Will, "You're overthinking things. There is a much easier way to get back at your sister."

He glanced at me in confusion. In response, I grinned at him and shifted. Those present were aware I was a runt, although they didn't seem to care. From the curious glances I was getting, I suspected none of them had seen a runt before.

It hadn't occurred to Tiffany or anyone else that I could sit on Will's lap in wolf form, mostly because they wouldn't have been able to do so. That was an odd thing about people; just because something was impossible for most, they never took the possibility into consideration.

I trotted over to the chair and jumped onto the foot stool. With a smug grin, I sat down and tilted my head cutely at Will. Tiffany's eyes were as wide as saucers—she definitely hadn't expected that.

Relief was clear in Will's stride as he walked over to sit in the big rocking chair. I jumped onto his lap and lay down as Will started stroking my fur.

Tiffany shook her head. "That is *not* fair."

I mindlinked her and everyone else in the room, *"Perfectly fair and completely logical."*

Will was now completely relaxed, which had been my primary goal. Shocking Tiffany had just been a great perk. We all talked and bantered well into the night.

We finally headed to our room, and like I had last night, I curled up on the pillow and waited for Will to return from the bathroom. The second he got into bed, he pulled my wolf form against his chest.

We swiftly fell asleep.

# Chapter 10

I woke up and realized I was in the same predicament I had been in yesterday morning. I simply enjoyed the warmth of all of the sparks for some time. Eventually, I sensed others in the house stirring and getting up.

I tried to free myself, but like last time, he simply pulled me tighter to his chest. It was time to pull out a new trick. Well, mindspeech wasn't exactly new, but this was my first morning trying to rouse Will with it.

*"Will. Will, wake up."*

He groaned in his sleep before burying his face into my fur.

My senses let me know he wasn't truly awake, so I tried again. *"Will. Come on, the cooks have already started the pancakes."*

Still no response.

*"Will..."*

Grasping at straws, I pulled up the memory of two people smiling at me. The warmth in the man's and woman's eyes was unmistakable. I pushed the image into his mind.

I didn't expect him to wake up in a split second with a snarl of fury. He rolled so his chest was above me with his arms braced to either side of my small wolf form. He quickly scanned the room as he hovered over me in a defensive position. If anyone else had been in here, I would have been blocked from their sight.

I blinked in shock when I noticed his eyes were nearly solid black. Without trying, I could pick up the fury that a mate possessed if someone else showed improper interest in their partner. A second later, he realized no one else was in the room, and he looked down at me, still mostly out of control and not awake enough to clear the fog from his mind.

"Who was he?" he demanded, his voice nearly a growl as he tried to discover which man would dare look at me with such love in his eyes. He didn't understand why I would share such a thing with him like this.

I blinked at him, still shocked at his reaction. "*Those were my parents.*"

I re-shared the image of them sitting on a bench as they watched me play in a patch of daisies as a young child. Realization dawned on his face, and his eyes faded back to brown. He must have been so focused on the male in the image that he hadn't noticed the lady or how they held hands.

"*Sorry,*" I said, "*I didn't think you'd react so strongly. Nothing else I said or did woke you up.*"

He sighed and rolled onto his side, finally relaxing now that the mate bond was easing up.

"In the future, please wait until I'm awake before doing things like that. It might also be best to warn me. I'm having a hard time predicting my own reactions, and it's got me off balance. I didn't even notice there were two people until you shared it again."

I nodded before shifting and giving him a hug. He returned it, and I pulled away as I sensed his emotions straying into areas we weren't quite ready for. Mine were also trying to escape my control. How on Earth did most couples last a couple of weeks before finalizing the bond? It was the morning of the third day, and we were both having control problems.

Will sighed and ran his hand through his hair. I eyed up his hair discreetly; I still had some weird obsession with it, and I hadn't taken my chance to play with it. I would have to rectify that tomorrow morning.

"I'll be training various fighters throughout the day," Will said. "Tiffany also has to work until lunch. I hate leaving you alone, but you can explore the packhouse or town if you want."

I tilted my head in consideration. "I have to do something for my keep. Would there be any problems with me going mushroom picking? I won't go far, and I have the mindlink if I encounter any difficulties."

Will frowned in concern. "Will you be okay by yourself?"

I nodded easily. "I did it for years in no man's land. If anyone crosses the trail of a cougar or bear, I'd appreciate a heads up so I can avoid that area."

A normal wolf had nothing to fear from them, and Will's eyes darkened as he realized the danger that such predators posed for me. His eyes lost their focus for a short time.

He raised his hand to gently brush the back of his fingers across my cheek. The familiar sparks followed in their wake as he said, "I've mindlinked everyone patrolling today, and they know to keep an eye out for large predators. Please promise me that you'll stay nearby and mindlink me regularly so I know you're okay."

His worry and concern were endearing, but I knew the mate bond would make him paranoid with little reason or incentive.

"That's easy enough to promise. It isn't easy for me to travel long distances, and it would take me several hours to reach the border on my own. Giving you updates will also let you keep track of me in case I get lost."

The words were more to reassure him than anything else. The chances of me getting lost or disoriented were non-existent. I had been a rogue for too long for that to happen. I *was* surprised he was letting me wander around the forest by myself with so little fuss or worry, but I could sense his conflicted emotions flickering along the edge of my awareness. He was having a hard time, but he was trying to let me do what I wanted.

I mindlinked Will for what had to be the twentieth time today. *"How is training going?"*

I felt his relief at hearing my mindvoice over the pack link. *"Same as last time. Where are you now?"*

*"Taking a break for a few minutes."*

I was sitting in a hole halfway up a tree. The sunlight shone between the leaves in golden rays and created a beautiful dappled effect on the forest floor. I took a mental image and shared it with Will.

His voice was slow with disbelief. *"Why are you so far above the ground?"*

*"I'm pretending to be an owl."* I leaned out of the hollow and looked straight down, sending that image to him as well. *"I'm actually not that far up. If no one else is around, I tend to find someplace off the ground when I want to rest. It's an old habit. Apart from a few deer, I think the biggest critter I've seen so far is a rabbit."*

I felt his shock roll through our private mindlink. *"I can see your paws in that image. You're in wolf form. How did you climb so high?"* His voice grew more worried, *"Tell me where you are, and I'll help you get down. A fall from that height could kill you."*

Most people couldn't shift in trees without falling to the ground, and Will wasn't aware this hazard didn't apply to a practiced runt. I decided to nip this paranoid mate moment in the bud and quickly left the hollow.

I carefully shifted on the branch before climbing down. *"Don't worry. I've done this more times than I can count. I'm small enough to shift in a tree without losing my balance. I climbed up in my human shape, and I can get down just as easily."*

Will's voice was still worried. *"Please just tell me where you are so I can come help you down. Please don't shift in the tree."*

I sent my amusement through the link at the same time I sent an image of my shoes standing in the leaf litter. *"Too late."*

I could feel his wordless frustration through the link. In response, I sent an image of him training people yesterday. I felt his shock and momentary distraction as he likely inspected the treeline around the arena.

He quickly realized it was a memory image and said, *"That isn't from today. I'm training different fighters."*

*"I know. That was from yesterday."*

*"When were you watching me?"*

*"About an hour before I stuck the leaves in Tiffany's hair."*

He was silent for a moment. *"How long were you watching?"*

My amusement was evident in the mindlink as I replied, *"Long enough for Tiffany to get bored and drag me away."*

I started walking through the forest as I searched for more mushrooms. I picked another one and put it in a shoulder sling bag Tiffany had lent me.

Our conversation ceased as we slowly dropped the mindlink.

I sat on a log on the small rise that overlooked the training area. My shoulder bag rested beside my feet, so full it couldn't possibly hold another mushroom. I was right on the edge of the forest, so I had a good view.

I hadn't seen the fighting training during my stay with the Black River pack, and I didn't remember any details from my original pack, so I wasn't sure if this was standard or not.

Even though I had never stepped foot in a pack's training arena, several rogues had been happy to give me self-defense lessons. One of my closest friends had been a fighting trainer, but he had a serious issue with the power Alphas could wield and had gone rogue.

I kept watching. Both Enforcers were present, and they used slightly different techniques. My eyes seemed to have a mind of their own and kept straying to Will.

It was late afternoon, and he had been training nonstop most of the day. A light sheen of sweat reflected the sunlight off of his skin. His muscles rippled with ease as he sparred with another fighter. It was mesmerizing. Simply mesmerizing.

I wasn't sure how long I sat there. Oddly enough, they never spotted me even though I wasn't hiding well. Will kept glancing at the forest to the east and seemed to be getting worked up. I took a deep breath but didn't pick up any odd scents. My senses didn't pick up anything in that part of the forest, although my range didn't reach far.

Will took a break and walked to the side of the field, once again gazing at the eastern forest. Even from here, I could pick up his growing tension and worry.

His voice entered my mind, his calm words at complete odds with what I could sense from my seat. *"How is it going?"*

I grinned when I realized he had no idea I had been within earshot the entire time. *"Pretty good,"* I said. *"I have a big haul of mushrooms. That bag Tiffany lent me is full."*

His voice was curious. *"Are you heading back?"*

*"No, I got distracted."*

My senses let me feel the worry rolling off of him as hints of jealousy arose, although his mindvoice only let a bit of worry and mild curiosity leak through as he asked, *"Distracted with what?"*

I sent amusement down the mindlink and shared a mental picture of him staring at the forest to the east. His shock echoed through my senses and our mindlink. He spun around to scan the treeline, finally spotting me. A relieved grin broke out on his face, and he started to sprint towards me.

Others looked over to see where he was going. When they spotted me, they smiled and went back to what they were doing. I stood up as Will approached. Moments later, I was engulfed in a hug.

"How long have you been here?"

"I'm not sure, although I saw the six fighters leave for their patrol shift."

He blinked slowly. "That was nearly two hours ago."

I shrugged with a shy grin. "Like I said, I got distracted and lost track of time."

Tilting his head in curiosity, he asked, "What was so distracting about it?" He obviously couldn't figure out how I had watched for so long.

I grinned and sent the image of him from half an hour ago, when he had stretched his hands high above his head. His muscles were quite visible despite the distance, and the sun glittered off his sweaty skin. I had carefully committed that one to memory.

I was startled to hear a faint rumble come from his chest. I glanced up at him to see his eyes darken. His emotions were a jumbled mix of pride, love, and possessiveness. My cheeks heated in a blush when I sensed his desire rising despite his attempts to suppress it.

I ducked my head and wrapped my arms around him in a hug, leaning my head against his chest so he couldn't see my rising blush. He wrapped his arms around me tightly and took a deep breath. I could sense his struggle to master his emotions and the mate bond's influences, as well as his frustration at having to fight for control.

After a few minutes, he sighed deeply. "I didn't think it would be this hard."

I rubbed my hand across his back. "It is hitting you harder than it's hitting me. Some of the things I'm occasionally sensing are pointing to your Enforcer role." He was silent in thought, so I let go and stepped back, saying, "I can sit on the sidelines if you want to practice more."

He glanced back at the training area, where the others continued their practice. I felt a faint shimmer of jealousy and protectiveness roll across his mind. He didn't want me near the men down there.

He ran his hand through his hair in renewed frustration. "Would you mind accompanying me as I visit someone? I'm hoping he might have some advice on how to control some of my reactions before I do something I regret."

"Sure. Let's drop these mushrooms off with the cooks first."

He picked up the bag for me and started walking.

I gave a small, uncomfortable cough to catch his attention, and he glanced back at me in confusion. In a wry voice, I clarified, "As much as I'm enjoying the view of you wandering around without a shirt, the jealous side of me doesn't want the younger cooks to stare."

When he smirked, I shrugged helplessly. There had never been a reason for me to be jealous before I met Will, and I was also trying to come to terms with these new emotions. He seemed to get a kick out of my reaction.

He nodded toward the main trail leaving the meadow. "If you want to head to that path, I'll meet you there."

I started walking as he jogged back to the training area to grab a shirt. Even though he had twice the distance to cover, he beat me to the wide path that led through the trees. We walked hand-in-hand as we took the mushrooms to the packhouse and left them with the cooks.

Will guided me to some cottages along the treeline and knocked on a door, which was opened by an older man. His gray hair and the faint ringing quality around his presence let me identify him as a retired Enforcer.

His lean frame might be a bit slower than the younger, active Enforcers, but his years of experience made him their equal. While he was technically retired, he would join a serious fight if it threatened the pack's safety. He just wouldn't do much of the smaller day-to-day stuff.

He smiled. "Will, it's good to see you again. What brings you here?" His eyes drifted over to me in curiosity. "And who's this?"

"It's good to see you as well, Tony. This is my mate, Jade. I'm here because I'm hoping you might have some advice or tricks. The mate bond is stronger than I expected, and I've had some control issues lately."

With an easy nod, Tony said, "Let's go to the reinforced training room and see what we can do."

Tony closed the door behind him and walked with us, asking, "When did you two meet?"

"Three days ago," Will replied.

Tony looked at me closely. "You're not marked, and the bond hasn't been completed, correct?"

I turned a bit red at the topic but nodded. Tony turned his attention to Will. "What kind of control problems have you encountered so far?"

Will made a face but honestly answered his mentor. "The very first day, I almost attacked Fred when he snarled at her. Since then, I almost lost control four times, and of those four, a couple occurred when no one else was even around."

I glanced at him in surprise. Four times? I knew about our game of keep away and the image of my father, but I couldn't think of any others. At the training arena, his control had been strained, but he hadn't come close to losing control. What other times had there been?

Tony gave him an odd look. "Have you been trying various techniques in case one is more effective?"

"I've tried them all. I've never had problems with my control before, and it has me severely off balance. I'm beginning to worry I might injure someone."

"Have you had any indication that you might harm Jade?"

Will shook his head violently. "No, the need to mark her is strong, but the control problems are occurring if I worry about her safety or if she's away from me."

We approached a brick building, and Tony opened the door and went inside. I followed behind Will. The padded walls and floors marked it as some sort of training room.

Tony led us to the side and down a staircase. I looked around the large basement room as Tony closed the heavy metal door behind us. The entire room was lined with some sort of metal plates, covered in numerous dents and scratches.

Will quietly told me, "This room is used for training Enforcers. The steel plates can usually handle any damage that may result from a slip in control when we are learning or trying something out."

I nodded in understanding.

Tony looked at me and said, "If you don't mind, I want to try a few things just to gauge Will's reaction."

"What do you want me to do?" I replied.

"We'll just try some basic stuff first. Can you please go to the far side of the room?"

I walked across the room and waited. Tony walked into the middle of the room between us while keeping an eye on Will.

"Will?" he quietly asked.

Will remained relaxed. "I would prefer her closer to me, but it's nothing that worries me."

Tony walked over to stand beside me. "Now?"

"I don't like it," Will said, with a frown. "Even just the thought of a guy standing beside her doesn't sit well with me. It's irritating, but controllable, although that's possibly because I know you so well. I'm not sure how I would handle it if it were a stranger." Will's emotions were starting to simmer as the mate bond made its presence known. It was barely noticeable, but I could sense it affecting his surface emotions.

Tony nodded and turned to me, holding out his hand for a handshake. I reached out, and even before I made contact, Will let out a low growl. Tony pulled his hand back and regarded Will with a raised eyebrow.

Will rubbed his forehead and apologized to the man who had trained him. "Sorry. It wasn't too bad when she was just standing there, but the instant she reached out to you, I couldn't help it."

Tony walked back to the middle of the room. "That reaction is actually quite typical for most higher-ranking males while their mate is unmarked. Which four times did you almost lose control?"

"I was chasing her and couldn't get through a bramble bush," Will said as he leaned against the far wall, relaxed now that Tony wasn't near me. "I couldn't get to her and that knowledge nearly made me lose it. This morning, she was trying to wake me up and showed me a memory of her parents. I flipped until I realized there were two people in the image and the man was her father."

Tony listened intently and remained silent.

With a sigh, Will continued, "I almost bolted today when I realized she was in a tree. I was scared she would fall, and the only reason I didn't run to her was because I didn't know where she was. Then, when she didn't contact me after several hours, I was ready to run through the forest searching for her scent. Thankfully, she responded when I mindlinked her, and it turned out she was watching me from the forest."

"Has there been any change in the severity between these events?"

Making a face, Will admitted, "It's taking less to push me to the breaking point. I can feel the difference in how paranoid I'm being, even from this morning to this afternoon. Just yesterday, we were both surprised at how little trouble I had with others being near her, even unmated males I knew well. Yet, today, I didn't even want her near any of the people on the training field."

Tony regarded him silently for a few minutes while thinking, then he mindlinked me. *"There is one technique that may help. Do you happen to have a rather harmless memory that is likely to make him struggle for control?"*

I considered his suggestion for a moment. *"Is this wise? I don't want you to get hurt. I did have a visiting rogue offer to buy me a dress yesterday, and from what I have seen, that's enough to make him fight for control."* I shared the memory with Tony so he could evaluate it for himself.

*"If he has control issues, his fighting technique will become sloppy,"* he replied. *"His strength may increase, but he won't be able to concentrate enough to form a strategy. That memory will work perfectly. You weren't interested, and Tiffany was there to protect you. The rogues lost all interest and left after they learned Will was your mate. The event is over and those two are not in the pack's territory. Give me a few seconds."*

Tony turned to Will and said, "I'm going to ask Jade to share a memory of a past event. She was in no danger, and those present left after learning you were her mate, so they pose no threat to the mate bond. Keep that in mind. I will stand here, Jade will remain where she is, and you are going to try to stay where you are."

Will looked uneasy. "I'll try..."

Tony glanced at me and nodded. I gazed across the room at Will and shared the memory of the rogue offering to buy me the dress before Tiffany sent both of them packing.

Will's snarl echoed off the walls at the exact moment I felt his control snap like an overtightened guitar string. He began racing across the room, only to be intercepted by Tony. They went tumbling across the floor until Tony managed to mostly pin Will.

With the mate bond spurring him on, Will wasn't going down without a fight, and the experienced Enforcer was having obvious difficulties restraining him. I froze, not entirely sure what to do.

How had that memory set him off? I expected him to have difficulties controlling himself, but not for him to completely lose control. From his expression, Tony hadn't expected it either, although he had been prepared just in case.

It wasn't safe for me to try approaching two fighters in an all-out brawl, so I watched as Tony struggled to subdue or pin Will. As an older and more experienced Enforcer, Tony shouldn't have had this much trouble containing Will.

Will looked at me and saw my wide-eyed gaze. His emotions flared with rage and protectiveness at the forefront. He let out a vicious snarl and broke Tony's hold with a visible surge of strength.

A swift kick sent Tony flying to the side, and Will practically blurred with speed as he raced over and slid into a fighting crouch in front of me. His back was to me as he faced his teacher. Vicious growls rumbled unceasingly from his chest, a clear warning for him to keep his distance.

Tony cautiously got to his feet and backed a few steps away to give Will some space to calm down.

"*Be careful,*" Tony told me. "*Please stay there until he regains control. I didn't expect his reaction to be so severe. If he feels the mate bond is in danger, there's a chance he may mark you by force. He isn't thinking straight, so we'll just wait it out.*"

I nodded and remained where I was. Tony backed up until he was against the far wall, where he waited with a patient expression. Will's growling slowly grew quieter as the seconds passed.

I could feel his emotions slowly subsiding and noticed when he started to fight against the mate bond's influences. Once he was getting the upper hand on it, I stepped forward to hold his hand and lean my head against his arm, hoping the direct contact would lend him strength to regain control.

Will used my handhold to pull me to his chest for a big bear hug. He buried his face in my neck, using my scent to calm himself. His emotions gradually returned to normal, almost as if the recent events hadn't happened.

He finally lifted his head and looked at Tony with worry, asking, "Are you alright?"

"Just bruises," Tony replied, shrugging nonchalantly.

Will released me from the hug but didn't relinquish my hand. With a sigh, he ran his other hand through his hair and apologized to Tony. "Sorry about that. That was *exactly* what I was scared would happen. I don't recall Roland being this bad when he first met Emily. Every unmated male simply had to keep their distance until things settled down. I'm losing it over memories and plants."

Tony's voice was quiet as he confirmed, "Roland wasn't this bad. Your first reactions were the mate bond, plain and simple. Those were normal and controllable. That last one somehow tapped into your Enforcer abilities and shattered your control. It was at that point where we encountered the problems. So, we simply have to figure out what is triggering your Enforcer role."

Will looked confused. "What could have triggered it? And why would it be getting worse?"

Tony rubbed his chin, deep in thought. "When you first lost control, you weren't trying to attack me, you were trying to get to Jade. I was having difficulty holding you back, but I was managing it. I was hoping I could pin you until you came to your senses, which would have created a buffer in the mate bond.

"At that point, it was mostly the mate bond, but something happened just before you broke my hold. It was like your Enforcer mindframe and the mate bond somehow short circuited with each other and joined forces. Do you recall what happened at that point?"

Will spoke as if the answer should have been obvious. "Jade looked concerned and scared, and I wasn't beside her."

Tony furrowed his eyebrows in thought for several minutes. Eventually, he asked me, "Do you have children, or is there any possible chance that you might be pregnant?"

"No. Why?"

"Such behavior is sometimes seen among higher ranking wolves if their mates are with child or have young children. Even if he wasn't aware of it, the mate bond would cause such instability and overprotectiveness." He shook his head before examining me again. "Do you have any sort of injury? Such a thing might create a vulnerability and cause similar overreactions, especially since the bond hasn't been completed."

I blinked as something occurred to me. "I'm not injured, but would being a runt count as a vulnerability? Now that I think about it, most of Will's control problems occurred when we were apart, almost as if he *had* to be beside me."

Tony's eyes widened. "You're a runt?"

He stared at me in shock and disbelief. I nodded and shifted so he could see it for himself. He stared at my wolf form until Will gave a light warning growl.

Tony shook his head to recollect his thoughts. "Well, that explains it," he said, massaging his temples.

I shifted back, although I wasn't sure what Tony was referring to. Will also gave him a confused look.

"What do you mean?" Will asked, reclaiming my hand in his.

Tony replied, "The mate bond knows she's more or less defenseless, and it's amplifying the protective tendencies that come with being an Enforcer. So, on one hand, we have an overactive mate bond. On the other hand, as an Enforcer, you would normally defend any member of the pack, but particularly the weaker or defenseless ones."

Tony turned his gaze to me as he continued his explanation. "If the already-amplified mate bond somehow convinces Will your safety is at stake, it also kicks in his role and drive as an Enforcer, and they join forces. That's when the problems start. Essentially, until everything settles down, Will's control is like a loose cannon where you are concerned."

I tilted my head. "Once I'm marked, will things begin to settle down?"

Tony nodded. "Yes, but from what I've heard, things won't truly stabilize until the bond is completed. Even then, he'll always be a bit touchy when it comes to your safety, just because he's an Enforcer."

"What have you heard?" Will asked. "Has this happened before?"

Tony crossed his arms and regarded Will. "When I was younger, my teacher told us about an Alpha who ended up with a runt for a mate. His control was even worse than yours since he was an Alpha. By the end of the day, the two of them went to a secluded part of their territory for a week to let things settle down."

Will ran his hand through his hair, not at all reassured by what he'd heard. "How much worse is this going to get? Do you have any advice?"

My eyes were drawn to his messed-up hair, but I forced myself to focus on the conversation at hand.

"Hopefully not too much worse," Tony said with a shrug. "Make sure she's with other women you trust during the day. It's just when her safety is in question that you have trouble.

Otherwise, you're simply dealing with the mate bond, which you are handling quite well."

With the experiments over, we headed back upstairs to discuss other possible options to help Will if he started having problems with his control.

Thankfully, Will didn't have any issues the rest of the evening. He flopped backward onto the bed with a groan. I shifted into wolf form and pounced on his chest to gaze down at him, tilting my head semi-innocently.

He opened his eyes and smiled up at me. "You have no idea how hard it was to not feed you that dessert."

I wolf-grinned and wagged my tail. I had sensed his internal struggle during dinner, but it was just the mate bond being its usual pushy self. He grinned at my expression and linked his hands behind his head, apparently unbothered by my weight.

He took a deep breath and closed his eyes, quite relaxed now that we were alone. I slid halfway off his chest before shifting back to human form, now leaning on his chest while the rest of my body rested on the bed. As I expected, his eyes flew open in surprise.

"Yeah," I said, "I felt it while I was eating. I didn't pry, but it was quite clearly reflected in your surface emotions, although you maintained your composure remarkably well, even when John passed me the salt."

Reaching up to caress my cheek, he asked, "What exactly can you sense? I know Omegas can sense emotions to some degree, but I'm not exactly sure how much they can pick up."

"It depends on how strong one's ability is, and mine is pretty strong in that area. I can pick up a person's overall mood if they are in the vicinity. If they are close by, I can look deeper, so to speak, and sense the weaker emotions or if someone is trying to hide an emotion. I generally don't look below the surface, nor do most Omegas."

"What do my surface emotions show at the moment?"

"Mostly contentment, some curiosity, and an undertone of love," I replied with a grin.

With a faint smile, he raised an eyebrow. "Just an undertone?"

I chuckled and admitted, "It pretty much leaks through your other emotions like water through a sieve."

He rolled over and propped himself up on his elbows with me underneath him. "Let's see if this has any effect on that undertone."

He leaned down to kiss my lips. Sparks exploded from our kiss, traveling straight from my lips to every nerve in my body. Like a powerful drug, it was addictive, and I instantly wanted more. I reached up and ran one hand through his hair as our kiss deepened on its own accord.

His hands gently cupped my head as a low possessive growl rumbled through his chest. His emotions were as chaotic as my own. Desire and want were the most noticeable emotions in Will's aura at this point. I wasn't much better.

Will gently broke the kiss as we breathed hard. His eyes were dark as he panted, "It might be best if you shifted. Your wolf form doesn't provoke such emotions."

I swiftly shifted before leaning up to lick the side of his face. He relaxed and rolled to the side so he was lying beside me.

He exhaled heavily before saying, "I hadn't expected that, and from your reaction, neither did you."

I snuggled closer to him without answering. He chuckled at my lack of response. His desire and want swiftly receded now that I shifted, replaced by a protective mindset. He scooped me into his arms before sliding under the covers. He held me close as we slowly fell asleep.

# Chapter 11

As was becoming our new habit, I woke up curled against Will's chest. It was like he was scared of me disappearing as he slept. I thought about simply relaxing while the last traces of sleep cleared from my mind, but I had my own priorities this morning.

I turned my head to examine his brown hair. Stretching my neck up, I nuzzled my nose deep into the disorderly strands. I exhaled slowly in contentment, resisting the urge to lick it like I had the other day. He might think there was something wrong with me if I did it again.

I extended my senses to examine Will's emotions while he slept. It wasn't easy since sleep created a barrier in the mind as the subconscious took over. I wasn't entirely sure I would be able to do it, although our direct contact gave me a chance.

A few moments later, I picked up flickers deep in Will's mind. I concentrated on them, trying to identify what they were. I had never delved so deep into someone's mind before. It was an odd feeling, like swimming down through pitch black water as I strained to see the bottom.

His emotions were like dozens of small glittering pebbles. Now that I was closer, I could guess their identity: the brightest ones were love, contentment, protectiveness, and possessiveness. I was surprised to see small glimmers of jealousy and fear. All of these small pebbles were scattered around a larger golden stone that gave off a soft and steady glow. It was oddly familiar, but I couldn't place it.

I pushed myself deeper into Will's mind for a better look. I hovered right above the stone as I examined it, still confused by its presence. It was somehow influencing all of his other emotions. Even though the others simply flickered or glittered, this one gave off a steady, faint glow.

I was having great difficulty remaining this deep in Will's mind, and my ability to sense emotions was being taxed to the utmost. Despite the short distance between me and this weird stone, my senses weren't able to identify it. I didn't recall ever seeing anything like it before, although I'd never delved this deep into someone's mind either.

I reached out to gently touch it, marveling at the faint glow that was almost hypnotic. A bolt of light slashed through my mind and body as I was blasted back into my own head by the force. I winced as my head pounded with the worst headache I had ever experienced.

Will jolted awake with disorientation, concern, and confusion washing over his mind. With my senses still recovering from the mental whiplash, his emotions were like bright sunlight during a major hangover. I quickly shielded my bruised and battered senses, which provided some relief.

Will glanced around the room groggily. "Did you try mindlinking me?" he asked. "Something woke me up, but my Enforcer disturbance-sensing abilities are quiet and no one is mindlinking me."

It was so strange to not be able to know what he was feeling. I kept my mindvoice quiet so he wouldn't be able to detect just how bad my headache was. *"Sorry. I was trying to identify an emotion in your mind, and I think I accidentally touched the mate bond. Simply coming into contact with such a powerful thing overwhelmed my senses and has given me a nice headache as a souvenir."*

That was one thing the other Omegas had warned me about when my ability to sense emotions had turned out to be stronger than average: Don't come into contact with a mate bond or attempt to influence it.

An established mate bond was a link of incandescent energy between mates, and it could be found if one dug that far into someone's mind. If someone touched it with their senses, the backlash would usually knock them out cold for days.

Our bond wasn't completed yet, so I hadn't recognized it for what it was. The only reason I was still conscious was because Will was my mate and I had only touched it, which had temporarily flared it to life from its semi-dormant state. Its sheer power had caused my headache, although I suspected that if I had tried to damage it, it would have flattened me.

Will looked at me in worry. "Are you okay?"

*"Yeah, my senses are just a bit bruised, and I have shielded them for the time being. They should recover quickly enough, but don't expect me to sense your emotions or level of control while I have my shields up."*

"Are you sure you're okay?" Will double-checked, tilting his head in concern.

I grinned at him despite my pounding head. *"Yes, I'm fine. The headache should fade soon. I just have to make sure my senses don't brush against it in the future."*

Will sighed and leaned his head against mine before muttering, "You really have to start sleeping in so I wake up first."

*"Is that even possible?"* I asked, sending my silent laughter down the mindlink.

When my stomach growled, he sat up and stretched. I couldn't figure out how he didn't have kinks in his back and neck after curling around me all night. I shook my fur out, which didn't help my headache any. I yawned and shifted so I was sitting on the edge of the bed in human form.

Will looked at my face, obviously trying to see how much my head hurt. I had been expecting it and carefully composed my expression so he wouldn't be able to see the battering ram pounding merrily in my head.

"Feel like a run before breakfast?" he asked.

I really felt like curling up in the darkest corner I could find while waiting for my headache to fade, but that would give me away. It was either help out in the kitchen or go for a run, and I didn't think my head would be able to take the clanging and banging of heavy pots.

"Why don't we check out the trails to the north?" I asked. The trees grew close together there, and the dim light under the dense canopy would hopefully keep my headache from getting worse.

Will nodded and grabbed some clothes. Selecting one of my new outfits, I headed to the bathroom to change.

By the time we returned to the packhouse, my headache had faded somewhat. It hadn't relented *that* much though, and my shields were still up since my senses felt rather battered and sensitive. Will didn't say anything, but he must have figured out my head still hurt. He stayed very close to my side as we filled our plates.

We went to sit with Samantha and John. I put my plate down, but before I could sit, Will pulled me onto his lap before placing my plate in front of me.

He gently rested his chin on top of my head as he declared, "This is a much better arrangement in my mind."

I flushed, unsure of how to react to this sort of thing. Had we been by ourselves, I wouldn't have minded, but I wasn't so sure about it with an audience.

Shaking his head, John said, "You guys may claim the mate bond made me annoying until it settled, but you have to admit I never did that."

Samantha grinned at us. "True. If I didn't have a mate, I would find these two almost intolerable while trying to eat."

Will's voice was amused as he replied, "It isn't as if we were kissing. You're getting worked up over nothing."

Deciding to humor Will, I remained on his lap and picked up my fork. Thankfully, our friends stopped talking in favor of eating. I savored my food, enjoying the things I simply didn't get during my time as a rogue.

One perk of sitting on Will's lap was that he was unable to stare at my face for most of the meal. He often glanced down, but I was short enough that he only saw the top of my head. His plan had apparently backfired on him, much to my amusement.

I looked up at him with an innocent grin and impishly inquired, "Is something wrong?"

He made a face. "I didn't think this through. I can't see your expression, and it's driving me crazy."

I laughed at the predicament he'd put himself in. He seemed fascinated by my smiling face so close to his. He tilted his head and held a slice of strawberry near my lips. I opened my mouth, and he popped it in. I closed my eyes as I enjoyed the sweet fruit.

Even without my senses, I could feel his gaze. I opened my eyes to see him staring intently at my face. When a blush heated my cheeks, he grinned and held up a bite-sized piece of waffle. I smirked but let him feed me that as well.

Before too long, Will glanced down at the table. "Your plate is empty," he said, sounding surprised. I glanced down and saw he was correct. He had fed me most of my breakfast.

John started snickering. "I was wondering how much time was going to pass before you looked away from her."

Samantha swatted John's arm. "Let them enjoy themselves in peace. It was kind of amusing to see the big, bad Enforcer acting like that. But if they start kissing during meals with that kind of intensity, I'm out of here."

I ducked my head as another blush heated up my cheeks and neck. With my senses shielded, they couldn't warn me if others were watching, and I had forgotten about our audience.

Samantha smirked, then commented, "On a more serious note, I hear the cooks used all the mushrooms you gave them, and Sylvia is hoping you might be able to find more truffles since she's traveling to a large multi-pack market next week and they should fetch a good price there. So if you don't mind collecting more today, they'd appreciate the help."

Will tensed up slightly, and I easily guessed the cause of his concern.

"The mushrooms are easy enough to gather in human form," I told her, "but I'd need to shift to smell the truffles. If I'm going to be spending that much time in wolf form, I'd like someone else with me, just in case a large predator shows up."

A low rumble echoed from Will's chest, and I rubbed his arm in reassurance. His eyes unfocused as he mindlinked someone. Before long, he looked down at me. "I just spoke with a couple of people who can accompany you. One woman usually scouts along the border, so it'll give her a chance to familiarize herself with the closer trails. The other one pulled a muscle in her leg, and it'll be a few hours before it heals enough for her to rejoin the patrols. Both are willing to help you pick mushrooms."

"That works for me," I replied. "They can pick mushrooms while I check the area for truffles." With a grin, I added, "You should finish your breakfast though. You seem to have forgotten it in your distraction."

He smiled at my change of topic and picked up his fork. Between bites, he inspected my expression and said, "Please stay near them and don't go climbing any trees. I don't think my nerves could take another stunt like you pulled yesterday."

I glanced at Samantha and idly commented, "I guess this means I should wait before telling him about the time I lived in the mountains and climbed cliffs on a daily basis."

She laughed when Will grumbled, "I am *so* glad there are no cliffs nearby . . ."

He made short work of his heaping plate of food.

The black-haired lady paused and carefully inspected the surrounding forest before bending down to pick a mushroom. She was quiet and reserved, and every one of her movements practically screamed she was a strong fighter.

Had I seen this aloof fighter when I was a rogue, I would have hidden myself in a fashion that only an experienced rogue could manage. I should have guessed Will would have managed to find actual fighters to accompany me.

The brown-haired woman was more relaxed and easygoing. Her slight limp wasn't bad enough to prevent her from joining the patrols, which only proved that the overprotective mate bond had taken Will for another scenic detour. He'd also forgotten to introduce them, so I didn't know their names.

I trotted through the area between them with my nose near the ground, trying to find the scent of a deeply buried truffle. It wasn't truffle season, so I wasn't sure if I could find another of the rare and coveted objects, but I was trying.

I kept an eye on my two guards since they had obviously never picked mushrooms before. When we started, I had showed them how to identify some of the common ones, and they were just picking those.

I mindlinked the brown-haired woman, although I let the other one listen in. *"That might look like the one I showed you* earlier, but it's actually an uncommon poisonous look-alike. If it grows at the bottom of a pine, you can generally assume it's inedible. I wasn't aware they grew in this area, or I would have mentioned it."

She turned the mushroom over in her hand as she examined it. When she spoke, her voice was curious. "I don't see any differences in appearance. Is it just caution speaking or are you sure it's toxic?"

I trotted over and dug up the small base from the leaf litter. "See the pink tinge? That's a sure sign it's the toxic lookalike. The toxic one also only grows on pine roots."

She looked at the base I had dug up before nodding and dropping the mushroom that would have given the consumer a nasty stomach ache. I didn't bother mentioning that my Omega abilities had tipped me off. My people and emotion sensing abilities were still shielded, but I could use the others to an extent. My headache also lingered, although it was easing up as the day went by.

I scooted under a bramble bush and dragged out a large orange-capped mushroom. The black-haired lady was the closest, so I took it over to her. She put it in her basket without a comment.

We slowly made our way through the forest. The two women walked within eyesight of each other while I zigzagged through the area between them, sniffing around for the faint earthy scent of a truffle and dragging back any hard-to-reach mushrooms.

We hadn't found any truffles, but the cooks were going to be delighted with our haul of mushrooms.

Pausing, I lifted my head and sniffed the air as I told my companions, "I'm picking up the scent of a bear, although I'm not sure which direction it's coming from."

Both of them took a quick sniff, and the brown-haired woman said, "I don't smell anything, but that might be because I'm in human form."

The black-haired lady gave me a measuring look before shifting into a sleek black wolf and darting into the under-growth. I resumed my search while remaining alert. A minute later, vicious snarls split the silence. It wasn't close by, but it wasn't that far away either. I glanced at the brown-haired lady, who was facing that direction.

She saw my curious look and said, "Well, there was a black bear. She's chasing it away."

I nodded and squeezed under a bramble bush where another big mushroom was growing. As I emerged, the black wolf trotted over and shifted.

"How did you smell a bear from that kind of distance while you were upwind?" she asked, watching me intently.

I shrugged, which wasn't the easiest motion in wolf form. *"I was a rogue for quite some time, and I'm used to watching for very faint scents. There isn't much wind in this area, so the bear might have passed by not too long ago."*

She didn't reply although she kept glancing at me with a speculative gaze when she thought I wasn't looking. My headache was almost gone, but it could easily return, so I didn't want to lower my shields to figure out which emotions were going through her head. I shook out my fur and kept going.

# Chapter 12

I took a deep breath, and both women glanced at me while also testing the air. I grinned internally at their reactions as I snuffled along the edge of the shrub to try and catch the elusive scent again. The faint aroma guided me to my left, and I started digging underneath a fallen tree.

A few minutes later, I backed out of the fair-sized hole I had dug. The brown-haired lady had been clearing away the dirt, and she stopped to reach into the hole. She carefully pulled out the fist-sized truffle and put it in a transport box. I wagged my tail happily and scooted under another bush to keep searching.

A few hours later, both women could barely squeeze another mushroom into their large shoulder bags. I'd found two decent-sized truffles and four small ones, so Sylvia would be happy. This pack's land seemed ideal for truffles, even out of season.

As we began heading back, I trotted along in wolf form, trying to see if I could locate another truffle. I paused, then turned to circle around a patch of leaf litter and pine needles.

Looking up at both of them, I asked, *"Do you mind shifting? I want to see if you can pick up this scent."*

Both of them immediately shifted. With their noses near the ground, they walked through the area I had circled.

The tawny wolf asked, *"What are we supposed to be smelling?"*

I tilted my head. *"Do you smell anything out of place in that patch?"*

She lowered her head and followed my original tracks before regarding me once more. *"No."*

The black wolf watched us silently as she kept sniffing the ground.

Blinking slowly at them, I tried to be more specific. *"Do you smell the faint trace of water willow?"*

The tawny wolf sniffed once more. *"I suppose, but it's extremely faint. Why is it important?"*

I spoke slowly and softly, *"There are no water willows near here. That scent doesn't belong. A rogue with a masked scent passed through here, and it couldn't have been more than a couple of hours ago or a scent that faint would have faded by now."*

Both wolves pinned back their ears with growls as they swiftly scan the trees.

I reassured them, *"Whoever he was, he isn't nearby, or I would have picked up his scent instead of just his trail. My guess is that he passed through about an hour ago. From how patchy his trail is, he was moving quickly."*

In a tight voice, the black wolf said, *"We've already alerted the sentries and scouts. We're heading straight back to the packhouse, just in case."*

I sighed at their overreaction, and somewhat dreading the answer, I asked, *"Does Will know?"*

The tawny wolf shook her head. *"Tony advised us earlier to keep anything odd from Will if it wasn't an emergency. He says you get to break the news to him when you two are alone."*

I sighed in relief. *"That's probably a good idea, especially with how he's been going overboard lately."*

Both wolves looked amused, so I guessed they agreed with me and didn't feel like having him race over here in a panic.

Picking up my pace to a lope, I headed toward the distant packhouse as the other two stayed close to me. Not far from the first location, I picked up another faint scent, one of pine and alder bush. I knew this scent and didn't mention it since he wasn't the type to cause problems.

No wonder the first rogue's trail had been patchy with speed. Jisk may not start trouble, but he would surely finish it, and it would probably take an Enforcer or an Alpha to bring the fierce rogue to a standstill. Nor did I want to meet the other rogue. If Jisk was chasing it, it was one of the nasty types.

By the time we reached the packhouse, my two guardian shadows were fidgeting with impatience. They were on high alert and itching to go help search for the trespasser, but they still carried the mushrooms into the kitchen.

The moment the women set the mushrooms and truffles down, they disappeared out the door with a speed that wasn't entirely due to the discovery of the rogue. I highly doubted Will would ever be able to convince either fighter to go mushroom hunting with me again. With a grin, I started washing the mushrooms as a small group from one of the other kitchens came to help.

We were about halfway done cleaning the mushrooms when Will mindlinked me and asked, *"Where are you?"*

He had been contacting me every hour or so to see how I was doing. His calmness meant no one had informed him about the rogue yet—and I certainly wasn't about to tell him right now, not if Tony and Evan were keeping quiet.

*"I'm in the kitchen, helping clean the mushrooms."*

His relief radiated down the mindlink, happy I was in the packhouse again. *"How many did you find? Any truffles?"*

I sent my amusement down the link, along with the image of the two guards having to walk carefully to avoid spilling their overloaded bags of mushrooms. *"Quite a haul, actually. You can expect mushrooms with supper. And yes, we even found a few truffles, although I had to dig halfway to the center of the Earth to get one."*

He chuckled, and I could almost picture him shaking his head in disbelief.

"*Alright,*" he said, "*as long as I know you're okay. I'm going to chase these new patrol trainees around the field a few times.*"

"*Have fun.*"

I felt his amusement and guessed the trainees were younger wolves who were just starting their training, and they would not be considering this "fun".

We were just dicing up the last few mushrooms when the Alpha mindlinked the entire pack, "*Please keep close to town and keep your eyes open. We found a dead rogue in the western forest, but it looks like he was killed by a second rogue whose whereabouts are still unknown.*"

The rogue's fate didn't surprise me, nor was I worried they'd find Jisk. If he didn't want to be found, it'd take an Omega with a strong wolf-sensing ability to notice his presence.

Jisk had been the one who taught me how to use the forest highway and how to mask my scent properly during my early days as a rogue. I considered him to be a father-figure after all the time he spent teaching me how to survive in no man's land when other packs weren't interested in accepting me. I hadn't realized just how far he wandered between his visits to check on me in my old camp.

Will's worried voice entered my mind as he immediately checked on me. "*Are you still in the packhouse?*"

"*Yes, still in the kitchen with a dozen others in the same room,*" I replied, my voice calm to keep him from worrying.

"*Please stay in the packhouse. If you want to leave, please let me know. I'm going to help our other fighters check the forest and try to track down whoever killed that rogue. We have no idea where the killer went, so they could be anywhere.*"

"*I'll stay here and call if anything seems amiss,*" I reassured him. "*One perk of my small size is that I can fit in the gap under some of these counters. No one can easily reach me under there, and that's if they even think to look in such a strange place."*

He sighed faintly. *"Thanks. Please don't leave the packhouse until we get things sorted out. The Alpha is waiting for me, so I have to go."*

*"I'll stay inside. In fact, I think I'll see if someone will help me bake. Stay safe."*

I felt his wordless acknowledgment as our mindlink faded.

Once we finished the mushrooms, most of the people took them to a different kitchen, but four stayed to help bake desserts. I was glad for their assistance, not because the recipes were hard, but because the stoves had over twenty buttons on them.

After a quick discussion, we settled on honey butter cakes. It was an easy dessert, and in no time, we had about thirty pans cooling in the walk-in fridge. We moved to another kitchen to cut up lettuce and other greens for tonight's salad.

It was almost time for dinner when Will and the others returned. I picked up his scent before he entered the room since I still had my shields up. My headache was almost gone, but lowering my shields would probably undo some of the progress I'd made. I turned to smile at him as he entered the kitchen.

His eyes lit up when he saw me, and he quickly came over to give me a hug. He breathed in my scent with a contented sigh, saying, "I'm glad to see you. We still don't know who killed that rogue, and we haven't made any progress in locating a trail, which means it was likely another rogue masking their scent. Please don't go into the forest without talking to me first, okay?"

I didn't need my senses to know he was worried about this rogue possibly harming me if we crossed paths. Pulling back to look up at him, I said, "Don't worry, I'll let you know if I go outside. Remember, I was a rogue for years. I would probably know if one was around before anyone else did."

He nodded reluctantly, accepting that detail as truth. "I know that in theory, but facts don't mean much to the mate bond. And I have an odd feeling some of the scouts are keeping quiet about something, particularly the two that were helping you."

With half a dozen people wielding knives nearby, I didn't need the mate bond flipping into overdrive. To distract him from that train of thought, I grinned and said, "They're probably trying to hide the fact that I nearly drove them crazy. Honestly, asking two experienced fighters to accompany a slow runt and pick mushrooms? What were you thinking? After that experience, they're never going to want to accompany me again, let alone even look at a mushroom."

He grinned unrepentantly. "Actually, Ruby mentioned that she'd like you to show her how to hide her scent and how to recognize a masked trail. Several others are also hoping you will hold a training session one day."

It never occurred to me that I would ever be in a situation where I was training someone.

"Which one was Ruby?"

"The black-haired one."

I made a face as I connected the name to the fierce and focused black wolf. "I have no idea how you managed to convince someone like *that* to collect mushrooms."

He made a wry face. "It took some talking, but she owed me a favor, and I was pretty sure you'd surprise her in one fashion or another. When she came back, she said I was right. It takes a lot to pique her interest or take her by surprise, and you managed it, so that's pretty impressive."

I furrowed my eyebrows. "How did I surprise her? All I did was run around and grab mushrooms. I think she only spoke once the entire time."

The only thing I could think of was when I had picked up the rogue's scent, but this wasn't the place to mention that, so it'd have to wait until we were alone.

He shrugged, dismissing the aloof warrior. "That's Ruby for you. But it's almost time for dinner and most of the food here has been carried out, so let's head to the dining area."

After dinner, we sat under a tree and watched the sun set. Will's arm was wrapped around my shoulders while I leaned against him. His finger swirled absent patterns along my arm, leaving trails of sparks and heat. He leaned the side of his head against the top of mine.

I snuggled closer to him and lifted my face to kiss his cheek. He quickly caught my lips with his own. I inhaled slowly as our kiss deepened, awakening emotions I had only felt since I met Will.

His tongue brushed lightly against my lips, sending electricity shooting through me. The sensations were much stronger than they'd been last night, rendering the sunset a distant memory.

My arms circled around his neck while he pulled me onto his lap. I couldn't think straight as desire and love washed across my mind, and considering my shields were still up, the emotions were my own.

Without breaking our intense kiss, Will slowly lowered me to the ground and once more braced himself on his elbows above me. I hung onto Will's neck, not willing to break the intoxicating kiss. His hand caressed the side of my face, leaving a trail of heat as my nerves tingled with an invisible fire.

Our lips parted as we both breathed hard. Will's eyes were nearly black as he looked into mine. "Jade, may I mark you?"

I nodded and tilted my head to the side to give him easier access to my neck. He kissed my lips softly before skimming his nose above my collarbone. He put another featherlight kiss on my skin before biting down hard. I winced in pain as his teeth and elongated canines easily broke through the soft skin and pierced the muscle beneath.

A lightless flash from the mate bond crossed my senses and the pain disappeared. Will released his hold and put light kisses over the wound that was healing rapidly under the mate bond's influence. The kisses on my mark made my toes curl with a new wave of sensations.

I leaned in to kiss his neck, and he quickly reclaimed my lips with his own. He gently pulled away and leaned his forehead against mine as we panted.

Will's voice was rough with desire. "I think we better stop. We are much too close to the kid's playground."

The mark had strengthened the mate bond considerably, and after our heated kissing session, the scents coming off us weren't something I wanted others to smell.

I brushed my thumb along his cheek and asked, "Do you have any plans on how to get us to our room without passing by someone? By the way, no amount of leaves will cover the scent of a fresh mark." Or my arousal...

His eyes darkened at the thought of someone coming close to me right now. With the mate bond ready to take him for another scenic tour of its strengthening abilities, I examined our options.

I finally went with the one that gave us the best chance of getting into our room undetected. "Give me a moment to lower my shields, and I can use my senses to find a clear path."

Closing my eyes, I controlled a wince as information once more poured into my strongest sense. The emotions coming off Will were *not* helping me keep dirty thoughts out of my mind.

I extended my senses toward the packhouse and tried to locate a clear path before my head started to pound. Even if my senses weren't fully recovered from my brush with the mate bond, Omegas were usually skilled at locating a route where no one would notice them. My mind scanned over the various areas and mindsparks of the pack members, finally locating a safe route.

I raised my shields in relief. "The back door facing the garden has no one near it. The stairs the Omegas often use for laundry is also vacant. We'll just have to wait until the hallway between the stairwell and our room is clear."

He nodded and leaned in for another kiss that sent tingles throughout my body. With a groan, he pulled back and sat up. Before I could move, he scooped me into his arms as if I weighed as much as a feather. He held me close and rested his head against mine momentarily.

Lifting his head, he started jogging through the forest to get to the specified door. Thankfully, the path was clear, and we got into our bedroom undetected.

Will gently set me on the bed before tossing his shirt on the floor and lying beside me. I idly traced patterns along his chest with my finger, watching the muscles shift in reaction to my touch.

"I love you," he murmured as he leaned in to place a gentle kiss on my forehead.

"I love you too."

"By the way, I'm never letting you go."

As he transferred his light kiss to my lips, I reached up to feel if my mark had finished healing. The instant I touched it, sensations shot through the mark and our kiss.

Its intensity took my breath away. In a flash, Will once more pinned me beneath him. His kiss deepened, igniting a fire within me that rapidly built in intensity. I kissed him back, barely noticing how tight his muscles were.

His hand dropped down to trace patterns along my sides. My stomach tightened with the desire that followed on its heels. A faint moan somehow appeared in my throat.

Will leaned in and whispered softly, "Will you be mine forever and always?"

"Yes," I replied with certainty.

Reaching up to kiss him once more, a faint rumble of possessiveness echoed from his chest. It mirrored my own swirl of emotions. I traced my fingers over his back, and he shuddered faintly. He leaned down to plant a solid kiss on my mark, pushing our need and desire past the point of no return.

# Chapter 13

I blinked sleepily as I woke up. When I moved my arms, I realized I was still in human form. Will's arm was slung across my body as he held me close to him. I shifted my legs and winced at the dull ache. After the events last night, the soreness wasn't a surprise. Hopefully, it would fade quickly.

I lowered my shields and let my senses roll out. More people were awake than usual, so we must have slept in. Breakfast was almost ready.

My sensing abilities had recovered enough for me to handle today without shielding. I probed deep into my own mind and saw the mate bond shining brightly as it pointed to Will. I looked at it in curiosity. The bond was pure energy, and it was actually very pretty. It was too bad only someone with an Omega's sensing ability could see it. Well, there was one way around that . . .

It took a bit of squirming, but I managed to roll over so I faced Will. His bare chest and peaceful face distracted me. I gently ran my fingers through his hair, taking advantage of having hands instead of paws this morning.

To my amusement, he didn't even stir, still sound asleep. I leaned closer and gently kissed his lips. The mate bond glowed brighter, and I sensed Will's faint flickering emotions stir to more vibrant life as he started to wake.

"Mmmmm . . ."

I pulled back to wait. Moments later, his eyes fluttered open sleepily. I located the private mindlink the mate bond provided and sent Will a closeup image of the mate bond.

He blinked, trying to comprehend the image while more than half asleep. I chuckled and leaned in to kiss him again. He returned the kiss swiftly enough.

His voice was thick with sleep as he murmured, "Okay, that I can understand. I still need some time to make sense of the image."

I leaned my head against his chest contentedly. Will hugged me closer and buried his face in my hair.

A while later he said, "I really can't find the ambition to get up."

"Well, breakfast has already started, and if we don't hurry, all we're going to get is dry toast and tea."

"That's fine by me if I get to stay here and cuddle with you," he mumbled.

It had been over two years since I last had bacon, and I really wanted some. My voice held a teasing tone as I said, "I've had dry toast for breakfast almost all year. Someone is making bacon and hash browns down there, and I really need a shower before I go anywhere."

He raised his head in disbelief, unable to believe I was choosing food over him.

I tilted my head innocently and informed him, "Besides, if we don't get moving, Tony and Tiffany are going to come drag us out by our ankles. Tony is after payback for whatever you did to him on the training field yesterday, and Tiffany is getting way too excited about makeup for my liking."

Will groaned as he sat up. "I'm up, I'm up . . ."

I slowly sat up and stretched, trying to loosen any stiff or sore muscles without it being too noticeable. I didn't want Will to start worrying. The presence of a sock on the end of the bed made me look around. My shirt was on the chair, but I couldn't see the rest from where I sat.

"I think this is the first time I've ever had to hunt for my clothes," I muttered as I got out of bed.

Will chuckled, and I glanced at him, once more marveling at his bare back before focusing on the difficult task of locating all of my clothing.

A few minutes later, I was dressed and presentable enough to walk to the showers. The hot water was still an amazing luxury.

As I dried off, Will's voice came through the mate bond. *"I'll meet you downstairs."*

I sent back a silent confirmation. It wasn't long before I descended the stairs two at a time as the smell of food filled the air. I hoped there was more than just toast left, but as long as I got something to eat, I wasn't fussy. I heard familiar voices as I approached the dining room door.

"Aw, come on. It's the last of the bacon. Surely you can share some of it."

"Nope. Hands off. It's my bacon."

Will must have managed to get some bacon, and from the discussion, it was among the last few slices. I was pretty sure I could convince him to share a piece with me, even if he was giving John the cold shoulder.

"Please . . ."

"Nope."

"Come on, I'll trade a sausage roll for a piece of bacon. I know you love these things. Besides, there's too much food on your plate even for you to eat."

"Nope. My bacon."

I could sense John's shock from here as he gasped, "Did you just turn down a sausage roll?"

"Yes."

"Who are you and what have you done with Will?"

I entered the room, which was mostly empty since breakfast was over. Will sat at a table with Samantha and John as he guarded a heaping plate of food.

Will grinned when he saw me and patted the bench beside him. "Come on, I saved you some bacon."

I headed over eagerly.

John gave in with a sigh. "Well, that explains it. Now I know why you aren't sharing."

I laughed at John's woebegone expression as I slid onto the bench. Will wrapped an arm around my waist and pulled me closer.

Holding up a piece of bacon, he told me, "I went through a lot of trouble to guard this while you were away." He offered it to me, and I took it with a beaming smile.

"Thank you." I quickly kissed his cheek before taking a bite of the warm and salty bacon. Will wore a smug smile and nibbled on a slice of toast as he watched me eat.

I noticed he had two forks, and I used the clean one to steal some hash browns. Will and I kept working at the pile of food adorning his plate. Halfway through, we uncovered a couple of sausage rolls, much to Samantha's amusement and John's exasperation.

My senses picked up something, and I glanced over my shoulder, noticing a woman a few tables away. She nursed a cup of tea and looked like she was feeling under the weather. Will turned his head to see what I was looking at.

"Is something wrong?" he asked, sensing my faint alarm through the mate bond.

I said quietly, "I'm not sure if she knows she's pregnant, but that tea is known to cause miscarriages during the first couple of months."

Will frowned as his eyes unfocused, and the lady froze with a horrified look.

I barely heard her voice as she whispered, "Are you sure?"

Emily happened to walk in at that moment, and her Luna senses alerted her to the sudden mood change in the room. She looked between our tables in confusion before asking, "What's going on?"

Will quietly said, "She was drinking tea, and I asked her if she knew that kind was known to potentially cause miscarriages. She hadn't been aware of it or her pregnancy."

"Which tea is it?" Emily asked with a concerned frown.

Will shrugged, and the other lady answered, "It's an herbal tea I usually drink if I don't feel well. It's in a big blue box in the kitchen. It didn't have any warnings on it."

Emily blinked, obviously knowing which tea she was referring to. She asked Will, "How do you know it can cause miscarriages?"

"My senses can detect the herb," I said. "Most Omegas should be able to identify it."

Emily nodded slowly. "When you're done eating, can I please get you to join me in the kitchen? We'll label any tea with that herb in it."

"Of course," I replied.

Emily left the room, and the rest of the meal was quiet. The woman went to see the pack doctor and make sure the few sips hadn't caused any damage.

We finished eating, and Will headed to the training area while I went to the kitchen. When I entered, I saw hundreds of boxes of tea had been lined up on the counters. Emily was holding a box of red stickers while talking quietly with a man and a woman. A quick check with my senses confirmed they were Omegas.

The Luna looked up. "Jade, the Omegas separated the teas that they thought could cause issues, but they've never tried to determine if something could cause a miscarriage."

"It takes a bit of practice. An Omega's sensing ability is better suited to determining if something is edible or if it's gone bad. Tea normally doesn't cause any harm, so it takes a certain knack. Let's see how they did."

I went to the end of the counter where they had piled anything suspicious. After checking each box, I said, "Yes, all of those can cause miscarriages, particularly during the first month or two of pregnancy."

The Omegas promptly began placing red stickers on the boxes. I carefully went through the rest of the collection on the counter, occasionally pulling out a box that contained overly strong cleansing herbs. Using the mindlink, I "showed" the Omegas what I was looking for in my senses. They went through the long row again as I followed behind them. In the end, they managed to detect all but two boxes.

Emily stared at the boxes with red stickers. I tilted my head in worry as her emotions swirled into distress that almost bordered on despair, and the feelings were rapidly building in strength. The two Omegas gazed at her in concerned confusion, also detecting her inner turmoil.

I walked forward to gently touch her arm, tentatively inquiring, "Emily? Are you okay?"

Her breath hitched in a sob. "I've drank at least one of these teas every day for as long as I can remember . . . To think they may be the reason I have no children . . ."

I opened my arms, and she came forward for a hug. One of the Omegas began using their calming ability. It was quite strong, and I could already feel Emily relaxing.

I patted Emily's back. "Well, now you know. You still have a chance." I added a bit of humor to my voice as I said, "You aren't that old yet."

She chuckled weakly at my attempt to lighten the mood. "Sure, bring my age into it."

My senses alerted me to possible trouble, and I shifted my weight uneasily. "You might want to calm the Alpha down before he gets here. If he gets any closer in the mood he's currently in, I'm disappearing."

The Omegas glanced at each other in worry. We were the only ones in the room with the Luna, and an Alpha was prone to attacking a possible threat first and asking questions later. Such powerful emotions would have echoed through the mate bond and alerted him to her earlier extreme distress. He was coming at full speed, likely hellbent on thrashing whoever had caused her such heart-wrenching anguish.

Emily's eyes got distant before she told us, "I'll meet him by the door and take him to his office to calm down."

We nodded, and I helped the two Omegas put the tea away as Emily left the room.

A glint of eyes in the fading light made me freeze. With a sinking feeling, I slowly turned for a closer look. My heart started racing as the cougar stared at me, not at all intimidated by my human form. For some reason, I didn't have my bow on me. I was also missing all the other weapons I usually carried.

It took a step forward, and I took a slow step backward. A twig snapped beneath my shoe, and the cougar charged. I jumped to the side and shifted into my tiny wolf shape as the cougar's leap flew high above me.

Its eyes locked onto me, far more interested now that I was snack sized. My heart sank as I realized there were no dense shrubs or rabbit holes in sight. The cougar sank into a stalking crouch and took another step forward.

Shifting, I snatched a large branch off the ground and held it tightly. It wasn't the best weapon, but it was better than nothing. My other faint hope was that my sudden change in size would deter the creature. The cougar paused, but resumed its stalk, vanquishing that faint hope.

Holding the branch like a bat, I backed up, only for my back to bump into a tree. I quickly glanced up, but the branches were too high for me to reach. Climbing wasn't an option.

The cougar slowly crept forward, and in the distance, I heard a faint whisper. "Jade . . ."

The cougar stopped, but it sank into a deeper crouch and shimmied its rear end side to side as it prepared to pounce. I held onto the branch so hard my knuckles went white. Small tremors of fear ran through my muscles as adrenaline flooded my system. It was as if the forest was shaking as well . . .

*"Jade!"* Will's loud mind shout broke through the dream, and I opened my eyes with a gasp. My heart continued racing from the nightmare even though Will's arms were wrapped tightly around me. I exhaled a shaky breath of relief when I realized I was safe in bed.

As my muscles slowly relaxed, I said, "Thanks for waking me. It was just a nightmare."

His intense worry and concern continued to hum across the mate bond. "Just a nightmare? You were terrified and panicking. It was so strong I could feel it clearly through the mate bond even though you were asleep." He took a deep breath as he also tried to calm down. "What was it about?"

My heartbeat was finally slowing down to something closer to normal, and I leaned my head against his shoulder. "I have a severe problem with cougars. They're obsessed with me, and I don't feel like becoming cat chow." I whispered, "The only four times I thought my life was truly in danger was when a cougar was after me."

Will's arms tightened around me protectively with a low growl. "I'll never let that happen. The pack members have always kept large predators away from the town just in case a child went wandering. Since you came, all of our fighters have been keeping an eye out for bears and cougars. We've also been chasing them off the pack territory."

That was a relief, but considering I had stumbled across a bear the other day, I wasn't going to be traveling carelessly.

"I know. It's an old fear."

He lowered his head to my neck and inhaled slowly, his muscles relaxing slightly. "Please don't go into the forest without letting me know. I'll become paranoid if I constantly wonder if you went out for a run. And we still haven't figured out where that rogue went or why it killed the other one."

I could sense his internal struggle. He didn't want to be controlling, but he also didn't want me to be traipsing into possible danger with him unaware.

I nuzzled my face into his hair and reassured him, "I already promised to tell you if I went into the forest. Even if I *did* go out without someone accompanying me, we do have the mate bond connecting us." I sent a feeling of humor through the mate bond before mindspeaking him, *"In other words, if I yell your name in a panic, it means 'get your butt over here right now.'"*

He chuckled weakly and lifted his head. "You have no idea how glad I am that you're so easygoing. I know far too many fighters who would ignore my requests and probably wouldn't even let me know if they were in trouble until they were at death's door."

"That's the difference between a fighter with an over-inflated ego and a runt who has spent a few too many years as a rogue."

I felt his relief and amusement, and I decided this was the best opening I was going to get.

I cuddled up against his chest and murmured, "Besides, you wouldn't have wanted to meet the rogue that was killed. We actually picked up his old scent trail while collecting mushrooms. We promptly headed back to the packhouse, but his scent had an undertone of old blood, so he would have been one of the nasty types. I also managed to catch a whiff of the one chasing him, and it was clean."

Will stiffened. "I don't recall any mention of this earlier . . ."

I sighed heavily. "I was told to save it until we were alone, and I really didn't want to kill the mood the last two nights."

Will remained silent for some time, stewing over the discovery and the fact that it had been kept from him. "Who told you to remain silent?"

"Tony. And the two guards agreed. They didn't feel like being near me if you overreacted and came running."

"So that's what they were keeping from me," Will muttered, not exactly impressed, but not as upset as I'd feared.

I rubbed his arm. "There shouldn't be any need to keep secrets like that now that the bond is completed and has stabilized. You might overreact, but you shouldn't lose control."

He sighed and dropped his head against my neck again. I kept silent, debating if I should tell him more than I'd told the others.

"What are you thinking about so hard?" Will murmured.

In a contemplative tone, I said, "How badly will you react if I told you that I knew the rogue who evaded you?"

Will's breath caught as he stiffened again. I could feel his overprotective tendencies rising as he tried to restrain them. I waited patiently.

Eventually, he asked, "Can you expand on that comment?"

I traced my finger absently over his arm as I replied, "He was more like a father than anything else. I met him about a month after my pack was destroyed. Until then, I had been traveling with a group of rogues who'd found me, but a pack had invited them in. They didn't want a runt, so I had to keep going.

"I stumbled across Jisk shortly after, and he traveled with me for years. He was the one who taught me most of my survival skills. Everything from smoking meat to masking my scent, including any little trick he could think of to help me evade anyone who may pursue me.

"He showed me how to climb trees to evade ferals and how to detect a rogue's hidden scent. On two different occasions, he killed a cougar that had me trapped in a rabbit burrow. He was actually the one who helped me join the Black River pack, although he had no way of knowing the Alpha would pass away so soon. He travels a lot since we parted ways, but I see him every month or so. He's the type of rogue that hunts down unlawful ones. I was surprised when I picked up his scent."

Will was silent for some time before he said, "Oddly enough, I think it would be interesting to meet him. I'd be curious to hear his stories."

I snickered, knowing Will was more interested in stories about me than Jisk's adventures. "Oh, I'm sure he has more stories about me than I care to contemplate. I was quite clumsy when I was younger."

When I yawned, Will hugged me closer and said, "Sleep. We can talk more tomorrow."

# Chapter 14

Tiffany was describing some sort of fancy dress she asked a seamstress to make her. Despite trying to listen, I kept zoning out. Had she been discussing something like how it held up to the weather, I might have been able to pay attention, but things like lace and ruffles just didn't jive with my fashion sense or survival skills.

She froze mid-sentence as a wave of shock rolled across her mind. I had actually been pretending to pay attention, so I saw her eyes widen as she stared at me. Will, Samantha, and John all looked up at the sudden silence.

Tiffany reached over and gently tugged the wide strap of my tank top to the side, revealing the mark on my shoulder.

"When did this happen? I thought Will was oddly relaxed, but I didn't expect this yet." She took a deep breath, and a wave of frustration crossed her mind. She huffed, "I can't even pick up your scent under Will's to see if it changed. Did you roll in a pile of leaves? You smell like the forest again."

Samantha and John also gazed at the mark in surprise, so they must not have noticed it either.

With a shrug, I said, "I ran around with it all day yesterday, and no one commented. Will's scent overwhelms mine fairly easily, and as short as I am, my fur rubs against leaves and grasses during our morning run."

Tiffany shook her head. "No one tells me anything important. I have to catch it myself every time. At least I have the morning off so we can catch up on gossip. What are your plans for today?"

"Not much. One of the Omegas asked if I could help make lunch in the smaller kitchen, and this afternoon I have to put together some sort of plan to teach people to mask their scent and detect those who are doing it."

"Great, I can help you in the kitchen this morning."

As Tiffany dried a cooking pot, she groaned and asked, "Why did I agree to this again?"

"I have no idea."

She perked up. "Oh, right. Gossip! So, is your bond completed?"

I dropped the pan I was washing into the sink of water in shock, splashing both of us. "Is that really the first question you came up with?"

She grinned unrepentantly. "Since I can't figure it out on my own, I have to ask."

I sighed. "Yes, although I'm not sharing any details."

With a snort, she said, "He's my brother, I don't want those kinds of details. But I do have to ask if he's seen those gray temptations we bought."

"What's it with you and lingerie?"

She pouted. "I dream of a mate of my own to drive insane one day. The worst part is that I haven't had any luck in finding him—and I made sure to see every guy who visits the pack or passes through. I've even gone to the worst parties in the creepiest packs, but I still haven't had any luck."

"Hopefully you'll find him soon."

She glanced over at me in speculation. "You seemed to know who Mark's mate was even though they hadn't met yet. Do you have any idea who my mate might be? You've been to dozens of packs." Her mood shifted to hope and excitement.

"Mark was mostly coincidence since I had met Cassie a couple hours before. Nothing is standing out in my mind at the moment."

I passed her the last pan, and she sighed as she dried it off, her hands moving slowly in disappointment. An old memory came to mind, one that might lift her sadness or at least give her some hope.

I slowly said, "There might be a chance I can give you a lead, but I'm not sure if my Omega abilities are strong enough to pull it off."

She spun around to face me. "What? How?"

I gestured to the doorway. "Let's go to your room. It will be quieter, and we won't be disturbed."

She quickly led me upstairs. We sat on her bed, and I took her hands as I told her, "I've never attempted to do this before, and I'm running off what someone once told me a long time ago. You have to sit still, close your eyes, and try to quiet your mind. The fewer emotions I have to sift through, the better. Okay?"

She nodded eagerly before closing her eyes and taking a deep breath. While she worked at calming herself down, I mindlinked Will, *"I'm testing out one of my Omega abilities with Tiffany, so don't be surprised if you feel a few weird tingles across the mate bond. We're in her room, and her door is locked if you come looking for us."*

*"Thanks for the heads up."* He didn't seem concerned, possibly because I was with Tiffany in the safety of the packhouse.

I stretched my senses toward Tiffany and went below the surface. Her energetic mind was swirling with emotions that she chased around and tried to force into an inner peace. The varied colors of the emotions were distracting. It was like watching a hyper teenager try to meditate after drinking four or five espressos and two energy drinks.

With an internal sigh, I dove deeper. What I was looking for would be hidden in the depths of her mind. Our hand-to-hand contact was needed for me to go this far into someone's mind. It was much harder with her than it had been with Will. The emotions this deep were like a heavy fog, deeper and more primal. I kept straining to push through the miasma.

Like with thick smoke, just beneath the emotions was a clear area. I circled around it in curiosity. The elderly Omega had been right; each wolf had about a dozen potential mates. This was why most found their mate so easily.

Once they met one of their mates, the other connections would disappear. Those who were rejected or lost their mate still had hope of finding their second chance mate since the remaining stones would re-appear.

Tiffany had six potential mate stones at the moment, although the dull lifeless rocks were a far cry from the glowing stone I had seen in Will's mind. From what I had been told, the stones were inert and shouldn't have any dangerous energy since she hadn't met any of her potential mates.

I gingerly reached out to touch one, wary of a backlash. Nothing. I could feel the faintest wisps of emotion through it, likely coming from her potential mate, but that was it.

I backed up a bit to regard the six stones. Well, she definitely had a mate out there. But where were they? Since I could dimly sense the guy through the stone, that meant there had to be some sort of link.

Was it at all possible to see which direction it led? I tried pushing my senses into the stones, but I was already at the edge of my abilities, and I could feel the strain. Even a hint of a direction or distance would help...

My attempts at figuring it out with my senses were about as successful as asking a rock for the time of day. My frustration built as my thoughts became impatient. *Come on, stones. I'm trying to help you here. Who do you belong to?*

Chills ran up my spine as the stones stirred at my internal muttering. They began shimmering and somehow reflected my power back at me, temporarily holding me captive. Like a mirage, I could see each stone's link leading to a distant location.

The illusion zoomed out, and I could see foggy patches of color scattered across the landscape like a map. Everything in the image was made of light. The fog was territory held by various packs, the rivers were a pale blue sparkle, and the forests were various shades of green depending on the dominant flora in it.

I eyed up the links. Four were more than a quarter of the world away, so I concentrated on the other two. It was hard to focus. Between my growing exhaustion and using my abilities at this extreme level, I wouldn't be able to do this much longer.

Taking a deep breath, I forced myself to concentrate. One link went far to the south, past the mountains. I noted its location and turned to the last stone.

This link was closer and headed to the northwest. I examined the rivers and lakes near it, committing them to memory. It would take someone like Tiffany about ten days to run that far. Oddly enough, neither of the last two links were inside a pack's boundaries. Her mates were likely rogues.

I had what I needed, and as if the stones were eavesdropping on my mind, they released me and returned to their dormant state. I sighed in relief, but I wasn't quite done yet.

After my last couple brushes with the stones, I wanted to see if I could get an idea of what her mates were like. I went up to the stone that pointed south and put my hands on it.

I gently pushed my senses into the stone, being careful to let it know that I just wanted to get an idea of who he was. The emotions became stronger, and I got a vague sense of anger and irritability. My eyes widened, completely baffled as to how Tiffany was a match for this grouchy rogue.

The other stone's link had been closer, and I went over to it. The faint ringing of laughter came through, along with an undertone of sadness. He seemed like a better fit for Tiffany and would likely adapt to pack life more easily than his more distant competitor.

I let myself float away from the creepily aware stones and quickly pulled myself back into my own mind. With a sigh, I untangled my hands from Tiffany's and flopped back on the bed. It was almost strange to only feel my own emotions after being submerged in her subconscious for so long.

Tiffany opened her eyes and stared at me, holding her breath. When I grinned at her, her unusually quiet mind suddenly roared with excitement.

"Did you find him?" she demanded, her entire body practically quivering.

"You need to fetch a map showing the nearby packs and the land to the northwest," I said. The exhaustion was hitting me hard now, and I yawned. "I managed to pick up where he was, but you're going to have to move fast in case he's traveling. I advise taking a few fighters along with you, just in case you encounter trouble in no man's land."

She leapt off the bed and took off running. I closed my eyes to rest for a moment. Even if he was traveling, his scent wouldn't fade too much if she left soon. The mate bond would make his scent stand out like a beacon, regardless of whether or not he was masking it.

Hopefully, he wasn't traveling too fast or going too far.

"Are you ready?" Will asked as we walked through the forest. "Do you need help setting anything up?"

"I got everything done this morning. A couple of pack members helped," I replied as we ambled toward the meadow where I was going to show people how to mask their scent.

Will gazed at the trail ahead. "I'm looking forward to this. So many people were interested in joining that we actually had to turn people away to keep the class small enough. You could be doing this a few times."

I shrugged. "I have no problem with that. The classes really do have to be kept small. If we have more than fifteen people, it'll just create a chaos of scents that will impede their learning."

"Even Tiffany wanted to join, but considering how fast she left yesterday, I doubt she'll be back for a couple of weeks."

"I hope she finds him," I murmured.

Tiffany was currently racing toward the circled spot on her map with two fighters accompanying her. All three had agreed to remain silent about my strong sensing abilities since I didn't like having that sort of attention.

In theory, any Omega with a really powerful sensing ability should be able to do it, but I had tested my ability in the past, and it hadn't been strong enough to pull it off. I suspected my bond with Will had strengthened it somewhat. For all we knew, Tiffany was on a wild goose chase. She was aware of that too.

We rounded a bend and saw the meadow ahead. We were early, but there were already half a dozen people standing along the edges. They chatted among themselves while looking at the various bags and piles scattered in the roped off areas.

I recognized a few of them from watching Will's training sessions. A motionless black-haired fighter leaned against a tree, staring intently at the setup in the meadow. I hadn't expected to see Ruby here, so this was a surprise. I knew she'd never hurt me, but her intensity was the sort that set off warning bells and would make any rogue avoid her.

Before long, everyone had arrived. I took a deep breath and steeled myself to try to train these people. I'd never done anything like this before, and I was flying blind. I was used to avoiding attention for my own safety, not trying to tell a bunch of fighters what to do.

"Good morning," I called, feeling odd for speaking so loudly when I was used to being quiet. "Thank you for joining me. I'm going to show you how to mask your scent, and then we're going to try and detect such camouflaged scents."

I walked over to a section of grass where a large variety of plants lay. "Can you please gather around?" When they did, I continued my lesson. "In the forest next to us, which of these plants are most common and which ones are not found at all?"

A guy spoke up. "Mostly oak trees with some pine. If I recall correctly, there is lots of that sage grass and clover. I don't think I have ever seen those white flowers in there though."

"When you go running, start watching for those kinds of details and keep them in mind as you scent the air," I told him. "Take a deep breath. What does my scent smell like at the moment?"

Ruby watched with piercing eyes as she took a deep breath, although she didn't comment.

A woman to the side replied, "Mostly like Will, although I'm picking up a hint of fern if I try. I actually can't detect your personal scent though."

With a nod of approval, I replied, "I asked that just to point out that my scent won't behave quite like yours. As a runt, my scent is weaker and is easily overpowered. Please watch and track my scent as I do this."

One by one, I picked up handfuls of various leaves and plants and rubbed them onto my skin and clothing. I used a lot of the common plants and avoided using the ones that didn't grow in this clearing.

Once I was done, I asked the woman, "What does my scent smell like now?"

They had been keeping tabs on my scent as I worked and most kept sniffing the air with shocked expressions.

The woman slowly replied, "I can't pick up your scent at all. It's like you aren't even there . . ."

"Balancing the plants is important. Let's go over here." With the group in tow, I walked to a nearby roped-off section that was long and narrow. "I'm going to run down this, then you're going to spread out and each take a section. Cross your section in wolf form and see if you can pick up the things in my scent that don't match the normal smells."

I jogged down the length of grass slowly, making sure to scuff my feet a bit. They shifted and sniffed the area I had crossed. The group mindlink was filled with chattering as they discussed the lesson at hand.

It took them a few minutes, but in the end, they realized that some of the plants I'd used to cover my scent simply didn't match the meadow grass in that exact spot. Once they discovered that, all of them were able to pinpoint the path I'd left.

I confirmed their consensus. "Exactly, no matter how hard we try, it isn't possible to get the exact ratio of plants perfect. The smallest of plants can faintly influence something. Technically, you're not trying to smell a person, you are watching for any inconsistency or odd plant scents. Now, let's see how well you can cover up your own scent."

Everyone was eager to learn, and the morning flew by. Their attempts to mask their scents were humorous as they quickly realized that balancing the scents was harder than it looked. They helped one another as they learned which plants stood out and which subtle ones were needed for faint undertones. At the moment, all I could smell was plants.

"Okay," I said. "You have the basics down pat. At this point, all you really need is practice. I have one last test before we begin practicing. Go over to those two stumps, take a sniff, and decide which one had someone stand on it this morning. Keep your decision a secret until I give the answer."

It wasn't an easy puzzle. Both stumps were pine and had been cut this spring, and their pungent scent was still quite strong. I had spent a lot of time carefully masking the scent of a volunteer so her scent was as close to the meadow as possible. It was even hard for me to detect it, but there were a few small differences that made it possible.

They shifted to their wolf forms and quickly circled the two stumps that had been roped off. I had to keep a straight face as a swirl of bewilderment and confusion touched my senses. A flash of success made me focus on an individual in the group. Ruby's intense scrutiny had found something amiss, although her focused appearance gave no hint of it.

Before long, all of the wolves sat around the stumps waiting for the answer. I walked between the two stumps and told them, "That was actually a trick question. Two people actually walked across this stump, and no one touched the other one."

Surprise crossed the minds of all wolves present, including Ruby's. Her focus intensified even more as I caught her off-guard yet again.

I gestured to the forest. "You know what you're looking for, so all you need is practice. We'll stop for lunch, and afterward, we'll all go into the forest between here and the river. Mask your scent and try to find the other's trails. Keep in mind that you'll likely have to alter your scent as you go into different areas. Since we'll all be in this section of forest, try to find everyone at least once by scent alone. I'll be out there too, so please alert me if you see any big predators."

They scattered to the sidelines to grab the bagged lunch we'd brought with us. Most of them continued chattering excitedly about our lessons as they ate.

I slipped between various shrubs and stopped to sniff a recent trail. The rest of the group were somewhere in this section of the forest as they tried to hide their scent and locate their companions' trails

The group was sharing a separate group mindlink at the moment, and most of the discussion was about whose trail they had found.

I sniffed the trampled leaves and said, *"Jones, you have too much pine in your scent. Try diluting it with some grasses and shrubs."*

*"Are you sure it was me? I haven't used pine yet."*

I sent humor down the link. *"Some pine sap has been stuck on your paw since we started."*

The mindlink rippled with people's amusement, slightly muffled by an undertone of distraction as they also checked their feet. Their skills had advanced by leaps and bounds as the afternoon passed, both in masking their scent as well as determining the identity of someone else's scent trail.

I continued to provide various tips and corrections for each person's scent. They were nowhere near as good as an average rogue, but they were better than most packs at this point. None of them had found my trail yet. Will would have been able to, but he was training in the fighting area.

I eased into a raspberry patch and crouched down as I watched a black wolf trot by without noticing me. Ruby paused to sniff a plant growing at the side of the trail.

Using a personal mindlink so the others wouldn't hear, I told her, *"Lily of the valley has a pungent scent. Personally, I wouldn't use any of it at all."*

She jumped and looked around, trying to spot me since I could obviously see her. I wiggled out of the thorny raspberry canes and made it halfway out before she spotted me. After blinking in surprise and sniffing the air, she trotted closer. When she reached me, she leaned down to sniff my fur. Frustration laced her emotions, so she must not have been able to pick up anything that stood out.

I gazed up at her. *"Try again, but concentrate on the earthier, more subtle scents. People who frequently do this usually have a certain signature in their scent. As everyone noticed, Peter likes cedar and Jill tends to favor red clover. It's a scent that they are simply drawn to and it sticks really well to them. I have one too. See if you can pick it up. The trails left by those with subtle signature scents tend to fade faster."*

She brought her nose so close to my fur that the hairs shifted as she sniffed. Her eyes narrowed in concentration, before suddenly widening. *"Fern. It's the same scent you had this morning, just weaker."*

I nodded. *"Exactly. Now head to the east and see if you can find my trail. I didn't try to hide it, so it's just a matter of locating it before it fades."*

She took a step back and looked at me like she had never seen me before. I felt surprise and respect briefly cross her mind before she refocused on her hunt. With a sharp nod, she trotted in the direction I had specified. I was surprised by the tinge of respect I had sensed, especially coming from a fighter like Ruby.

She was sharp. If she kept practicing, she could become a very good tracker. Jisk might actually have his trail discovered if he passed through again, which amused me to no end. But he was experienced enough that he regularly used the forest highway to break his trail, and it was nearly impossible to track someone like that from the ground.

I scampered in the other direction in search of another scent trail to critique.

Eventually, we gathered back in the meadow to discuss whose trail had been the most noticeable and what they could have done to fix it. It was almost time for dinner, but they were still lingering in favor of the discussion at hand.

Jill asked me, "How far did you go? I don't think I found your trail."

"I wandered between the river and the meadow three times using different routes that were far apart. Anyone going east to west would have crossed them."

She pursed her lips. "I guess that's a reflection of experience?"

I nodded. "Yes. Once you get better, you'll notice that it's impossible to completely cover up someone's scent. All you're doing is making it harder to find. I can easily pick up another rogue's scent, and if they know what they're doing, they'll be able to detect mine as well."

One of the men asked, "I assume it'll take at least a few weeks before we get to that level, right?"

"Yes. Just like when learning a new fighting style, it takes time and a lot of practice. That being said, unless you plan on missing out on a steak dinner, we should head back."

I felt shock roll across the group as they sniffed the air. The mouth-watering smell of barbequed steak was strong enough to easily smell in human form.

"How did we miss that?" the man asked in bewilderment.

"You were so focused on small details that your mind excluded the other scents to help you concentrate," I replied.

"Just keep that in mind so you don't forget about it in the future."

He nodded, and everyone began heading back to the pack-house to make sure they got a steak.

# Chapter 15

I stared at Ruby in shock. "I'm not sure I heard you right. You want to go mushroom hunting?"

"Yes," she replied easily, unfazed by my confusion.

I couldn't comprehend it. *She* had come to *me* to ask if we could go *mushroom hunting*. She hadn't liked it last time. In fact, Will had called in an old favor before she grudgingly agreed to the unpleasant guard assignment, and he wasn't involved this time.

Ruby seemed to feel the need to press her case. "The cooks haven't had mushrooms for several days, and I know Will doesn't want you to go deeper into the forest without a fighter nearby."

She waited as if her suggestion was an easy everyday task she didn't mind helping with. Even though she looked calm, I could sense her excitement and determination. This was the first time I'd ever seen her hide her intent focus, although it shone through her other emotions.

I finished folding the tablecloth in my hands as I looked under the surface of her mind. She was obviously after something, but there was no treachery or anything like that. I wondered if she wanted more lessons in scent detection, but she seemed a bit too excited for that. She wasn't the kind to answer direct questions, so there was only one way to find out what was on her mind.

"Sure, we can go," I replied, placing the tablecloth in a basket. "When do you want to leave?"

"I'm free now."

I chuckled in spite of myself. "Well, help me fold up this monstrosity of a tablecloth, then we can grab the collection bags."

She briskly helped me fold up the massive tablecloth and guided me to the shed where the collections bags were stored.

I trotted under a bramble bush to fetch several mushrooms. Even though my back was to Ruby, I could feel her human form watching me like a hawk. There was no threat in her gaze, but it was definitely unnerving.

As best I could tell, she was trying to discover something. There weren't many things I might know that her pack members wouldn't, so it was a short list to guess from.

*"Was there something in particular you wanted to discuss or learn during this outing?"* I asked idly.

Her surprise flickered along my senses, but her voice didn't show it. "Not really. I wouldn't mind learning how to smell a truffle, but I'm mostly out here to help the cooks."

I snorted my amusement and kept my tone light. *"Liar."*

She stiffened, likely at getting caught so easily, although her voice remained cool. "What makes you think I'm lying?"

*"When someone has been a rogue for a long time, a lie is as obvious as a masked scent trail. On top of that, you've been staring at me with the intensity of a coursing hound waiting for the restraints to be removed so it can be loosed on the hunt."*

She frowned but didn't reply. I grabbed the mushroom and brought it over to her. She bent down to take it from me, although she still didn't say anything. I had a sneaking suspicion she wanted to learn some rogue tricks but refused to admit it aloud. With that in mind, I decided to give her something to think about.

I looked up at her with a serious expression. *"I have met those who favor letting their body language announce that they are experienced fighters. Yours is extremely obvious, and you must have trained yourself to do it. Such a tactic has its uses, but it also eliminates the ability to launch a surprise attack since an opponent would have already marked you as trouble."*

She blinked and regarded me in confusion, unsure of where this conversation was going or what had prompted such a comment. Her mind swirled as doubt and pride warred with one another, as if she was rethinking some long-held assumptions.

From what I'd seen, she prided herself on being known as a fierce fighter at a mere glance, but such fighters were rarely underestimated by opponents. I wasn't sure if her body language was a conscious decision or not, but my words were at least making her think about it.

I glanced around to make sure I had my bearings. We weren't far from where I had first played catch-me-if-you-can with Will, and there were plenty of bramble bushes and other sprawling plants in the area. Perhaps she needed something else to think about as well...

I sat and tilted my head at her. *"Can you please shift?"*

She instantly shifted and tested the air, possibly assuming I had smelled a predator or was going to give another tracking tip. Unfortunately for her, I had something else in mind.

I dropped every hint of puppy behavior and body language I normally used. I had learned over the years that others had an easier time with my runt size if I included some puppy-like nuances, and I rarely dropped them all, even if no one was around.

Her eyes widened as her head pulled back at the sudden change. Instead of facing a runt that reminded her of an innocent, defenseless puppy, she clearly saw a cautious, experienced rogue in miniature.

My voice was quiet but serious. *"Any wolf out there can outrun me."* I put a bit of humor into my voice. *"But let's see you catch me."*

With zero warning, I bolted under a bramble bush and took off at full speed. Ruby stared after me, her mind completely stunned. After a few seconds, she got over her shock enough to begin running around the sprawling bramble bush, although I was already out of sight.

I lay on a patch of grass and happily regarded the pile of mushrooms in front of me. I could sense Ruby's frustration off to the side as she tried to locate me. When I had first run through this area with Will, I had been running through unknown territory and had done fairly well. This time, I knew the lay of the land.

Ruby had been trying to catch me for a couple of hours with no success. I had lost her well over a dozen times, only to appear from the side and yip at her before taking off again.

To her credit, she hadn't given up, but she prided herself on being a top fighter, so discovering she couldn't catch a runt wasn't a pleasant realization.

Admittedly, I had been forced to use almost every trick I knew to evade her after showing myself. She thought I was just running and hiding, but I had actually been collecting mushrooms. It was good evasion practice for me, and the pile of mushrooms was bigger than I was. I couldn't wait to see her expression when she saw it.

When Ruby finally located my latest scent trail, I laid down and fluffed up my fur while putting on my best cute puppy expression. She charged through the bushes, only to slide to a stop in surprise when she saw me.

I smiled at her as if the last few hours hadn't happened and kept my voice innocent. *Do you think there is room in your bag for these? I also found two truffles, but I need help digging one up.*

She stared at me as if I had grown two heads, simply unable to merge the innocent puppy runt act with the sly rogue that had evaded her time and time again.

She could see the puppy-like traits now that she had seen me without them, but she still couldn't make her heart believe what her head knew. Her heart and instincts saw the puppy-like characteristics in my petite size and wanted to protect me.

I tilted my head and colored my mindvoice in feigned confusion. *Is something wrong?*

She blinked slowly. Her reply sounded like each word was being pulled out of her. *How did you do that? It shouldn't be possible.*

I chuckled and shook out my fur as I sat up, dropping all but the couple of puppy traits I usually wore. Surprise flickered across her mind as she saw the change again. I shifted back to my human form and started loading the mushrooms into my own collection bag. Ruby also shifted and came to join me, watching closely in case I had more surprises up my sleeves.

As we worked, I spoke contemplatively. "Most of what I just did is only possible for a runt. Things like running where most wolves can't, sneaking down rabbit burrows, running through hollow logs, and such. Some things simply wouldn't occur to most wolves. During a hunt, most people rely entirely on their wolf shape and don't think outside of the box."

We started walking through the forest side by side, and I could feel her burning curiosity as she asked, "How so?"

I glanced at her in amusement. "When chasing another wolf, the average wolf would never consider shifting, but our human shape can do things a wolf can't, such as climbing trees."

She was somewhat confused. "What good would climbing a tree do?"

I handed her my collection bag. "Can you hold this for a moment?"

She took it and watched me as I climbed the tree beside us with the ease of practice. The leaves quickly hid me from view, and I silently swung from branch to branch and ran along the larger boughs in the dense canopy. I climbed halfway down a different tree and silently grinned at Ruby, who was still staring into the first tree as she waited for me.

"I'm over here."

Ruby jumped and whirled around with wide eyes. She glanced at the tree above her, then back to me, unable to figure out how I had appeared over here. She took a step closer to the first tree to peer up into it before stepping back and muttering, "Nope, I'm not going to look any harder just in case there are two of them . . ."

I laughed and climbed down. "To the best of my knowledge, I don't have a twin out there. But if you think that is impressive, there are other tricks most rogues can do that I can't simply due to my smaller size and lack of strength."

She looked intrigued, and now that she was no longer surprised or confused by my actions, she no longer sported that super-focused hunter look. Her body language also seemed more laid-back. She'd probably been thinking about my earlier statements while searching for me the last few hours and made a few decisions.

"You're much easier to talk to like this," I commented. "The way you acted before would have made most rogues avoid you."

"Huh. I guess that's why I never saw any rogues in no man's land. Well, other than ferals."

With a grin, I started to reply before a mindvoice blasted across my senses. *"I FOUND HIM!!!"*

I jumped in shock, and Ruby immediately fell into a fighter's crouch, scanning our surroundings for danger. With an annoyed sigh, I replied to the mindspeaker while letting Ruby listen in.

*"Tiffany, have you ever heard of knocking? You almost gave me a heart attack!"*

Her reply was immediate, but my comment hadn't dampened her enthusiasm. *"Sorry! But I found him! I found Nathan! I can't believe it! He is SO hot!"*

I laughed at her high spirits and swooning. *"Is he part of a pack?"*

*"No, he was a rogue in no man's land. They had a camp close to where you thought he was. He was exiled because of something his father did. He's coming back with us! Just wait until you meet him!"*

I sent humor down the link. *"Uh-huh. I know the power of a mate bond. You aren't going to be so perky when any female so much as looks at him."*

Ruby grinned as we picked up Tiffany's shock and realization.

She recovered quickly. *"Well, you're marked, so I doubt I'll have too many problems with you, but yeah, any unmated female is going to be my new nightmare."*

My reply was thoughtful. *"Well, it'll take you at least a week to get back. That should give you plenty of time to realize he won't look at anyone else. Remember his reactions towards other males will be stronger as well, and he won't be used to having a lot of people around."*

*"Hmmm . . ."* Tiffany faded out of the mindlink.

I exchanged an amused look with Ruby. "Let's go get those truffles."

Ruby helped me move a log away from where one was hidden, and I showed her the scent before digging it up. It didn't take us long to collect the second one and head back to the packhouse.

As Ruby and I walked down the hallway, Will came down the stairs and paused when he saw the overflowing bags of mushrooms we carried.

Ruby gave Will a long-suffering look. "You're lucky you have Enforcer stamina. Your little mate is a handful to keep up with once she gets going."

"How did she convince you to go mushroom picking again? I thought you hated it."

She groaned and set the bags on the floor. "I don't like picking mushrooms, but it gave me a chance to discuss masked scent trails without distractions—or so I originally thought. The biggest problem is simply keeping her on track. You can be in the middle of a conversation, and she'll disappear under a bush or change the topic with lightning speed if she smells a truffle or unusual plant."

Will blinked slowly, as if he had never heard Ruby talk so much at once. She had really loosened up throughout the day. I wasn't walking beside the same werewolf that helped me fold the tablecloth this morning.

I grinned at Will. "Next change of topic, what are you doing here so early? You usually train for several hours longer than this."

Ruby's frustration rose when she realized she had missed something unusual that stood out to me. She was getting quite irritated at herself for not noticing such things, but she was determined to improve. Her intense focus was now hidden deep. I could sense it, but couldn't see it.

From some of her earlier comments, her newfound dream was that any foe would underestimate her, which wasn't surprising after how I had tormented her all morning and afternoon.

Will smiled at me, although he still seemed unsure of what to make of this new Ruby. He said, "Alpha Mike and Beta Trevor should be arriving shortly and will probably stay overnight. They are a neighboring pack we're on good terms with. From what I heard, they're hoping to also trade for a few truffles."

"Well, they have good timing. We found two more."

With a shrug, Will replied, "I'll let the Alpha know. It's up to him and a few others to decide if we want to trade them or take them to the auctions. He'll probably let Alpha Mike trade for these two. The ones that went to auction were fetching very good prices since they're uncommon this time of year, but the fact that we sold over a dozen in a few weeks is attracting attention."

Ruby took my bag of mushrooms and hefted all of them over her shoulders as she said, "I'll take these to the kitchen. We'll have to do this again in a few days. See you later."

"Thanks for the help. Let me know when you want to go again."

"Sure. When I drop these off, I'll ask the cooks when they want more mushrooms," she said before walking down the hallway and disappearing around the far corner.

Will watched her go in shock, then turned to me with wide eyes. "What did you do with Ruby? I've known her since we were little, and the person who just left is not Ruby."

I felt Ruby's amusement and sense of achievement as she overheard his comments from her hiding spot down the hallway. She was looking forward to seeing other people's reactions, and I figured she shouldn't be the only one to have some fun.

I shrugged innocently. "Nothing really. We ran through some bramble bushes, climbed a few trees, splashed around in a creek, and dug up a few truffles."

He rolled his eyes and replied in a dry voice, "Of course . . ."

In a low, evil voice, I said, "And I drove her crazy too."

He chuckled and shook his head. "I'm curious to see how long these changes stick."

I grinned at him mischievously. "That depends on how much longer I can keep tricking her into thinking that she actually dislikes collecting mushrooms."

Will roared with laughter, and I felt a jolt of emotions pass through Ruby's mind from her eavesdropping location. The reverse psychology would likely drive her crazy all night while she tried to unravel my words. She didn't know I could sense her presence and emotions. So far, only a handful of people knew I had been an Omega and still possessed those skills.

Until Ruby came along, no one else had ever bothered to examine me carefully enough to realize there was more under the surface than met the eye. At the moment, she was the only one who could see the rogue I had carefully concealed. I was kind of looking forward to messing with her head in the future.

Will took my hand in his and guided me out the front door to enjoy the sunshine before our guests arrived.

I sat in a rocking chair on the porch while sewing up the frayed hem on my coat. Alpha Roland guided two strangers onto the path leading to the packhouse. Their tour had been fairly laid-back and informal since these two visited frequently.

When Roland invited the Alpha inside for trade talks, the visiting Alpha told his Beta to relax for a while. I paused to watch the larger man follow Roland inside while a leaner guy sat in a lawn chair to enjoy the view of the town. Furrowing my eyebrows, I reached out with my senses before considering the invisible man inside and the relaxed one still in my view.

My fingers flicked the needle in and out of the fabric as I mindlinked Will, *"What does the visiting Alpha look like?"*

He sent me an image of the larger man. *"Why do you ask?"*

The mate bond was powerful enough for me to open my mind and let him see my conundrum.

His wordless shock rolled through the link as he asked, *"Is there any way your senses could be incorrect?"*

*"No, Roland and Emily are showing up properly. There is no haze of confusion, so my senses are working perfectly. They also seem quite used to this. If you think about it, it certainly gives them an edge and an element of surprise. How often do they visit?"*

The man who had just gone inside had a Beta's aura, while the man in my sight was clearly an Alpha as far as my senses were concerned. He was trying to suppress and hide it, but my senses weren't deceived. The Omegas would have been busy and keeping a low profile out of sight, so they wouldn't have tied a face to what they were sensing. That was assuming their sensing ability was strong enough to detect such things, and if they happened to be using it within sight of these two.

Will was still trying to wrap his head around the idea I had just dumped on him but replied, *"These two actually visit fairly often, at least six times a year."*

I considered the amount of power they gave off before asking, *"How did your Enforcer senses miss this? You can sense the fighting ability of anyone you come across."*

His voice was sheepish. *"I have to concentrate to use that ability, and I only ever scoped out the Alpha. I never bothered with the smaller guy since Alphas are always more powerful than the Betas."*

I was amused but didn't say anything since he was already kicking himself for his oversight. Will faded out of the mindlink to go talk with Tony. I kept sewing as I felt the visiting 'Beta', Trevor, approach and sit in a nearby chair.

Glancing over, I politely greeted him. "How are you enjoying your stay so far?"

"I always enjoy visiting this pack," he said, quite relaxed and at ease. "Your group is always so welcoming. How have things been around here lately?"

He was crafty and had obviously gotten lots of information simply from talking to various pack members like this in the past. He had an aura that made you want to trust him and talk openly. I was also able to prevent it from overly affecting me because I could sense it.

"Pretty good." I kept fixing the frayed hem as I spoke. "I haven't heard of any real problems. From what I hear, it's been a good year for the gardens."

"That's good. Our carrots and beets did well this year. Was it the same here?" he asked as he absently gazed at the town. His voice had just the right amount of interest to engage anyone even semi-interested in that topic.

Most people loved to brag about their gardens, and prideful wolves loved to show how great their pack was. They wouldn't have even noticed the subtle pull this man's aura had on them. I felt his aura strengthen a fraction more, although it was still a very light influence. I raised an eyebrow at him and used my passive ability.

His aura slid off me, and even as he turned his head to glance at me in shock, I dropped the ability. His aura focused on me again, more alert since I had caught him off-guard.

I pretended to not notice anything as I replied, "I'm not entirely sure since I only joined this pack a few weeks ago."

He shook his head as if to clear it. "How did you do that?"

"I could ask you the same question."

"I thought the sociable abilities of Betas were well known?" he asked in confusion.

I turned my head to examine his expression like a parent who was doubtful of their teenager's story. His emotions stirred as he began to squirm internally. I was somewhat impressed he didn't growl at my stare since most Alphas couldn't tolerate anyone doubting or challenging them.

"Most people who've lived as a rogue for a long time can identify Alphas and Betas at a glance as easily as they can pick up lies, half-truths, and deceptions," I said, keeping my voice fairly neutral, but letting the trace of a challenge lace my words.

It was true enough, which would keep him from wondering if I might have an Omega's sensing abilities without the rank, but it also guided his mind down a different path that revolved around his true identity instead of my little focus-evasion trick.

A stunned look crossed his face as he realized he'd been caught, then he burst out laughing. After a few moments, he shook his head and said, "We've been doing this for over three decades, and you're the first one to notice."

I grinned at his easy-going manner, relieved he wasn't as stern as many Alphas were. The "Beta" Trevor was actually Alpha Trevor, while Mike was truly the Beta. For some reason, they had pretended to be the other rank.

I had never heard of an Alpha who could swallow their pride enough to consider that, but this easygoing man had obviously done it many times. Just as surprising was his ability to not respond to the challenging tone in my earlier words.

"Why did you pretend to be a Beta?" I asked. "I thought I was losing my mind until I watched you for a bit."

He leaned back in the chair with a grin. "Mike looks more intimidating than me, and he's very good at trading negotiations. People find it easy to talk to me, so I tend to wander around and collect information on what the pack might have in surplus. Who have you told about your discovery so far?"

"So far, just an Enforcer, and he's talking to an older one to see if he noticed it in the past."

His eyes drifted to the mark on my shoulder. "You didn't tell your mate first?"

"Will *is* my mate," I replied with a grin.

"Good for him! I bet you keep him on his toes."

"I try my best."

He laughed again. "What gave my rank away?"

I tilted my head as I examined him for a moment. "Lots of tiny things just kind of added up. You pretended to be respectful of Mike's position, but some of your body language still proclaimed who was truly in charge. Alphas have an unconscious attitude and body posture. You managed to hide most of it, but some is still there for those who know what to look for."

"I guess I had better work on that later. In the meantime, I better go let your Alpha know before he hears it from another source." Trevor got to his feet and headed inside.

*"Will, Alpha Trevor is heading inside to let our Alpha know the truth."*

*"Thanks for the update. Neither Tony nor Evan noticed, so I don't feel quite so bad now, but I think it's safe to say we'll be paying closer attention in the future to any visitors."*

*"Well, no harm was done, so it was an easy learning experience. And Trevor said he did it at other packs without getting caught, so their Enforcers must not have realized it either."*

*"How is Roland taking it? Some of my Enforcer senses are shifting slightly, but nothing that makes me think a disturbance is brewing."*

I shared what my senses were detecting. *"It looks like Roland is taking the news well. There was a bit of tension at first, but they must be good friends since I'm now picking up more amusement than anything else."*

*"That's good. Let me know if anything changes."*

I sent confirmation down the link.

# Chapter 16

The days settled down and passed by seamlessly as I learned more about the pack I had joined. To my relief, it wasn't as hard to fit in as I had feared.

I carried a pail of vegetable peelings outside to the garden compost. After dumping them in, I stretched in the warm sunshine. Since my shift in the kitchen was over, I was tempted to wander over to the training area to spy on Will.

My mind easily pictured how his focused expression would transform into a heartwarming smile if he spotted me. It wasn't often he noticed my spying hobby, but if the wind shifted, even the faintest whiff of my scent was enough to catch his attention.

I wandered through the garden and saw Tiffany kissing a guy in a remote corner of the garden. They had just arrived last night, so I hadn't met Nathan yet. I altered my path and went to greet them.

When they didn't notice my approach, I paused to wait for their prolonged kiss to end. After a while, I crossed my arms and leaned against a tree, wondering if I had become invisible or something. I hadn't covered my scent, although the wind wasn't in their favor right now.

I debated leaving, but since I could sense some children nearby, it was probably wiser if I made them aware of their surroundings. Startling a former rogue could be even more dangerous than catching a trained fighter off-guard.

With that in mind, I smirked and asked, "How long before you two come up for air?"

They both jumped, and Nathan automatically spun into a defensive position in front of Tiffany with an instinctive growl.

I chuckled and waved a dismissive hand at him. "I'm not interested in competing. I hope we all make it out of this life alive."

He blinked, taken aback by my lack of concern and bizarre greeting.

Tiffany groaned at the interruption, then reassured her new mate, "You can ignore her, Nathan. She's mostly harmless. Besides, her mate is an Enforcer."

Nathan blinked and his stance relaxed as he sat beside Tiffany again.

She introduced us. "Jade, this is Nathan, my mate. Nathan, this is Jade, my brother's mate."

Keeping an eye on Tiffany in case the new mate bond gave her issues, I walked closer to the duo.

"How did you sneak up on us like that?" Nathan asked. "No one has gotten that close in years without me knowing about it."

I sat cross-legged on the grass. "I lived as a rogue for a while and move silently without thinking about it. You were also quite distracted."

They glanced at each other with guilty, smitten expressions. I glanced over my shoulder as a black wolf trotted along the treeline with her nose to the ground. I remained silent as I watched her disappear into the forest, searching for the runt she knew would be spying on Will shortly.

Watching her in confusion, Tiffany asked, "What is Ruby doing?"

"Don't talk so loud, or she'll hear you and notice me," I responded quietly.

Nathan regarded my still form with a faint frown. "Why are you hiding from her?" As a former rogue, he'd always want to know about any potential threat or trouble.

I grinned at him, much to his surprise and confusion. "In theory, I'm not hiding from her. In reality, she simply hasn't found me yet."

Tiffany looked even more confused after my explanation. "Why is she looking for you? I don't think I've ever met a fighter less interested in regular life."

"She turned over a new leaf," I replied with an innocent shrug.

Tiffany snorted. "Yeah, sure. I'll believe that when I see it."

"Just wait and see," I said, grinning in anticipation. "She's been hanging out with me a lot this week."

"I thought Will was easing up in the protection area. What happened?"

"It wasn't Will. For some reason, she decided that collecting greens, mushrooms, and truffles was more fun than being in the fighting area."

She shook her head. "Now I know you're lying. That simply isn't possible."

Nathan eased into the conversation. "Speaking of impossible things, how did you know I was in that valley?"

With a faint sigh, I replied, "It's actually an ability some Omegas have."

"You aren't an Omega . . ."

Tiffany quickly interjected, "She was designated as an Omega when she was with a different pack. Then she was a rogue before she came here."

"Since it was just a designation," I added, "the rank faded, but the abilities remained. My sensing ability is pretty good, but the rest are weak."

"Well, I'm in your debt for sending her in my direction. I'm glad I was still there when she ran into the camp looking for me." A smile appeared on his face at the memory.

Tiffany blushed and ducked her head, leading me to guess that she had single-mindedly charged right into a rogue camp in her excitement.

"Well, she gets to take you shopping now," I told Nathan. "I went through one torture session and that was enough for me."

Tiffany defended herself with a scoff, "Torture . . . You survived. Did you ever even use the lingerie?"

"That is for me to know and for you to never find out."

She mock-scowled at me, then her face lit up as she turned to Nathan. "Oh, that reminds me. What kind of lingerie do you think would look best on me?"

I laughed at his wide-eyed look. The mate bond was more than ready to help him with dirty thoughts, but the question was like a double-edged sword, and he was fully aware of it.

"Don't worry, Nathan." I snickered. "Just tell her that you have to see her in every piece she owns before you can give her your honest opinion. She probably has every type in existence so that could take a while."

Nathan's eyes darkened as Tiffany's cheeks and neck flushed bright red.

"Jade!" she exclaimed. "You aren't supposed to be helping him!"

I shook my head and muttered, "Well, that did it . . ."

Seconds later, a black wolf bounded into the garden. She barely spared Nathan and Tiffany a glance as she trotted over.

*"There you are,"* she said, apparently ignoring the other two, although she let them listen in. *"Sylvia says there's an auction in a couple of days, and she's hoping we can find some truffles since there is a cooking competition coming up and numerous chefs with*

*deep pockets will be there. Do you have time to go truffle hunting with me today?"*

Tiffany's jaw dropped, and I felt Ruby's triumph and amusement even though she gave no sign of it.

I nodded eagerly and swiftly got to my feet. "These two are about to discuss Tiffany's current collection of lingerie, and anything that gets me out of the immediate vicinity is more than welcome."

Tiffany's face flushed even redder as she exclaimed, "That's it! You're so dead!"

She lunged toward me, arms held wide to catch me in a tackle. I quickly shifted and dodged out of the way, taking her by surprise as she flew over me.

Ruby chuckled as she darted in and gently grabbed the scruff of my neck. Turning on her heels, she bolted full tilt out of the garden with me hanging from her jaws.

As we entered the trees, Tiffany gaped at us from where she was sprawled on the ground, her shock at Ruby's action overriding her vengeance. Poor Nathan looked between us and her, completely bewildered by what he had just witnessed.

At the dinner table, Tiffany eyed up Ruby, who was sitting beside me, before turning her attention to Will.

"So," she said. "If I told you Ruby grabbed Jade by the scruff of her neck and dragged her off, what would you say?"

Will continued to calmly butter his dinner bun. "If you're referring to the event earlier today, then I would thank her."

Nathan glanced at Will in confusion. "How can you be so calm when someone grabs your mate by the scruff of her neck?"

He was honestly curious, whereas Tiffany was still attempting to get revenge. I let Will feel their emotions through the mate bond so he wouldn't make an incorrect assumption about Nathan. Ruby lacked this knowledge and bristled at the question.

"In the beginning, before she was marked, I probably would have flipped. It's a bit different now. For one, Jade doesn't mind it too much. Two, it got her out of reach of my sister—which is something you'll appreciate one day. Three, Jade can't really defend herself, so Ruby's intervention was welcome."

Nathan nodded slowly, still not quite understanding.

Tiffany asked Will, "Are you sure this is Ruby? This is not the Ruby that was here when I left to fetch Nathan."

I snickered at her question. She hadn't been the only one to ask it lately; many people were equally bewildered by the changes in the formerly fierce and aloof black wolf. She had gotten much better at hiding the tell-tale hints of her elite fighting abilities.

She was no longer the die-hard fighter obsessed with patrols and training. Instead, she now spent no more time than the average wolf on the training field, and she was enjoying her new laid-back lifestyle.

Much to Will's amusement, she had arranged her free time so she could accompany me into the forest most days, regardless of what I was looking for. In truth, she was eager to learn any rogue secrets or skills I could show her. Since she was normally the only one helping me, she more or less had my undivided attention, so she was learning quickly.

Several days ago, she had managed to pick up the subtle scent of a truffle while patrolling and had been so excited she'd immediately mindlinked me. She could also pick up my scent if she crossed it, but I could go places she couldn't. I still lost her easily enough, much to her chagrin.

Will shrugged as he replied to Tiffany, "As far as we can tell, it's still Ruby. Jade was teasing me that she was driving Ruby crazy, but at this point, I think Ruby might have made a few round trips to that destination."

Ruby glared at him over my head, and Will smirked right back, knowing he was trying to get a rise out of her.

I sighed and put a hand on each of their arms as if separating them. "Alright, children. Settle down and get along."

They both gave me a disbelieving look at my attempt to intervene when I was powerless to stop them. I felt a jolt of recognition from Nathan and glanced over at him.

"You mentioned you were a rogue for a while, did you ever meet a man named Jisk?" he asked. "That was one of his favorite sayings, and he said it exactly how you did."

I grinned in pleasant surprise. "Was it that obvious? Yes. I knew him, and that's where I picked it up."

Will's eyes widened in recognition of the name, and Tiffany asked, "Who's Jisk?"

With a shrug, Nathan replied, "I only met him a couple of times. Fierce-looking guy, although he seemed fairly laid-back. He's one of the rogues that hunts the unlawful ones. Ummm . . . has a nasty grudge against Alpha commands; he never did explain it, but it's the reason he refuses to join another pack. If two people started trying to rile each other up, he would say the exact same thing Jade just did." He turned to me. "How did you meet him?"

I grinned at that memory. "It was quite a few years ago. He walked by without noticing me napping under a shrub, and I yipped at him right as he stuck his head into a cave. Needless to say, he jumped and banged his head. The most amusing part was that he blamed the cave roof instead of me."

Nathan shook his head. "There's no way you could have gotten close enough to that guy to startle him. He would have noticed you."

"I wasn't full grown," I said, "so I was pretty tiny. He heard the rustling, but he thought I was a rabbit. It didn't occur to him that a runt would be in no man's land. How did you meet him?"

Nathan looked dubious but accepted my claims. "He stumbled across our camp a few times and stopped to gossip for a while."

Ruby was listening attentively. I was pretty sure she would be tracking down Nathan for other stories from his days as a rogue, which would drive Tiffany to distraction.

Right on cue, Ruby started asking him questions. I leaned against Will as the two of them talked. He wrapped his arm around me as he listened to stories from a world he had never known.

I leaned against a tree and silently fumed, although none of the dozen people on the training field likely noticed me. Unaware of my mood, Will continued training an older teenager on how to correct his stance.

To his credit, the sandy-haired woman was to the side, and he hadn't noticed most of her flirting attempts. The few poses he had caught sight of, he ignored. His disinterest was the only mollifying thing in this situation.

I couldn't act like the jealous mate I was, particularly when I wasn't able to win a fight with anyone here. No amount of training could correct that. As a runt, my speed, strength, and stamina would never be equal to a normal wolf. Sure, I had a few tricks up my sleeves in case unpleasant rogues cornered me, but those generally involved serious or possibly even lethal injuries.

Seriously harming a packmate out of jealousy wasn't something to even be considered, *especially* when my mate was ignoring the perpetrator. I didn't really want her dead; I just wanted her to leave my mate alone. Why couldn't she go flirt with Evan? He didn't have a mate yet, and as an Enforcer, his odds of ever finding her were extremely low.

I took a deep breath to control the jealousy and gave a low whistle of greeting to the person hiding in a nearby tree. Even in my distraction, the faint whiff of pine and alder hadn't gone unnoticed. My senses had also been tracking him while he circled closer. My eyes remained on Will as Jisk dropped out of the tree and leaned against the trunk.

He regarded the fighters silently for a while before quietly saying, "Do I have to give him a lecture on the exclusivity of the mate bond?"

It didn't surprise me that he knew who my mate was. I'd sensed Jisk's distant presence dozens of times, so he had undoubtedly scoped out the pack and the people in it. I hadn't managed to dodge Will and Ruby to get far enough into the forest to say hello the few times he had ventured close to the packhouse, and he was likely aware of it.

"Not really," I replied with a deep sigh. "His eyes have never wandered, and I couldn't have wished for a better mate. That woman is getting on my nerves though. I didn't realize what an evil beast jealousy is. I have no idea how Will managed to control himself when we first met."

He chuckled lightly, although I could sense his serious mood beneath. His appearance wasn't a light thing since anyone who looked this way would be able to see him. Even though he normally preferred to remain unseen, his building irritation easily let me guess why he'd come out into the open.

Jisk considered the mate bond to be sacred, and the fastest way to anger him was for someone to intrude upon it. If anyone tried to entice someone who was already mated, like this blonde was doing, he'd get upset.

If someone who was already mated tried flirting with anyone other than their mate, he got livid and generally tried to take a chunk out of the offender. And heaven help the person who was contemplating rejection or mentioned rejection as a possibility within his hearing.

He crossed his arms and asked me in a loud voice, "Exactly how long is your mate going to let that woman flirt with him before telling her off?" His eyes never left the training field.

Every head on the field whipped in the direction of the unfamiliar and irritated voice. The training area fell silent, the lessons at hand forgotten.

I shrugged and replied in a monotone voice, "I'm not sure, but I'm hoping she stops soon."

If anyone hadn't noticed the flirting before, they were aware of it now. Will's eyes went nearly black when he noticed the trespassing rogue beside his mate. I felt his worried mind-probe through the mate bond as he checked if I was okay, only to be surprised when he realized I wasn't the least bit uneasy in the stranger's presence.

*"Relax, it's only Jisk. At the moment, that promiscuous woman is the only person he wants to pick a bone with."*

My words partially reassured him that I was in no danger, but they made him worry for the woman's safety. That irritated me, and I sent the emotion and its cause down the link.

His chagrined wordless response acknowledged my point, but also reminded me that as an Enforcer, he'd have to intervene if Jisk attacked her. I wasn't entirely certain if Will, even though he was an Enforcer, was a match for the experienced rogue, but I heavily shielded that thought, lest he catch it.

People began glancing between Jisk and the woman. She looked uneasy with all the attention she was getting, but she squared her shoulders and told me, "Having a runt around makes our pack look weak, especially when the runt is paired up with an Enforcer. You should run off with that rogue since he seems interested in you. I can look after Will. He needs a strong mate, not a runt, and it will be less of a burden on the pack."

My insulted growl was drowned out by an enraged roar from Will and a furious snarl from Jisk. Numerous other growls cut off as people stared at the two furious males who radiated power. The woman's eyes widened when she realized all of the sounds had been directed at her.

My head pounded as dozens of minds radiated outrage and disbelief at the woman's callous words. I partially shielded my senses to block out the stomach-churning emotions.

Jisk stalked forward, his smooth movements revealing him to be the deadly predator he was. His continuous growl shook the air around him as he glared at the woman.

His voice shook with cold fury as he demanded, "How *dare* you infringe on a mate bond? What of your own mate? He's out there somewhere waiting for you, unaware you're trying to shatter his heart."

The woman took a shaky step back toward her fellow fighters, but her packmates made no move to protect her. From their glares and lack of support, I had a feeling they hadn't been aware of her opinion, nor were they willing to tolerate her behavior, even if it meant letting a trespassing rogue attack someone on their territory.

"She's a *runt*. She makes our pack look weak. An Enforcer needs a strong mate," she pressed. Despite her strong words, she began edging away from both Jisk and her packmates as she took in their expressions.

Will's hands shook with his crumbling self-control, only to be distracted when Jisk lunged forward with snarl. Jisk didn't touch her, but he snarled right in her face as she scrambled back in a panic.

He matched her step for step as fury burned in his eyes. "You disgust me. Trying to tempt one already claimed in front of his own mate? You probably won't even remain faithful once you find your own partner."

When Jisk paused in his pursuit, she shifted and raced for the trees, bolting into the undergrowth. After what had just happened and her packmates' refusal to help her, she'd probably move to another pack, or so I hoped.

Jisk turned his unimpressed glare to Will and slowly advanced toward him. Will eased into a defensive stance, ready to defend himself against an attack.

Jisk snorted at his actions. "As if I would hurt an old friend by attacking her mate."

He stopped and crossed his arms as he studied Will. Through the mate bond, I could feel Will's conflicted emotions and confusion.

Jisk told Will, "In the future, I highly advise you to growl at anyone attempting to flirt with you. Your silence was encouraging that lowlife, and it was definitely ticking off your mate. Jade might not be able to fight off an interloper, but if you let someone encroach on the mate bond, she could certainly make you regret that mistake."

Will's eyes narrowed at his tone and the unexpected lecture, but I could feel his shame when he realized how Jisk saw the situation. Will's mind touched mine as he examined my emotions. His guilt echoed through the mate bond as he noticed the jealousy and faint traces of hurt from his actions. Will looked away from him, wordlessly admitting that the rogue had won this battle of words.

Jisk turned sideways, as if to leave, then paused and quietly told Will, "Never take your mate for granted. An understanding mate is worth more than gold. Never abuse the trust and faith a mate puts in you. If an Enforcer can't defend a mate bond, then we might as well just hand this world over to the ferals and be done with it."

Will nodded slowly but didn't reply. When the Enforcer didn't argue or try to make excuses, Jisk walked back to the forest. I turned my head to watch him as he went by.

"I'll see you later," I murmured.

He gave a barely audible whistle of agreement before disappearing into the shrubs. My senses tracked him as he climbed a tree and picked up speed, zigzagging through the canopy as he made his passage untraceable. Soon he was too far away for me to track with my shields in place.

Will jogged over to where I was still leaning against the tree and held out his arms, silently asking for a hug. His regret and wordless apology rang through our bond, so I stepped into his embrace.

"I'm sorry," he said, holding me close. "It never occurred to me that ignoring her would have bothered you. She's relatively new to the pack, and this was the first time she came to the training field, so I didn't know she was going to do that. Can you forgive me?"

Behind Will, the others on the field watched the forest in suspicion or curiosity, off-balance after the rogue had appeared in the heart of their territory without anyone noticing. Several of them shifted and ran into different sections of the forest.

When I cautiously lowered my shields, I could sense them circling the area as they tried to track and intercept the potential threat. Unfortunately for them, Jisk had a solid head start and they didn't have a hope of finding him.

I leaned my head against Will's chest. "You're forgiven. But please don't let others flirt with you." My voice took on a teasing tone. "I might have to do something rash, like find a bear and mindlink you a picture of it looking at me. I bet that would give me your undivided attention."

He took a deep breath and shuddered lightly at my idea. "How about we don't do that? You can just mindlink me and tell me to snap out of it."

"Or," I murmured in a contemplative tone, "I could send an image of my reflection in the mirror while wearing that set of silver lingerie I bought."

"You own lingerie?"

With a chuckle, I said, "It *was* your sister who took me shopping. There was no avoiding it."

Will's emotions were in a whirlwind. Training had dropped to the very bottom of his to-do list.

# Chapter 17

I flicked an ear back and tried to pick up my pace. There wasn't much undergrowth around here, and with the black wolf rapidly catching up, I sighed and came to a stop. I turned around and sat down, facing the way I'd come.

Within moments, Ruby bounded down the trail and skidded to a stop in front of me with a grin. I wolf-grinned back at her, impressed at how quickly she'd caught up to me today. At this point, she was just as talented as most rogues when it came to covering her scent or tracking a camouflaged trail.

I tilted my head innocently. *"Fancy meeting you out here. You seem to be in a good mood today."*

She chuckled, and her falsely over-enthusiastic voice sounded in my mind, *"A coincidence, I'm sure. How can one not be happy on a day like today? The sun is shining, and the birds are singing!"*

*"And the fact that you currently have Tony, Evan, Will, and half a dozen others struggling to track you down has nothing to do with it either, correct?"*

*"Nothing whatsoever."* She fluffed up her fur smugly.

*"That's good. Otherwise I would warn you that Will has realized you're with me, and they are heading this way with all the speed the Enforcers can muster."*

She blinked and darted into the trees. *"Got to go! See you later!"*

I snickered and trotted the other way. Since Will was out here chasing Ruby around in some sort of training exercise, he wouldn't be at the practice arena, so I wasn't too sure what to do with my free time now.

I spotted a black hole in the ground and decided to check out the rabbit burrow. There was no telling when I might need to take shelter in a place most predators couldn't follow.

A quick sniff of the rather prominent entrance revealed that a few rabbits called this burrow home. With nothing more dangerous lurking within, I crawled inside to investigate, idly wondering what Will would think when he realized I frequently crawled into rabbit burrows.

A few alarm foot thumps came from ahead as the rabbits fled down different tunnels. I noted which ways they went since those were likely the closest exits. I continued crawling through the network of tunnels as I sensed Will approaching.

*"Where are you?"* he asked as he slowed down, likely looking around.

I sent amusement and a childish sense of adventure along the link, sharing the feeling of dirt in my fur as I explored deep beneath the surface. *"I'm checking out this rabbit's burrow. You should see all the tunnels down here!"*

Apparently that was the wrong answer.

His worry flooded down the link even as I felt his heartbeat surge. Before I had a chance to reassure him, a soundless snap echoed across the mate bond as the bond and Enforcer abilities ganged up on him. His mind hazed over as he swiftly located the entrance I'd used and started digging for all he was worth.

*"Hey, Will. I'm okay,"* I assured him. When he didn't reply and continued digging like the world depended on it, I tentatively asked, *"Will? Can you hear me?"*

There was still no answer. The mate bond had hit him really hard this time, and he needed some time to calm down and regain control. Following the rabbits' earlier examples, I quickly squeezed out one of their emergency exits.

Will was so focused on digging he didn't even notice. With a frown, I shifted and climbed into a nearby tree to watch. Tony and Evan remained at the edge of the clearing to watch Will while the others continued chasing after Ruby.

I mindlinked Tony, *"He hasn't lost control since the bond was completed. It happened so fast there wasn't even time for me to mindlink him."*

Tony shrugged as he replied, *"Having you out of his reach has always pushed him over the edge. In the past, he could see you, but this time he couldn't, so that might have had a hand in it. It's uncommon for mates to lose control once the bond is completed, but it can happen if the mate bond overreacts sufficiently. With you being a runt and him being an Enforcer, the odds are much higher."*

I rolled my eyes and wished he would have warned me earlier. We watched as Will swiftly uncovered the entire network of tunnels, which was quite an impressive feat considering how deep some of them went.

When he ran out of tunnels to unearth and hadn't found me, he started snarling and lashing out at trees in a mindless rage as his control slipped further. I stared at him in shock. I'd never seen him like this before, and from Evan's and Tony's stunned expressions and how they backed partially into the shrubs, neither had they.

*"Will. Will!"*

Nothing. My words couldn't get through the mindlink. The mate bond had him in such a state that it had raised strong mental shields. Since I was the only person capable of approaching him without risk, I climbed down.

He spotted the movement out of the corner of his eye, and as he turned his head, his eyes widened in recognition. Spinning in my direction with far more speed than should have been possible for such a large wolf, he charged in my direction.

Even with the mate bond reassuring me that he'd never harm me, I took a step back. He slid to a stop in front of me and used his neck and chest to push me to the ground. Unsure of what to do, I dropped to my knees and rolled onto my side.

He crouched over me and glared across the clearing as a fierce snarl ripped out of his chest. Under his threatening gaze, Tony and Evan lowered their heads and backed into the undergrowth until not a single patch of fur was visible.

*"We can't approach him when he's like this,"* Tony said in frustration. *"Try to calm him down and let us know when he returns to the realm of reason."*

I rubbed my hands against Will's stomach. "Take it easy. I'm fine. I was never in danger."

His never-ending growling continued.

I mindlinked Tony, *"Calm him how? He's blocking the mindlink, and my spoken words aren't getting through."*

*"You're his mate. You'll manage. If not, he'll snap out of it eventually."*

His enigmatic reply was about as useful as trying to convince Will I was okay. I began edging out from under Will. The moment he realized I was moving, his growls turned to snarls and he lowered himself until he lightly pinned me to the ground.

I was out of the tunnel, so I wasn't sure what potential danger the mate bond was worried about at this point, but it didn't want me going anywhere. I sighed at the situation I had gotten myself into.

"Will? Can you please let me up? I promise I won't roll down another rabbit burrow. Will?"

The low growls still rumbled through his chest. My senses told me that he didn't even really hear me. I dug a bit deeper into his mind, but the mate bond's glow overwhelmed everything to the point where he was acting at an instinctive level.

With a sigh, I rolled onto my stomach and rested my chin on my arms while waiting. A rock dug into my ribs and dirt dropped out of Will's fur, courtesy of his frantic digging earlier.

I rolled my eyes and flicked a pinecone away. The rock continued digging into my side, which only added to my growing annoyance. I knew the mate bond was to blame, but this particular event was unexpected and a bit exasperating.

"Earth to Will . . ." I muttered as I reached over to his ankle and gently tugged on a tuft of fur. His response was to put a bit more weight on me and continue growling at the trees where Tony and Evan had disappeared.

His weight pinned me against the ground, making the rock dig in painfully. I tried to wiggle out, to no avail. With only one option left, I shifted into my wolf form and sighed in relief when the rock no longer attempted to drill a hole into my ribs.

My shift distracted Will but not in a good way. The absence of physical contact immediately goaded the mate bond into a frenzy, thinking I had disappeared yet again. He stepped to the side to check beneath him, and his murderous glare softened when he realized I had simply switched forms.

His protective and defensive mindset shifted rapidly into one of evasion and determination. In a lightning fast move, he grabbed the scruff of my neck and took off at speeds that left me frozen in terror. The smell of my fear pushed him into running even faster, determined to put as much distance between us and where we had been, as if his imagined threat was back there.

I could sense Tony and Evan trying to keep up, but they were simply unable to match his speed while the mate bond spurred him on. They fell back and simply tracked his scent.

Will blasted through the forest, weaving between trees and shrubs with some sort of destination in mind. He suddenly slowed down, but his mind was just as hazy as before. He trotted directly toward a large tunnel dug into the base of a hill.

Well, it was large by my standards, but I wasn't sure Will would be able to fit inside. Oblivious to my doubts, he ducked his head, and his paws scrabbled at the dirt as he squeezed down the tunnel, reaching a slightly larger den at the end.

He managed to curl up in the tight space before finally putting me down on his stomach, nuzzling me gently. With a bit more shuffling, he settled down with his shoulders completely blocking the entrance.

His side rose and fell under me as he breathed. It was like lying in the middle of a giant, furry donut. With a sigh, he buried his nose in my fur. A tongue almost half as big as I was ran down my back as he started licking my fur. I made a face but didn't bother commenting since his mental shields were still up.

Tony's voice entered my mind. *"How are you holding up? I can't believe Will managed to fit into that den."*

He was torn between concern for me and laughing at Will's accomplishment of squeezing his massive bulk into the narrow space.

The situation was just too ironic. *"For someone who freaked out when I climbed into a narrow tunnel, he shouldn't be allowed to pull a similar stunt. I'm currently getting a bath. Feel like trading places with me?"*

Tony sent his amusement along the link. *"Nope. Just keep hanging in there. Will would probably turn us into a scratching post if we tried anything."*

With a sigh, I dropped my chin on my paws to wait. The fur on my face, neck, and back went from dry to damp, then from damp to soaked. About the time my fur simply couldn't get any wetter, Will's mental shields faded out as the mate bond subsided. He blinked slowly at me as awareness finally appeared in his eyes.

*"What just happened?"* His mindvoice was slow and confused.

"*Good question,*" I said, nuzzling his cheek. "*I was exploring and having a great time with Ruby when you jumped off the deep end.*"

He huffed as my words triggered his memory. "*You were stuck in a rabbit burrow. I could feel the burrow walls pushing against you from all sides through the mindlink. What did you expect? And you can't tell me Ruby was in those tunnels with you.*"

I had known he would have felt the dirt in my fur, but he must have noticed my fur rubbing against the tunnel. Then the image of him attempting to somehow stuff Ruby into one of those tunnels made me chuckle.

"*No, you would have found her if she was down there, but, alas, she wouldn't fit. She was nearby though. I had more room in most of those burrows than you have in here. And I wasn't stuck. That's why you couldn't find me.*"

He huffed in irritation, and I shook my head until my ears flapped, sending small droplets flying from my fur. Will blinked when several hit his face.

"*Why is your fur soaked?*"

"*Gee, I wonder why?*" I said, baring my teeth in a wolf-grin. "*It surely couldn't have anything to do with the couple thousand kisses I got over the last five minutes.*"

His voice was slow in confusion. "*Somehow I don't recall that . . .*"

"*Well, there isn't anyone else in here.*"

Will lifted his head, only for it to hit the ceiling of the rather snug den he suddenly found himself in. "*How did I get in here?*"

"*That's a mystery for another day. Let me go out first so you don't have to worry about squishing me.*"

He squirmed around until he unblocked the entrance. I clambered over his side and trotted out the tunnel. Near the entrance, I reared up on my back legs but was unable to touch the roof with my front paws. Tony chuckled at my display from where he lay at the base of a tree.

I trotted over, prancing a little for extra effect. *"I made it!"*

He grinned at me as his tongue lolled out the side of his mouth. *"So I see. I'm waiting to see how Will manages to get out."*

*"He'll probably shift and crawl out."*

Tony shook his head. *"After losing control like that, he won't be able to shift for a while."*

I blinked slowly. *"Oh. This could be interesting . . ."*

Tony wolf-grinned in reply as I trotted over to him. We watched the entrance as scratching and muffled noises came from within.

Will eventually grumbled, *"This is impossible. There's no way I could have gotten into this tunnel in wolf form."*

*"Well, you did,"* Tony replied cheerfully. *"You managed it while carrying Jade too."*

Will snorted, unimpressed with his mentor's claim and amusement. *"How long will it be until I can shift? It might just be easier to wait."*

*"Not long. About five minutes."*

*"Then I think I'll wait."*

*"Hey!"* I exclaimed. *"That's no fair! You freaked out when I was wandering down a rabbit tunnel, but when you're actually the one stuck underground, it's a different story?"*

Will contemplated it for a bit. *"As odd as it seems, me being stuck doesn't bother me. You being potentially trapped is a different story."*

I shook my head. *"Unbelievable. You know the chances of a bear or cougar sneaking up behind me when I'm out here are far more likely than when I was down in the rabbit burrow, right?"*

Will's mindvoice went tight with that thought. *"I'm sure Tony can protect you from bears and cougars for the next few minutes."*

I snorted and my gaze strayed to a nearby tree, which gave me an idea to further torment Will. I shifted and quickly climbed the branches while Tony watched in suspicion.

*"What are you doing?"* Tony asked with misgivings.

I sat on a big branch and shifted back to my wolf form without replying. With a grin at Tony's wide eyes, I lay down on the wide branch. He must not have realized I could shift in a tree so easily.

*"I'm getting a good seat to watch the upcoming show."*

*"Jade, what are you up to?"* Will asked, sounding like he probably didn't want to know the answer.

*"Nothing I haven't done before, and no, before you ask, I'm not in any danger."*

That alone made Will worried. *"Jade . . . what are you doing?"*

*"Just laying down and watching the tunnel."*

He was still suspicious. *"Then why did Tony seem concerned?"*

I shrugged even though he couldn't see it. *"I guess Tony didn't realize I was actually part cat."*

Will gave up interrogating me and asked Tony, *"What is she doing?"*

*"She's fine,"* Tony replied calmly. *"You can see what she did when you come out."*

Will's growl echoed out of the cave and through the mindlink. *"You two are hiding something from me."*

*"Not really,"* I said. *"If you come outside, it's quite obvious."*

*"Jade . . ."* His voice held a warning tone as his patience rapidly waned.

*"Alright, alright. Just don't blow a gasket. I've done this thousands of times."* I shared an image of my aerial view of the tunnel.

*"If you look down, will I see shoes or paws?"* he asked, his voice shaking in worry.

*"I can show you whatever you want to see."*

*"That was* not *what I wanted to hear."*

With a few grunts and groans, Will squeezed out of the tunnel in a rather painful-looking fashion. He instantly spotted me and ran in my direction. *"Don't move. I'll come get you."*

I rolled my eyes but remained where I was. *"Fine, I'll let you play the knight in shining armor."*

I perked my ears as I waited to see how he planned to get me down in his current predicament. Right as he reached the tree, his fur quivered with the failed shift. With a thwarted growl, he turned his head to stare at Tony, possibly asking his old friend for help.

With a chuckle, Tony shifted and climbed into the tree. He carefully picked me up and carried me back down. Will immediately came over to nuzzle me as Tony set me on the ground. I shook out my fur and gave a big yawn. Will sighed as if he was as tired as I was.

*"Let's head back,"* he said.

I shifted and draped an arm over his shoulders as all three of us began walking back.

When Will finally managed to shift back into human form, he took my hand in his and grumbled, "You're going to be the death of me one day . . ."

I shook my head. "You were supposed to chase Ruby, not ruin my exploration."

"The dirt was pushing against your fur like you were stuck. It's dangerous down in those tunnels. If one of them collapses or caves in, we might not be able to get to you fast enough."

With a sigh, I replied, "Will, I've done this for *years*, and I've never gotten stuck in a burrow. Nor have I ever had one collapse while I was in it. When I was a rogue, I went into rabbit tunnels and climbed trees on a daily basis. I even slept in a rabbit burrow at night. You didn't have to destroy the rabbits' home like that. The poor things are going to be traumatized for life."

Will stubbornly defended his actions. "As far as I knew, you were stuck. I couldn't see you, and I thought something was wrong. I was worried I wouldn't be able to get to you fast enough."

Tony idly commented, "I'm thankful I never ended up with a runt for a mate."

I narrowed my eyes and poked him in the ribs. "What do you mean by that?"

The gray-haired man chuckled at my actions. "The fact that you can fit into places I haven't been able to since I was six months old still boggles my mind. I can't imagine having a mate who could literally disappear down a rabbit hole. I wondered if Will lost his mind when I saw him ripping up the ground like a madman. You were climbing a tree, so I couldn't figure what pushed him over the edge like that."

"How was I supposed to know she had gone out a different exit?" Will grumbled. "I was just following the various tunnels trying to find her."

Tony gazed at the leaves overhead, eventually telling me, "You should probably avoid places where he can't see or reach you. This seems to be a constant and major trigger-point for him."

"But keep-away is my favorite game!" I protested. "Are you sure we can't work on this slowly and see if we can wean him out of it?"

Tony tilted his head contemplatively. "You could try, but I doubt it's going to help. Please give us warning if you two attempt it."

Will shook his head. "And let me repeat myself, you're going to be the death of me one day."

We just grinned at him.

After dinner, Will and I went into one of the side rooms to relax in front of the fireplace. I curled up on the couch and leaned my head against his shoulder. He contentedly fiddled with a strand of my hair as we simply enjoyed the quiet crackling of the fire.

I was half asleep when Will sat up straighter with a groan. "I hate to say it, but duty calls once again. Why do they always wait until the evening to get into arguments?"

I leaned against the pillows and regarded him sleepily. "Because they're too busy during the day. I'm pretty sure if you dropped a few hints about how they're disturbing your time with your mate, they might take the warning. And if you tell them to save their clashes until they're close to the border and out of earshot, it'll give them alternatives."

"I think I'll do that. Be back soon." Will leaned down to place a soft kiss on my forehead.

With a stretch, I also stood up. "I'm going to find the washroom and come back to wait for you. If I fall asleep, it's your fault for being too slow."

He chuckled as he exited the room. I shook my head to clear it and went the other way. Busy days and big meals were exhausting, and bed was starting to sound better and better all the time.

I entered the washroom and paused with a sigh when I saw someone had used all the toilet paper and hadn't replaced the roll. Shaking my head, I crouched down to rummage under the sink for another roll.

When I noticed a small pink box, I narrowed my eyes and did a quick mental tally. I pulled a small object out of the box and checked for the paper instructions, which were nowhere to be found. The side of the box wasn't any more enlightening, but it couldn't be that complicated. I grabbed a roll of toilet paper and headed to the toilet.

As I washed my hands, I examined the stick. One line. That meant I wasn't pregnant. I wasn't sure whether to be relieved or disappointed. Considering how alive and well my love life was, it was only a matter of time until a child appeared.

I wasn't sure what protection or preventatives Will might have used, although he probably hadn't bothered. Enforcers seemed to have gotten the short end of the stick when it came to family life and rarely had more than two or three children.

I wrapped the test in more toilet paper and stuck it in my pocket. Some people would actually search the bathroom garbage for such things so they'd have something new and exciting to gossip about. I didn't want to be in the gossip chains and planned to dispose of it in a different garbage.

With another yawn, I headed back to the couch to wait for Will. It wasn't long until he returned, and when he sat down, he pulled me onto his lap. I leaned against his broad chest contentedly.

"I think this group finally got the message to conduct such annoyances away from the packhouse."

"Hmmm. What did you say?"

He grinned with a wicked glint in his eyes. "I told them that if they interrupted my cuddle time with my mate one more time, they'd be training with me all day for a solid week just to ensure they simply wouldn't have enough energy to bother anyone. Needless to say, they readily agreed with me after that."

I laughed. "Oh, that would scare them. Nothing like having an irritated Enforcer determined to work you until you drop from sheer exhaustion."

Will chuckled in agreement and wrapped his arms around me. I absentmindedly traced patterns along his forearm as my eyelids got heavier. Will began humming lightly, and the sound dragged me to sleep against my will. I dimly felt him carry me upstairs to bed.

# Chapter 18

I rolled over and poked Will's chest as I sleepily mumbled, "Why did you set the alarm clock so early this morning?"

"I have a meeting with the Alpha before he leaves for more trade talks," he groaned, barely awake enough to talk.

"Well, your alarm has been going off for almost ten minutes."

"What? Why didn't you wake me sooner?" He scrambled out of bed and grabbed his clothes.

I sat up and stretched. "It was your alarm clock. How was I supposed to know why you set it so early? Even I don't get up this early if I have any say in the matter."

Will disappeared out the door without replying. With a yawn and another stretch, I decided to get out of bed. Will had been kind enough to fold my clothes and place them on the dresser for me. The pants were still clean, so I grabbed them and shook them out.

With a clatter, the pregnancy test rolled across the floor, escaping from its toilet paper cocoon. I pulled my pants on and went to retrieve the items.

As I bent over to pick them up, I paused when I saw the second line on the display. I slowly picked it up with a frown. There had only been one line last night. Could it be defective? I'd never used one of these tests before, so I began wondering if I'd missed a step.

Still mulling over the test, I got dressed and headed to the bathroom on this level. A quick check under the counter revealed the same type of pregnancy test, but this one still had the instructions.

My eyes widened as I realized the results needed at least ten minutes to show the second line. I had definitely not waited that long last night. I read further. One line appeared immediately. The second line would indicate pregnancy and took time to react. If the test sat too long, the second line might appear anyway.

I grabbed another test and glanced at the clock on the wall to check the time. Twenty minutes later, I stuck both tests in my pocket before retreating to the bedroom with my mind whirling. No wonder I had been more tired than usual the last couple of days. I was pregnant.

This was not how I had planned to start my morning.

Since I was up so early, I peeled potatoes in one of the smaller kitchens to help the cooks, most of whom were still sleeping. Luckily, no one else was in the room since my mind kept drifting back to the three pregnancy tests hidden upstairs. I had found a different brand just to double-check, but all three tests told me that Will and I would need more than one bedroom before the year was out.

I focused my senses within myself. With a lot of concentration and searching, I finally located the light in my body that wasn't mine. Barely weeks old, the light flickered very faintly, almost invisible within the glow of my own body. A second flicker almost made me drop a potato. I paused to take a closer look with my senses. Yes, there were two flickers. Twins.

Still somewhat in a daze, I continued peeling potatoes. My mother had once told me twins were common in the maternal line of her family tree. It looked like my runt gene hadn't overridden that hereditary legacy.

I pursed my lips as I wondered how many people might have noticed. I lowered my nose to my shoulder and took a deep breath. Even at that close distance, I could barely pick up the faintest trace despite knowing exactly what scent I was searching for.

At a guess, I'd have at least three weeks before my scent shifted enough for the average pack member to notice. Possibly more, since my personal scent was easily overpowered by other scents.

Ruby might be able to pick it up in a week or so if she was paying attention. Considering she always tracked me when I left the packhouse in the afternoon, she'd likely be the first to notice. Thankfully, she wasn't the type to gossip about such things.

How was I going to break the news to Will? I knew he'd be thrilled, so that wasn't the issue. I just wasn't sure how to share my latest discovery.

The news might also worry a few others. Tony had already said he'd be moving to a different pack for a year as soon as he found out I was pregnant.

I was pretty sure he'd just been teasing Will, but he'd also taken the time to show us the history notes from when the Alpha's runt mate had been expecting. Both of them had to move to the edge of the pack territory for the last few months since the pregnancy combined with the runt gene sent the Alpha's mate bond into a protective overdrive.

I furrowed my eyebrows, suddenly wondering if yesterday's episode with Will had anything to do with my pregnancy. Even if the male was unaware, the mate bond would alter his behavior as the delivery time came closer. I shook my head and dismissed it since he'd assumed I was stuck in a tunnel.

If I recalled correctly, the knowledge of the pregnancy seemed to trigger the overprotective tendencies more than the subconscious awareness from the bond.

The moment Will found out I was pregnant would be the turning point, regardless of how much he tried to keep himself in check. Just like when he'd consciously realized I was in a rabbit tunnel, his concern for my safety and wellbeing would certainly end up messing with the mate bond and his mind.

I smirked when I realized Will's one wish would be coming true shortly. With twins, it wouldn't be long before I wouldn't even be able to fit into a rabbit burrow.

Eventually, I headed out for a run in the nearby forest. Even though Ruby had never joined my morning run with Will, it wasn't long before I sensed her nearby.

I wondered if Will had asked one of the Omegas to let her know if I left the building. If he had done so, at least Will's protective measures were subtle. The patrols continued to chase large predators outside of the borders, although that wouldn't stop Will from worrying.

Ruby crossed my trail and promptly changed direction, coming my way. With a grin, I waited until she caught sight of me before shifting and darting under a bramble bush. I took off full tilt while she attempted to catch up.

As per usual, she couldn't see me or easily follow my trail under the bushes, so I quickly lost her. My Omega abilities also gave me an unfair advantage that she still wasn't aware of.

Just to be helpful, I gave a yip and darted away, more than ready to practice my evasion skills in a game of hide-and-seek.

I drizzled syrup over my pancakes as I examined Tiffany's new shoulder accessory. Nathan was much more relaxed now that his mark resided on her collarbone.

"Well, now I know why you two were conspicuously absent last night," I commented.

Tiffany grinned unrepentantly. "We made it longer than you two did. Besides, Nathan told me that he loves my lingerie collection."

He leaned over to whisper into her ear, "Ah, but they are much lovelier when they adorn your body."

His whisper was soft, but we were right across from them.

Samantha shook her head and proclaimed, "No more of that at the breakfast table."

They both grinned at her before resuming their breakfasts.

Ruby wandered over and told me, "Sylvia is hoping we can check the eastern forest in hopes of more truffles. Care to join me? Half of that area is under bramble bushes."

"Sure, come find me once breakfast is over."

She nodded and went to go get some breakfast. Tiffany shook her head without a comment, still unable to figure out how the aloof, die-hard fighter was volunteering to go find valuable fungus.

My paws sent dirt flying as I dug a truffle out of the ground. Ruby sat nearby and watched since she couldn't fit under the bramble bush. I carried it over to her and continued exploring the undersides of the sprawling plants.

My nose was focused on scents, but that left my mind plenty of time to wander. I had managed to discreetly dispose of the tests in a dumpster, but I hadn't figured out how to tell Will.

I kept mulling over ideas. I kind of wanted to surprise him, but I wasn't sure how. This wasn't something I had ever considered, nor had I ever helped anyone with this sort of thing since I'd been a rogue for so long. Oddly enough, I suspected Tiffany would have some great ideas if I could catch her alone, assuming she didn't scream the secret out at the top of her lungs the instant she found out . . .

Evan's voice rang out across the pack-wide mindlink. *"We're under attack. All non-fighters retreat to the safe houses. On-duty warriors head to the southern border. All other fighters protect the safe houses and delay any intruders that get past us."*

I ran out from under the thorn bush, and Ruby grabbed me by the scruff of my neck and began racing back to town.

*"Jade, where are you?"* Will asked as the powerful ringing of his fully awakened Enforcer abilities echoed behind his words.

*"About ten minutes from town with how fast Ruby is running. We're heading for a safe house."*

He sighed in relief. *"Good. Stay safe."*

I had no intentions of dying anytime soon and sent wordless agreement and love down the link. His presence faded from my mind as he raced to the border to help with the threat.

When Ruby reached the nearest of the three safe houses, the gathered fighters parted to let her through. As she got closer, I saw the safe house was a large, fortified cave dug into the side of a rocky hill. She went inside before setting me down, immediately turning around and trotting back outside where her fighting skills might be needed.

I shifted back into my human form and looked around. The single room held chairs and a few large barrels of water. About three dozen people were in here, most of whom were elderly, teenagers, or children. A couple of pregnant women and young men were also present. All were non-combatants.

From the murmuring coming from outside the still-open door, those with minimal fighting training who didn't want to stay inside had to remain close to the door, behind their trained counterparts. As a runt, I wasn't good in hand-to-hand combat, and I had never shown my skills on the archery range, so I doubted they'd let me join the archers in the trees.

The door was closed and several people inside barred it. I sat on a chair in a corner while extending my senses. Those inside were mostly bored and simply waiting to be let out. I didn't think this was a practice drill though. Outside, the protective mindset of the fighters was a fierce glow, tempered with their anger and determination.

I recalled the ringing in Will's voice when we last spoke, and I became even more certain this was an actual attack. I pushed my senses further out, noting that almost everyone in the packhouse was in the main safe room. Anyone not near a safe room had a mindset similar to the fighters and were likely hidden archers.

The main packlink remained quiet. There had been no updates from those at the border. Nothing about the enemy numbers or their location. No calls for backup. No mates wailed about their partner being in a serious fight or getting injured. No children screamed as their family link with a parent disappeared forever.

Just unnerving silence.

My instincts and intuition had been honed in no man's land, and they were telling me something was very wrong. I strained my senses as I pushed my awareness past the town's edge. These senses had never been meant for long-distance use and this was about as far as I could extend them.

A few unfamiliar wolves raced through the forest around the town. Their mindsparks and invasive mindset marked them as the attackers. A dozen wolves weren't a serious threat to the defenders guarding the door. But how had they gotten this far when at least a hundred warriors were along the border? And why hadn't we heard anything from our fighters yet?

I touched Will's mind and tried to get a sense of what he was up to, but the bond was blocked. With a frown, I tried to find a way through it, only to realize this wasn't a normal mind shield. This was a blank unawareness that I had sensed once in the past when someone had been knocked out cold.

My heart dropped as I wondered if Will had been injured. The Enforcers would be leading any attack, and like any powerful fighter, he'd also be a main target as the enemy attempted to cripple the pack's defenses.

He was alive—the mate bond reassured me of that. Even if he'd been seriously injured, it would have alerted me. But the block and lack of communication weren't adding up, and I didn't like it.

I mindlinked Ruby who was standing guard outside, *"Something isn't right. I can't reach Will through the mate bond—it's like he is unconscious. I haven't heard anything from the fighters. Do you have any idea what's going on?"*

Her mindvoice was tight with strain. *"None of the Enforcers are responding. Most of the warriors are also silent. We have no idea what's happening at the border. Don't let anyone open the door until we tell you it's safe."*

That dashed my faint hope about the fighters creating a separate mindlink to avoid distressing the non-combatants.

*"That doesn't sound good. Do our fighters normally go silent? The last pack I was in, they always kept the pack members updated, even if it was bad news."*

*"No,"* she replied shortly. *"They're supposed to let us know where the enemy is and if they get into a fight. At this point, we're certain some attackers have slipped past them."*

*"Please be careful."*

She sent a wordless acknowledgment through the mindlink, and I let the link go silent so she could concentrate properly. My survival instincts were kicking in, and I was beginning to wish I had remained in the forest and hidden in a rabbit burrow. I was cornered in here, and the sheer number of fighters in the area outside more or less screamed that a safe house was in the vicinity.

I was also worried about Will. Most attackers would kill an Enforcer if they were given the chance. I prodded the mate bond but still got no response. My only consolation was that the mate bond *was* intact. It would have shattered if he died.

Several people started calling across the main packlink, asking the distant warriors for updates. A couple of the fighters near town replied that they hadn't seen anything yet, but there was no reply from those along the border.

A few women in the room began crying when they realized they were unable to reach their partners. An older woman sat with them and began asking questions. I listened intently as they confirmed their bond was intact but that something was blocking it.

I pushed my senses to their limits once more. The handful of strangers continued to circle the area but didn't approach the fighters. Their minds reflected more restraint than I expected, like they were waiting for something.

Our warriors still didn't reply, and no one had reported a shattered mate bond or broken family link yet, so all we could do was wait.

An anxious hour later, my head shot up as one of the fighters close to town shouted, *"They're coming! I see at least fifty of them."*

I pushed my senses out again, only to count at least a hundred people advancing. None of the mindsparks were familiar and their determination marked them as trouble. The safe house fighters readied themselves for the fight to come.

*"Fall back,"* one of the fighters told the sentry, who began racing ahead of the incoming attackers.

The other sentries also retreated to the groups around the safe houses. So far, anyone who'd gone farther out to scout had fallen silent shortly after they encountered the enemy. The strangest thing was that all of them were still alive. No one had died yet.

This safe house was right at the edge of town, and the approaching group was heading directly toward us. Anger and unease rolled through our defenders as the attackers appeared along the treeline in both wolf and human forms.

The invaders rearranged their formation as they slowly advanced. As they got closer, several defenders charged forward. Within seconds, their minds also dropped into dark glimmers of unconsciousness with only minor injuries.

I hesitated for a moment, then mindlinked Ruby, *"It's like they're putting people to sleep. Run to Trevor and Mike's pack to get help."*

*"The Alpha and Beta are already heading there for reinforcements. They were on their way back from a different pack and not far from Trevor's place, but it'll be at least five hours until we can expect any help to arrive."*

She was intently focused on the slowly advancing mob and their actions. Several attackers would close in until a couple of fighters charged forward, then they paused to examine the more restrained defenders.

*"Pull back to the door. Attacking them in small groups isn't working,"* Ruby told the others.

They eased back until they were right in front of the door, refusing to be lured into a fight like their unconscious comrades. I slowly got to my feet, too nervous to remain sitting when there were only a couple dozen fighters left standing.

Out of habit, I tried to scent the air, but it was useless in here. I kept tabs on the standoff outside. The attackers had stopped their advance now that the remaining defenders refused to be lured away.

Without warning, the defenders' mindsparks dimmed into dull shimmers—including Ruby's. The pack link—with all the updates from the fighters outside—went silent. I rubbed my sweaty palms against my pants as I tried to mindlink Ruby, to no avail.

Chills ran down my spine as I realized the attackers had neutralized our fighters at a distance. And to make things worse, they had done it quickly enough that our defenders hadn't been able to warn us.

The instincts I had picked up during my days as a rogue were screaming that something wasn't right. An attacking group had somehow rendered almost two hundred fighters unconscious without sustaining major losses. I had never heard of anything like this before.

As the intruders dragged the unconscious defenders away, I backed into the corner along the wall with the door. There was no other door or exit, so we were trapped in here. Others began murmuring among themselves, and a few started crying as they realized how bad our current situation was.

Dead silence fell as a loud bang echoed across the room. All eyes locked onto the heavy steel door as another bang vibrated through it. People shuffled as far away as they could.

The door was thick reinforced steel, specifically designed to slow attackers and give the fighters time to regain lost ground. However, no door could stop a force if they had all the time in the world to break it down.

The other two safe houses and fighters protecting them listened as several people in here gave them updates. The door slowly developed a dent and rattled more with each blow. Several people shifted into their wolf forms and stood with raised hackles in front of the children.

Minutes later, the door burst open as women and children screamed. The handful of wolves charged forward as bags of powder were thrown into the room. I swiftly held a tissue over my nose, even before I recognized the sharp scent as that of a rare herb capable of rendering the mindlink inert.

Three large, heavily-armored men pushed their way into the room amidst the ensuing chaos and used shields to deflect the wolves' attacks. I tensed, halfway expecting a pained canine scream as the fighters retaliated, only for them to bat the wolves with an odd paddle. The wolves staggered across the floor as their minds began to haze over, soon collapsing into furry mounds.

My eyes quickly examined the three men, only now realizing that lethal weapons like swords were absent. Several others shifted—mostly older teens and a few of the more mobile elderly—and likewise charged the men as panicked screams filled the air and everyone else tried to get away in a room with only one door.

The huge men continued to rely on their strength, size, and armor while swinging the paddles. Small barbs on the paddles glistened as if wet, and even through the tissue, I could smell the powerful tranquilizer.

As the men pushed farther into the room, I saw one potential escape route if I could catch them by surprise. If I misjudged or they expected it, I'd run right into their hands, but if they weren't prepared for it, I had a chance of getting away. With no way to attack them and nowhere else to go, it was my only option.

I used my senses to quickly note the locations of the men outside who were waiting to come in and grab my unconscious packmates. The three men slowly advanced as everyone moved against the walls to try and avoid them. A couple of people huddled near me, but most had gathered against the far wall.

Taking a deep breath, I readied myself to use all of the abilities I had picked up as a rogue and Omega. I shifted into my wolf form and turned my passive stance ability to the max so they would have a hard time focusing on me.

I darted between the feet of those near me and raced along the wall. I almost reached the door before one of the men noticed my tiny gray shape in the shadows.

"Catch the pup heading for the door!"

They hadn't been expecting anyone to approach, and it had given me precious seconds. I spread my senses around me as several people ran to the door to intercept me.

I launched myself at the doorjamb and ricocheted off at an angle. I darted between two men and ran full-tilt for the forest. The men followed, shaking their heads as they struggled to focus on me and my unexpected actions. They had expected to catch a clumsy puppy, not an agile runt, especially not one their eyes refused to lock onto.

Adrenaline surged through my veins as I felt something brush against my fur, but I didn't look back to see what had narrowly missed me. Several pursuers shifted and were hot on my trail as I reached the edge of the forest.

One jumped ahead of me, trying to cut me off, and I swiftly changed direction to run under low branches. If they valued their eyes, they would have to go around the tree, which they did. Two wolves quickly caught up in an open area, and I ricocheted off another tree to put a bit more distance between me and them.

I saw a massive bramble bush ahead, and I used all of my speed to race toward it. Paws thudded behind me, so close his claws brushed against my tail.

My heart hammered as I felt him reach down to grab my neck. I put on another desperate burst of speed and ducked beneath the leaves. His scream tore through the air as he realized moments too late that the leaves had concealed massive thorns.

While his friends were distracted, I changed direction and kept running. I was finally far enough ahead to pull the disappearing act that had frustrated Ruby so many times in the past.

# Chapter 19

I silently dropped onto the branch beside Jisk as we watched the invading group carry unconscious people to various locations along the town's main street.

"I've never seen anything like this before," Jisk murmured.

"Nor have I," I replied, equally as quiet. "Did you notice they are separating people by gender, age, and fighting ability?"

"Yes. I can't believe how many chains they wrapped the three Enforcers in."

"Don't remind me," I growled faintly. "If it weren't for the fact that those chains weigh more than I do, I probably would have attempted to free them once they woke up. The mate bond is giving me more than a bit of grief right now."

He also growled his frustration. "I'm somewhat handicapped in this situation as well."

My eyes moved to one of the groups who were currently being tied up. "That group is well to the side, and I can always untie them later so you don't have to go near her."

With a grunt, he replied, "It doesn't surprise me that you noticed. How long have you known?"

I rummaged around in my backpack and passed him a small baggie with a few leaves in it. "I connected the dots about two weeks after arriving here."

He examined the leaves. "Thanks. I might need them."

I nodded without commenting. The leaves were so potent that if someone rubbed them under their nose, it'd overpower any other scent, including the smell of their mate. It was more of a last resort if he had to go near her since he wouldn't be able to smell anything else.

Second chance mate bonds relied more on looking into each other's eyes, so their potential mate's scent didn't always stand out until after eye contact. He'd also been keeping high in the trees to prevent her from possibly noticing him, which had been one of my original clues.

Jisk flicked a finger at a large scar-covered man who was barking orders at everyone. "I think this group might fall into anarchy if we can remove the guy in charge. At least half of them don't look happy with what they're doing. He might be holding their mates hostage."

"I was thinking that as well, but we need to find the guy in charge first."

Jisk gave me an odd look. "You think the demanding loud-mouth down there isn't the one in charge? No one else has dared to contradict him."

"I'm positive," I said, once more looking at the town. "Look at how he pauses when a decision needs to be made. He isn't just thinking, he's mindlinking someone. I think he's the second-in-command."

Jisk growled as he came to the same conclusion I had. "He's a decoy in case someone wants to take out the leader."

"Exactly. Now we just need to figure out where the real leader is hiding. I doubt he's far away. I checked this half of the forest already, but my senses can't reach the other side from here."

Jisk smoothly rose into a crouch. "Let's go."

I followed him as we traversed the forest highway without a sound.

Jisk glowered at the stand of trees in the middle of the large meadow as he told me, "I don't like this plan."

With a shrug, I said, "There isn't any way for you to get across the grass unnoticed. Your part of the plan is riskier than mine."

He snorted. "If I thought you actually believed that last sentence to be true, I'd tie you up and take out both of them myself."

"Unless you have an alternative plan?"

He sighed and shook his head in frustration. "No, this is the best one we've been able to come up with. I just don't like the thought of sending you off alone." He turned to me, and his dark eyes stared into mine. "Do *not* take any risks. You aren't a match for any of them. Do what you have to do and run. Whatever you do, don't get caught."

With a serious nod, I shifted and scampered into the sprawling thorny bushes, disappearing from sight. We'd located the Alpha in a meadow just east of town. The trees were spaced too far apart to use the forest highway, and the long grass and low shrubs prevented a regular wolf from sneaking close.

I eyed up the tall grass before leaving the shelter of the thorns to crawl closer to the clearing ahead. My scent currently matched this clearing perfectly, so much so that even Jisk couldn't detect me.

My belly fur brushed against the ground as I crawled through the grass that was barely tall enough to hide me. I edged in closer until I reached a large tree, then waited for the pacing man to turn the other way.

I quickly shifted and climbed the branches, keeping the tree between me and him. When I peered through the leaves, the man was still pacing. His eyes faded out of focus frequently as he mindlinked people.

Keeping quiet, I climbed higher until I reached a hollow in the side of the trunk. A quick check revealed it was an old woodpecker nest. As I had hoped, it was also big enough for me to squeeze into.

Sitting on a nearby branch, I pulled a tiny vial of liquid out of my backpack. The mixture of deadly plant extracts and snake venom was an extremely nasty poison. This was the deadliest one in Jisk's arsenal and potent enough to kill an Alpha in less than five minutes.

I dripped the thick liquid onto the arrow, coating the arrow-head and part of the shaft. I carefully nocked the arrow and turned my attention to the Alpha below. He was still pacing in a circle he had beaten down in the grass. I had studied his habits earlier and waited for the perfect opening.

His eyes narrowed in thought for longer than usual while he concentrated on something complex. I slowly drew my bow. As soon as his eyes went vacant, he'd be relaying detailed instructions over the mindlink.

There! I loosed my arrow and immediately shifted to scramble into the woodpecker nest. I flattened my head so not even the tips of my ears would be visible.

A roar of fury came from below as he yanked the arrow out. The clock was ticking. I just had to keep out of his reach until the poison did its work. He probably wouldn't spot the hollow I was hiding in, and even if he did, the thought of a runt hiding inside probably wouldn't cross his mind.

I tracked him with my senses as he searched the nearby bushes, already starting to stumble. My senses could just reach the town, where the attackers milled uneasily, unsure why their Alpha was suddenly so furious.

The presence of several brightening mindsparks made me realize some people were starting to wake up. I prodded my mate bond, but it was still unresponsive. They had likely given the Enforcers a much higher dose to keep them down.

Below, the Alpha stumbled and fell as his legs gave out. His presence shimmered as his body fought a losing battle against the toxins. At this point, he wouldn't be able to catch me, so I cautiously peeked out of the opening.

He lay on the ground as blood trickled out of his ears and nose from the poison's hemorrhagic effects. I climbed out of the hollow and shifted before descending to the bushes on the forest floor. I made a face at the next part of our plan, but dutifully shifted and snuck closer to the Alpha.

Still in wolf form, I stepped on a few twigs as I emerged from the bushes. The Alpha's head turned in my direction as he tried to sit up. I tilted my head in a puppy-like manner at his incredulous expression, then turned and ran into the undergrowth.

He shifted into his wolf form and lunged to his feet with a furious snarl, but he only managed to stagger a few steps before collapsing once again. I didn't slow down until the trees were dense enough for me to use the forest highway to get close to town undetected.

When I got closer, I was surprised to see the Enforcers were awake. They were still quite groggy, but they were shaking off the tranquilizer with commendable speed. About half of the pack was also awake.

The tension among the attackers was almost visible as they milled around. They stopped mid-step as a slight tremor passed through them. Their Alpha had died. For an instant, silence reigned before loud snarls and growls echoed across the town.

Will struggled wildly against his bonds, realizing I was nearby via the mate bond. My mental shields were up to prevent distractions, so if he had been trying to talk to me, I wouldn't have noticed.

I lowered my shields slightly. *"Have you ever heard of a poker face? If they realize you have a mate running around, they'll use you to get to me. Then they'll use me to control you."*

Even though his muscles still quivered with pent-up emotion, Will reluctantly ceased his struggles. *"What are you doing here? Run away!"*

*"Not yet. Help is on the way, but I have to do one thing before I put as much distance between these attackers and me as I can. Please, if you love me, don't react to what I'm about to do in case they realize you're my mate."*

I felt his worry, but I raised my shields before he could reply. He could give me a scathing lecture later about the dangerous stunt I was about to attempt.

I'd probably even be in full agreement with him. I'd never had two hundred pissed-off wolves out for my blood before, and I *certainly* never imagined I'd be intentionally taunting them.

I readied another poisoned arrow and took aim at the milling group. Things in the attacker's organization were starting to fall apart, but just as Jisk and I had assumed, there were a couple of people who were continuing with the original plan, whatever it was.

My senses tracked Jisk as he got into place and readied himself. It was my turn again. I stepped out from behind the tree and loosed my arrow at the third-in-command, who had been preventing more than a few attackers from leaving.

I shifted into wolf form and hid behind a large log. The man screamed in pain as his hands gripped the arrow lodged in his stomach. Heads spun in his direction before turning to the treelines as they tried to spot the archer.

I took a deep breath to build up my courage. If I had been wearing boots, I would have been shaking in them. This was insane. Why had I agreed to this?

Before I could change my mind, I jumped on top of the log.

"There!" someone shouted, immediately spotting me.

I posed on the log as all eyes riveted on me. From the rising hackles on a number of the fighters, they knew I was responsible for killing their Alpha. I currently had the undivided attention of any loyal followers.

A dark brown wolf launched out of a window to land on the second-in-command. Even from where I stood, I heard the snap of the man's neck as he was caught completely by surprise. Jisk immediately attacked a couple of nearby fighters, and the snarling had everyone focusing on them.

In the distraction, I turned and darted into the undergrowth. Several fighters noticed me escaping and gave chase, although I sensed a few others taking their chances and running away. Footsteps grew louder as several wolves started gaining on me.

As I darted down a rabbit burrow I had checked earlier, I knew my pursuers didn't stand a chance of catching me. I squirmed through the tunnels in a fashion that would have had Will doing somersaults and went out the far exit, leaving the wolves sniffing at the entrance.

Once I was a safe distance away, I shifted and climbed a tree before heading back to the edge of town. I took care to remain completely hidden as I examined the chaos below. Jisk had disappeared, although judging by the half a dozen bodies, he had left his mark. Several of the attackers were in loud arguments over who was now in charge and what should be done.

I sensed Jisk's approach and glanced over as he climbed up the other side of the tree. A few minor scratches adorned his arms, but I didn't see anything more serious.

"Good job," I said. "Do you think anyone will be elected leader easily?"

Jisk grinned at my compliment. "I'm not sure. I wasn't paying much attention since I was trying to cover the scent of the blood spatter on my clothing. I assume you didn't have too many problems with the Alpha or those chasing you?"

"I got lucky. The Alpha didn't know where to look for me until I showed myself. These guys have obviously never been rogues, and the three chasing me were completely baffled by my journey down the rabbit hole."

"Do you have any idea who might be winning the loudmouth election down there?"

"Give me a moment." I pushed my senses out to examine the undercurrent of emotions, but something else caught my attention. "Wow. Will is absolutely furious. I have no idea how he looks so calm. I almost pity the one who unties him. Oh, wait a minute . . ."

I felt another faint brush against my mind shields and thought I recognized it. I lowered my shields and asked, *"Alpha, were you trying to contact me?"*

My mindvoice went through, and I felt his relief at finally getting a response.

*"What's going on? Why isn't anyone else responding?"*

I sent him a mental image of the scene in front of me. *"None of our pack are dead, but all were exposed to an herb that blocks the mindlink and many were tranquilized, although it's starting to wear off. It looks like about half of their force is here on threats and are quickly scattering in all directions. We took out the first four in command and several of their top fighters. They're currently bickering over who gets to call the shots. If you circle around and come up from the south, you'll catch them by surprise since they think they cleared that direction."*

The whiff I'd gotten in the safe house must have worn off, so the Alpha had been able to contact me even though the main packlink was still down. The Alpha was silent for a while, likely relaying my information to those he was traveling with.

He eventually said, *"In that case, we'll come up that way and catch them by surprise. Trevor and Mike are with me, along with a large group of their warriors. We're just crossing the border now, so we'll be there shortly. I know you aren't a trained fighter, so please stay safe until we take care of the intruders."*

"Alright. *I'll continue hiding near the town in case you need updates from someone with a vantage point."*

*"Thanks."* The mindlink faded out.

I told Jisk, "The Alpha is coming with a bunch of fighters from the neighboring pack, including their Alpha and Beta. They're going to loop around and come up from the south in about fifteen minutes."

Jisk sighed in relief. "Oh, good. They can finish up the battle. There shouldn't be much resistance at this point."

I stood beside Jisk just inside the treeline as the rescuers tied up several attackers who surrendered while others began untying and unchaining the pack members.

Jisk eventually sighed. "I'm glad the battle is over and no innocents got hurt."

"I fully agree. I was really worried about them for a while."

As Jisk gazed to the side, his emotions shifted to longing, with undertones of sadness, unease, uncertainty, and echoes of pain.

I spoke quietly, "If you want, you can wear a pair of Will's sunglasses and use those leaves to block her scent. I can make her do the same if you want to talk with her without the mate bond playing havoc with your minds."

Hope and anticipation started to rise as he thought about it. "I'd love to do that. Perhaps in three days? That'll let the pack have some time to recover and give her a chance to run for the hills if the thought of being with a rogue makes her think twice."

I chuckled at that unlikely event. "She won't run for the hills because of that. If you've been paying any attention to what she's been doing the last two months, you'd know a rogue's abilities intrigue her."

He wrapped an arm around my waist and gave me a quick hug. Sincerity rang in his words as he said, "Thanks, kiddo."

"You're welcome." I returned the hug. I was honestly happy for him. He deserved a second chance at love.

It was rare for Jisk to show emotion like this. His original mate had rejected him in order to marry an Alpha for power, and that rejection still pained him. To make things worse, the Alpha had used an Alpha command on Jisk to force him to leave the pack and never come back.

I was pretty sure I was the only person he had ever told, and I had never mentioned it to anyone. Jisk had been like a father to me in no man's land, so I truly wished the best for him. If his second chance mate accepted him, it would erase the scars and pain of the previous rejection.

With a sigh, Jisk dropped his arm. Then his body tensed slightly as he took a slow, deep breath, testing the air. He turned his head in my direction and took a second breath. As his wide eyes lowered to meet mine, his emotions formed a whirlwind in his mind.

Uh-oh.

His voice was tight as he said, "Please tell me you were unaware you were pregnant when you joined the fight."

Of all the people to notice . . . Letting someone expecting a child get in the way of any possible harm was right up there with rejection in Jisk's mind. There was no sense in lying since he'd pick it up instantly.

I sighed in defeat. "I knew a couple of days ago."

Jisk's anger grew, and I waited for his explosion with trepidation. Much to my surprise, it never came. His anger dropped into heavy irritation.

"If I'd known, I would have tied you up and hidden you deep in the woods while I took them all out. I can't believe you didn't tell me before I let you go off on your own." He crossed his arms and frowned at me, just like an irritated father.

I grinned shakily at my lucky break. "I can believe you'd do that. It kind of slipped my mind with Will tied up like a turkey. I'm not far enough along for it to slow me down yet."

He growled a reprimand at my idiocy before glancing over to where the Enforcers were tied up. "Does Will know?"

I grimaced. "Not yet. I've been trying to find a way to surprise him with the news. Luckily, no one else around here has a nose as keen as yours."

Despite his irritation, he chuckled. "You mean you've been putting it off to postpone the typical Enforcer overprotectiveness."

I stuck out my tongue at him. "You'll have to come by regularly and visit your niece or nephew, or I'll be most upset with you."

"You're letting me be an uncle?" he asked, looking at me in shock, although his excitement was rapidly building underneath.

With a grin, I said, "Well, it's either that or grandpa, but that makes you sound kind of old."

He laughed. "I much prefer Uncle Jisk. Although I never thought I'd have the chance to hear that from a child."

His mind radiated unshadowed joy, something I had never sensed from him before. I grinned at his excitement.

"It looks like they're about to start cutting the Enforcer's chains," I told him, "so I'm going to head down and make sure Will doesn't kill someone in his desire to get free."

"I have some loose ends to tie up, and I'll be back in three days. I'll meet you in that small meadow where you gave your first lesson in tracking masked scents."

"That works for me," I said, wondering what he had thought of my attempts to teach my packmates.

I waved goodbye as he disappeared into the trees like a ghost. Now that all the attackers were secured, I headed into the town to see Will.

As I approached, a couple of men from the rescuing group were trying various tools on the heavy chains while all three Enforcers were forced to wait impatiently for their freedom. Will kept struggling against his chains, reminding me I hadn't lowered the mindshields on the mate bond yet.

Trying to postpone the lecture I'd certainly be getting at some point, I lowered my shields and mindlinked him. *"Relax, Will. They'll have you free shortly."*

His panicked and worried voice immediately responded, *"Jade! Where are you? Are you alright?"*

His back was to me and the wind wasn't in his favor, so I put my hand on his shoulder and said, "I'm right here."

He jumped at the contact, but the sparks immediately let him know who it was. He let out a huge sigh of relief. "Don't startle me like that. I was so worried about you. Are you okay?" He struggled to turn his head around enough to check on me.

I walked forward and sat on the ground beside him. "I'm fine. I just shot two arrows and ran. Jisk was the only one who got close to the fighters."

"Why didn't you run away before that? You didn't stand a chance against those fighters! They could have caught you!"

I rubbed my hand on an unchained section of his arm to try and calm him. "I know. That's why I only shot two arrows that were loaded with poison. Other than that, I ran and hid. You know how hard I am to catch and track if I put my mind to it. I have so many tricks that I lost them within seconds."

Will took a deep breath and tried to calm himself, releasing it in a heavy sigh. "I can't wait until these chains are off . . ."

The two men testing out various hacksaws and cutters glanced up. "We're trying. You should be flattered they used such heavy-duty and expensive chains to bind you."

Will growled faintly and pushed his arms against the restraints yet again.

Rolling my eyes, I poked him in the ribs and said, "Be nice. They're trying to free you. If they leave, I wouldn't have a clue where to start."

Will pressed his lips together and refrained from commenting.

I glanced up as Alpha Roland approached, accompanied by Trevor and Mike. I nodded a greeting at them. "Thank you for coming to our rescue."

Alpha Trevor nodded, dropping his disguise of Beta. "I'm glad we made it in time. Luckily, we didn't lose any men in the attack and only a few were injured."

"I'm happy to hear that."

Roland bent down to touch the chains binding Will, asking the men, "Why are these so much more difficult to cut than the other ones?"

One of them responded, "They're a special chain designed to hold Enforcers if they show signs of going feral."

"Someone obviously came prepared," Roland replied with a frown.

Still tied up, Tony asked the Alpha, "Do you know why they attacked? I'm glad to be alive, but I've never heard of an attacking group simply chaining up Enforcers."

Roland and Trevor exchanged a glance before Roland said, "This pack was from the south. They tranquilized everyone because they were after one particular person, but they weren't sure who it was and they didn't want to risk killing them."

"Who were they after?" Tony asked, sounding just as confused as I felt. Why would they attack an entire pack just to kidnap one member?

Roland glanced at me. "They were after Jade, although none of them realized it."

"Me? Why?"

Will growled and his muscles shook as he battled for control. The chains prevented him from shifting into his larger wolf shape and were probably the only reason he was still human.

With a sigh, Roland said, "Greed. They figured out someone in our pack was able to smell truffles and realized just how much money they were worth. Our pack has made almost half a million dollars selling those truffles at the auctions."

Trevor spoke up, "We interrogated a couple of the attackers, although it wasn't much of an interrogation since they spoke freely. A number of them weren't here willingly, and their stories all line up. The Alpha planned on questioning people until he found out who was locating the truffles, even if he had to torture someone to get their mate to spill the secret. He wanted the money.

"The Alpha didn't have an heir, so I sent my second son and some fighters down there to take control of the pack until we figure things out. If the pack doesn't accept them, they'll let their neighbors know what happened and the pack will probably end up disbanding."

Pounding footsteps heralded the arrival of someone carrying a cutting torch. He knelt beside Will and slid a shield under the chains to protect his skin from the torch.

Will's eyes lit up. "About time. Get these things off me."

When I chuckled, Will mock-glared at me for having the audacity to make fun of him in this situation.

"Look away," the man warned us.

We complied, and it wasn't long until the clattering of the cut chain marked the beginning of Will's freedom. I turned back and helped unwrap the numerous loops of chain, only to be suddenly engulfed in a big hug once Will was freed. His hug was tight enough to pin my arms to my sides and prevent me from hugging him back.

Laughing, I said, "Will, take it easy. You're stronger than me."

His arms loosened, although he didn't release me. Instead, he buried his face in my hair and mumbled, "You have no idea how glad I am to have you in my arms again. Are you sure you're okay?"

"Yes."

With a sigh, he scooped me into his arms.

"Will, what are you doing?" I protested. "Put me down. I'm fine."

He held me close to his chest. "Getting a second opinion. You probably wouldn't admit to an injury even if you had one."

I rolled my eyes at his paranoia. "I'm a runt, not some prideful fighter."

Will started striding in the direction of the infirmary. As we went by the Alpha, I sent him a pleading look.

Alpha Roland grinned at my expression. "Everyone else got checked by the pack doctors, so you might as well too. Especially since I hear you were dodging wolves and running around in the forest."

With a sly glance at Will, Trevor added, "What he really means, is that if he doesn't agree, Will would probably flatten him and take you to see the doctor anyway."

I chuckled in spite of my situation. That definitely sounded like Will when the mate bond was in overdrive.

"I don't even want to know how many rabbit burrows you went down today," Will grumbled.

I raised my chin in defiance. "Just two."

He snorted in plain disbelief. "Right."

"It's the truth! The rest of the time, I was climbing trees and pretending to be a monkey!"

The others burst into laughter, although Will squeezed his eyes shut and took a deep breath. When he sent a glare over his shoulder, the sounds were quickly suppressed.

The doctor gently poked my ribs while Will watched from the other side of the room, sitting on the stool he'd been exiled to.

"One or two small bruises, but they'll heal by sunset," the doctor said.

He pulled out a stethoscope and he slid it beneath my shirt, pressing his hand against the cloth to listen to my heart. Then he moved it to the side for my lungs. He went behind me and slid it down the back of my shirt. When he applied some pressure, I flinched as he found a bruise I'd been previously unaware of. Will tensed and growled sharply at the gray-haired man.

"Sorry about that," the doctor told me. Glancing over his shoulder at my mate, he said, "That wasn't intentional. If you want me to stop the exam, let me know."

Will gritted his teeth and silently fumed. The doctor moved the scope to the middle of my back, and I sensed something pique his interest. Suddenly intent, he moved the scope down to my side. Coming back in front of me, he lifted the hem of my shirt to place the stethoscope on my stomach just above my belt.

"Well, congratulations on the new addition to your family."

Even though his mind had tipped me off, his words still surprised me. I thought their heartbeats would have been too quiet to detect yet. Well, there went all of the surprise planning I had been working on . . .

"What do you mean?" Will asked, tilting his head slightly in confusion. Then his eyes widened. "Wait, are you saying..."

The doctor smiled and nodded. "I can barely hear the heartbeat, so she can't be far along, but you're going to be a father."

Will jumped up with a whoop. Picking me up, he spun around in a circle. I'd known Will would be thrilled, but his exuberant display still had me laughing in delight.

The doctor shook his head with a smile. "Easy with her. She isn't a ragdoll."

Will put me down and wrapped his arm around my shoulders, asking the doctor, "Is the child okay?"

The doctor nodded. "There's no sign of a blow or injury to the stomach, and she didn't get hit with any of the tranquilizer, so we don't need to worry about possible complications from that. Come back for an ultrasound in three weeks or so. She's still able to exercise, but it's advisable to keep her from anything really strenuous."

Will looked down at me with a grin. "That means no more trips down rabbit holes or climbing into trees. Your days of pretending to be a rabbit or monkey are over for some time."

I grinned back at him. "You should be glad I never particularly wanted to try flying like a bird."

Shaking his head, he muttered, "You're going to be the death of me one day . . ."

With a grin, I watched Jisk give Ruby a rose, which he had thoughtfully removed the thorns from. She took a deep breath of the flower's fragrance and kissed his cheek. The tenderness and love in his eyes were unmistakable.

Jisk could barely be pried away from Ruby's side, and she was just as enamored with him. She had agreed to the odd meeting conditions with curiosity. Within the hour, the sunglasses had come off, and they rarely left one another's side in the two weeks since.

Will sat on the bench next to me and commented, "I simply can't think of mates better suited for one another. Except for us, of course."

A smile tugged at my lips. "They are so alike it's almost scary. You and I seem to almost be opposites in most things."

"We have plenty in common. I enjoy training people, and considering how often you come to watch, you enjoy it too."

"And we both enjoy our evening strolls and cuddle time," I agreed, "although Jisk and Ruby seem to prefer the forest. I think I've only seen them relaxing on a couch once."

Jisk heard me and glanced over in amusement. Hand-in-hand, he guided Ruby to the bench across from us.

"Getting tired of me yet?" I inquired impishly.

"There are one or two draws that shall keep bringing me back," he replied, sending a pointed smile at Ruby as he rested his arm around her waist.

She snuggled against him and glanced between me and him. "Did she really manage to sneak up behind you when you first met?"

He sent me a wry look. "Yes. Let's just say I never assumed footsteps belonged to a rabbit after that."

I snickered. "I tried a few other times but was never successful. He's a quick learner."

"How long did you two travel together?" Ruby asked.

"Quite a few years," Jisk said. "Even though she was just a teenager when her pack was wiped out by ferals, it was next to impossible to get another pack to adopt her."

"Because she was a runt?" Ruby quietly asked. When Jisk and I both nodded, she snorted. "Well, she's more than welcome here, and I'll bite the tail of anyone who objects."

"You wouldn't be the only one," Jisk muttered.

"You really care for her, don't you?" Ruby asked as hints of jealousy flickered through her mind.

He was silent for a moment before quietly replying, "After my first mate rejected me for power, I thought I was incapable of ever feeling love again. Even though she was just a teenager, her humor and good spirits were never crushed when packs refused to accept her. She didn't even seem particularly bothered by the fact that she would likely never have a mate. It was almost a year before I realized she had somehow become the daughter I never had but had always dreamed of. She allowed me to feel love once more, and her presence helped me begin to move on from the pain of the rejection."

I blinked away tears brought on by Jisk's story and at how no hint of pain came from the mere mention of the rejection. The second chance bond with Ruby had finally freed him from the pain caused by the first shattered mate bond.

I quietly said, "You never told me that before. I had always thought of you as a father. You taught me so much."

He laughed shakily. "And you constantly kept me on my toes with all your attempts to sneak up behind me."

"I still think I managed it several times, but you'd certainly never admit it."

"Nope. I'll be the first to admit I have too much pride for my own good, although those abilities of yours were a constant ego check. I hope people never learn how easily you could track me and sneak up behind me."

Ruby chuckled. "Oh, I can relate to that. She's evil. It was like she knew exactly where I was at any given time."

Jisk, Will, and I burst out laughing at her unwitting words, leaving Ruby to look between the three of us as if we'd gone crazy.

I stifled my laughter long enough to say, "That's because I actually *knew* where you were whenever you got close."

She blinked in confusion, still not understanding. "How?"

"I had been designated as an Omega for about a year, so I could actually sense your presence. *That* was how I evaded you so easily."

Her jaw dropped, and Jisk used his finger to gently close it again.

She recovered and exclaimed, "So that's how you did it! I thought it was a skill only an experienced rogue could develop!"

I shook my head, still grinning widely. "Good rogues are almost as observant, but it can't quite compare to those abilities."

Footsteps made us look over to see Tony approach.

"Which abilities?" he inquired, having just caught the last few words.

Ruby grinned mischievously and said, "We were just discussing what abilities Enforcers had when it came to escaping."

Roland and Emily rounded the corner behind the Enforcer.

Tony scratched his head in confusion. "Enforcers usually don't run. Our mindset is geared to stand and fight."

Seeing Ruby's knowing grin, Roland raised an eyebrow in amusement. "Which one of my Enforcers is running away?"

Ruby pointed her thumb at Tony. "He is."

"Huh? I've never had thoughts of leaving the pack, except if-" Tony froze mid-sentence and stared at me with wide eyes. "No. Please tell me she isn't saying what I think she's saying."

It was Roland's turn to look confused. "What is Ruby implying?"

I grinned at Tony's pleading tone, letting my silence speak for me.

With a groan, Tony sighed heavily and told Roland, "She's warning us that you're about to see firsthand just how overprotective an Enforcer mate can get."

Roland brightened and told me, "Congratulations!" He elbowed Tony's side lightly. "It can't be that bad. I remember when Evan's mother was carrying him, and his father was an Enforcer."

Jisk cleared his throat and raised an eyebrow at Roland like an old teacher faced with a dense student.

"Jade is a runt, and Will is an Enforcer," he said as if the meaning should have been obvious. "You may want to connect those dots with the mate bond in mind."

Roland blinked in confusion, then his eyes widened. "Oh no . . ."

Tony smirked at his Alpha, finally able to get some revenge. "Oh, yes. It'll probably be just like what that history record portrayed. I plan to visit another pack when she is close to delivery and will return once the child is born."

"And how will you know when it's safe to return?" Roland asked.

"Jade isn't that big, and Will *is* an Enforcer. Any kids will be huge. Once that kid has to come out, I'll probably hear her yelling at him regardless of where I am."

I glared at Tony, who unremorsefully grinned back at me. Pursing my lips, I glanced up at Will, who looked down at me.

With a mischievous tone, I asked, "Shall we tell them that we're actually expecting twins?"

Will's eyes widened in pride, excitement, and terror.

Tony turned and started running away as he called back, "That's it! I'm heading to Trevor's pack. Call me when it's over!"

Jisk leaned over and whispered in Ruby's ear, "How does a nine-month vacation sound? Under the guise of trading relations, of course."

I shook my head as my friends made plans to desert me. When the mate bond sent Will overboard in about six months, I'd be the only one who'd be unable to escape.

235

# Epilogue

"Nancy! Get out of that tree this instant! I don't care what Uncle Jisk tells you!"

I looked over as Will ran to haul our five-year-old daughter out of the tree.

She squirmed in his grip. "But Mommy does it all the time!"

"That's beside the point," he said. "If I had my way, she wouldn't do it either."

Jisk and Ruby rounded the corner of the house in time to overhear Will's words.

Ruby shook her head in mock sadness. "Nancy, don't you remember what we told you? Don't climb trees if your Dad can see you."

"Ruby!" Will exclaimed, bestowing a frown upon her. I laughed, and he turned to face me. "You're not helping."

"But Nigel gets to climb trees!" Nancy said, still sitting in Will's arms.

Will shook his head. "Not if I catch him, he doesn't."

As they walked over, a young pup ran around Ruby's feet while an older one stalked through the bushes. Their two kids were bundles of energy and quite determined to use it.

"Uncle Jisk! Catch me!"

Will jumped in surprise as Nancy's twin dropped out of the tree above him into Jisk's arms.

Will shook his head in exasperation. "What is it with you people and trees? We're wolves, not squirrels."

Nancy gave Will a big hug. "They're really fun to climb! You would love it if you tried it. Just like when you told me I would like brussel sprouts."

Jisk smiled softly at the child and said, "Nancy, your father is simply too heavy for most branches. They would break under his weight."

"That's terrible! You mean he's stuck on the ground?"

I started laughing at the face Will made at his daughter's perspective. Ruby stopped in front of us, and the wind stirred her hair. I paused and took a deep breath before saying, "Congratulations."

Surprise crossed her face, although she clearly knew what I had just scented.

Jisk put Nigel down and took Ruby's hand as he commented, "I told you so."

"What am I missing?" Will asked. He knew the three of us had a rogue's sense of smell and detected more than anyone else in the pack.

"It's a good thing Jisk chose a house with three rooms for kids," I said. "They'll all be in use by midsummer."

With a shrug, Ruby said, "I thought Jisk's claims were out to lunch when the pregnancy test came back as negative, but if you picked it up, then the test was obviously faulty."

Jisk looked amused, as if he couldn't figure out why she would even doubt his word.

"Congratulations," Will told her. He glanced around and asked, "Where did Tim get to this time?"

I had been keeping tabs on my two-year-old son with my senses. "In the garden, eating your carrots."

Will sighed as he put Nancy down. "Why do you three insist on teaching the kids to climb and hide? They could hurt themselves if they fall from that high up."

"You have three kids and a mate," Jisk pointed out. "If they happen to be in different areas when an attack occurs, you can only rescue one at a time. Being able to escape into the trees gives them an edge if trouble shows up. Your mate can run down a rabbit burrow, but your kids can't do that. We're simply ensuring they have the best chances of survival."

"If they fall out of a tree and break their arm, I'm holding you responsible," Will grumbled, not liking Jisk's logic. He had grown more tolerant of my underground explorations as long as he knew ahead of time and only if the burrow was unoccupied. He still didn't like it, but grudgingly admitted it was a safe place if trouble showed up.

Jisk wasn't bothered by the threat and grinned easily. "If they break their arm, then you have my permission to chase me down and take a strip out of my hide."

Will scrunched up his nose as Ruby and I snickered. If Jisk took to the trees, Will wouldn't be able to catch him and he knew it. Three kids kept Will too busy for him to wait for Jisk to come down, and Jisk was even better at pulling a disappearing act than I was.

Jisk walked over to clap me on the shoulder. "See, he gives in easier all the time. It'll be a breeze with the next kid."

Will shook his head. "That's going to be a long time in coming."

"Sure, believe what you want to," Jisk replied with a smug grin.

Ruby narrowed her eyes, tipped off by Jisk's tone. She took a deep breath before exclaiming, "No! How could you do this to us? We barely survived the last two times! I think you two need to visit no man's land for the next seven months."

Will's jaw dropped. "Jade, are you pregnant?"

I stuck my tongue out at Ruby. "Spoilsport." I glanced between the two men before asking her, "So, do you think our darling mates are going to get along since they'll be in the same situation, or will they be at one another's throats in a few months?"

"Uh . . ." She tried to visualize the potential outcomes of having two overprotective males in the same vicinity. "If they team up, all four of us are going to be exiled for some time. The pack might just build a house on the border and simply count on those two to annihilate any trespassers. Although if they're busy beating on each other, we can sneak off for some peace and quiet."

Will and Jisk narrowed their eyes at us.

Jisk glanced at Will speculatively. "Well, I count Jade as a daughter, so if you can see Ruby as part of your family, we won't have problems with each other."

Will tilted his head as he examined the idea. "I think it can be done . . . One perk is that we can take turns checking on them. Any threat would have a hard time getting through one of us, but between the two of us, we could probably flatten anything if we put our minds to it."

Ruby looked at me with wide eyes. "Around-the-clock surveillance? I think I'll go mad. Assuming those two don't drive everyone else in the pack crazy first."

Both Will and Jisk seemed at ease now that their mates would be better guarded if they worked together. How fortunate we were.

I glanced at Ruby. "I say we leave them on babysitting duty and take a vacation by ourselves. Have some quality girl time. We could even invite Tiffany along since she knows which nearby packs have the best stores. She probably wouldn't mind a break from her children."

Both Will and Jisk growled their objections to that idea.

"Alas, there goes that plan," Ruby said. "We might have to work on it over the next few months." With a shrug, she dismissed the concern for the moment. "Anyway, we were heading to the store and just stopped by to say hi. We'll see you at dinner."

"See you later," I replied as Ruby and Jisk wandered away with their kids chasing after them in wolf form.

Will twirled a loose strand of my hair as we watched them leave. The twins quietly snuck back into the tree, eager to see how long it would take their father to realize where they were. Tim was still using a carrot as a chew toy.

A smile touched my lips as I realized how happy I was. I couldn't think of anything that could make our lives better. Will still loved me as much as I loved him. Our three children were a constant delight. I enjoyed being able to see Jisk smile on a daily basis after all of these years, and Ruby had a mate that was always one step ahead of her.

The valuable truffles Jisk, Ruby, and I located provided more than enough money to support the entire pack and make sure every member was well off. The Alpha and Luna loved their own long-awaited children and were carefully raising them to treat the pack members with respect. No darkness was visible anywhere in our future.

I had finally found a place where I truly belonged.

# Bonus Chapter: Among The Trees

*Jade's youngest daughter is unable to shift. As the daughter of a runt, Avery has plenty of inspiration for rising above her limitations. As surely as trees grow in a forest, she's determined to overcome this unique challenge and find her place in the world.*

**Avery's POV:**

I watched the group of wolves cross the river below me, then eyed up the large gap between the trees before dropping silently onto a larger branch beneath me. Like a diving board, the branch flexed down under my weight, and then shot my slender body into the air.

I flew through the air like a projectile as I careened headlong toward a spruce tree. At the last second, my hand shot out to catch a branch and correct my flight. I skipped along a large branch to reduce my momentum. The leaves rustled a bit, but otherwise, I had barely made any noise. Unlike the splashing wolves below...

*"Good heavens, Avery. Are you trying to turn into a bird?"*

Having been discovered, I grinned in amusement as I looked down at the light brown wolf and called back, "Beats splashing around in the water like a beaver."

*"Hey! I'm not a beaver! You're the rodent in this pack, Squirrel."*

I chuckled and crossed to the next tree as I kept up with the slow-moving group who was enjoying an evening stroll. I snagged a pinecone and chucked it at her.

She easily dodged the missile, of course, before barking in amusement, *"That is not helping your case any, you little squirre l..."*

I taunted her back as our bantering continued, "Furball..."

*"Squirrel."*

"Soggy canine."

A large brown wolf shook his fur out. *"Okay, you two. Save that energy for the training field tomorrow."*

I grinned at Uncle Jisk and ceased tormenting my friend—who happened to be his daughter—with childish taunts. If I were able to use mindspeech, we could have kept our friendly bantering private, but I had never shifted.

I could hear the others if they deliberately mindlinked me, but I couldn't respond, nor could I sense the pack link. No one was sure why I hadn't managed to shift in all my twenty years of life. It was unheard of for someone to have passed the age of ten without shifting, and most shifted by the time they were a month old.

With a shake of my head, I banished the thoughts from my mind. I looked around, but didn't see my mother's human form lurking in the trees or a small grey wolf darting under the shrubs. Nor was there any hint of a massive dark grey wolf. A grin spread across my face. *With the parents away, the kids shall play...*

I snuck ahead of the group and climbed halfway down a tree, waiting in ambush above where I thought Tracey might come out of the forest. I heard the heavy footsteps of a wolf approaching and caught a glimpse of brown fur through the branches. The wind was in my favor, and my nose was just sensitive enough to confirm it was Tracey.

The footsteps paused. *"If you try and push me into that mud puddle, I'm chewing your climbing gloves to shreds."*

I quickly scampered higher. "You'd have to catch me first!"

She snorted and stared up at me. "If I send your brother up the other tree, you're trapped. None of the other ones are close enough for you to jump to."

Locking my knees around a branch, I hung upside down. "Tim doesn't stand a chance of catching me in a tree. I'm the best climber around, and you know it."

"Yeah, your brother inherited your Dad's fondness for climbing."

*"It wasn't as if I didn't try to teach him,"* Uncle Jisk said as he trotted out of the shrubs.

I grinned at him and dropped off my current perch, snagging a branch and swinging across to another tree. I let go and twirled in a midair flourish before grabbing on other branches to land securely.

My dad's voice entered my mind, muttering, *"You're not a bird. Keep those feet on the branches."* He came into sight, along with the rest of the wolves on this evening stroll.

"I haven't missed a landing in eight years. Give me some credit."

*"You kids are going to make me old before my time."*

"I thought that was my job," Mom commented, her teasing voice coming from a few trees over. She dropped onto lower branches, now visible.

Cheekily, I added, "You should be happy I only laid claim to the squirrel title. At least I don't run into rabbit burrows."

*"Thank goodness for small mercies."*

Snickering, I swung into the outer branches and alternated between handholds as I let myself descend through the branches. When my feet reached the ground, I opened my hands and let the branches whip up like fanfare.

My father rolled his eyes, although amusement danced through them. *"Get your ass back in that tree."*

I burst out laughing, along with many others who recalled Dad's long fight to try and keep his kids and wife from climbing. It was only once he realized his youngest child was safer *in* the trees than on the ground that he had changed his mind.

*"I'll help,"* Tracey told him, stalking forward in a crouch.

"Instead of chasing me up the tree, why don't you give me a lift and we can go for a run around the border at wolf speed?"

*"I'm all for that idea!"* My cousin rose out of her crouch and trotted over to let me climb onto her back.

Dad looked up at Mom, who was already climbing down to catch a ride since her wolf form wouldn't be able to keep up.

I grabbed onto handfuls of Tracey's tawny fur. "No big jumps this time."

*"I second that,"* Aunt Ruby said, pausing by Uncle Jisk's side.

*"Fine. I'll go around that tree this time."* She huffed as she smoothly sped up to a light run.

I kept my legs tight against her sides, feeling the powerful muscles ripple beneath me. The forest flew past us as we reached speeds only possible for those in wolf form.

It was almost like we were flying, and I loved the feeling. And truthfully, it made me a little jealous. The closest I could come to this was during some of my aerial stunts. I longed for four feet of my own, but at this point, it would take a miracle.

The other wolves branched away from our group, leaving just our two families to continue. Nancy and Nigel also left, opting to follow some of their friends.

Soon enough, we reached the beaten-down dirt trail that marked the border, worn down by the passing of countless patrols. The birds above sang of the coming sunset as we ran below. The gentle breeze stirred the leaves and created a peaceful ambience.

Ahead, Uncle Jisk slid to a stop as his hackles rose, his urgent voice telling me, *"Get in the trees!"*

Tracey leapt for the sky, and I managed to grab onto a branch sturdy enough to hold my weight, swiftly climbing higher. A glance below showed that Mom was nowhere to be seen, and Dad was standing near Uncle Jisk, his hackles also raised in a formidable display.

Several wolves slowly emerged from between the trees, drawing closer to the border. These weren't wolves I'd seen before. My heart raced, but thankfully, their hackles weren't up.

Two of them shifted, an older man and younger one. The older one took a step forward and said, "Hello, we're travelling from Harland pack. Would it be possible for us to spend the night here and buy some provisions in the morning?"

Alpha Roland was away on trading negotiations, as was the Beta, which left Luna Emily and Dad in charge of the pack. Dad's eyes were slightly unfocused as he mindlinked her.

Dad's fur shimmered for a split second as he shifted into his human form. "If you give your word that you come in peace and won't cause any trouble, you are welcome to stay the night."

"No trouble intended. We're just looking to sleep without worrying about a feral sneaking up on us. Ran out of bread yesterday, so we wouldn't mind buying some before we leave."

*"I'm not sensing anything worrisome,"* Mom mindlinked us, using her Omega abilities to judge the newcomers.

Dad relaxed, as did Uncle Jisk and Tracey. Movement farther in the bushes betrayed the presence of our patrollers who were waiting to see if their help was needed.

"In that case, welcome to the Nightwind pack."

"Thank you. It's a beautiful evening. Mind if we walk with you?"

Dad opened his mouth, then paused as his eyes went vacant for a few seconds. To my surprise, he nodded. "Sure, we can guide you to the village."

I remained motionless in the tree, wondering why he didn't let one of the patrol members escort them.

Dad gestured to a path heading in the right direction. "This way. How was your journey so far?"

The two groups below merged and straggled down the trail, half of them in wolf form while Dad chatted with the older man. The younger one remained silent and gazed around in curiosity.

I didn't see any trace of Mom, but I knew she was hidden in the canopy with me. Somewhat intrigued by the newcomers, I snuck along the branches and kept up with the group.

My eyes kept straying back to the young man. The more I looked at him, the harder it was to look away. There was just something about him...

He wasn't exactly tall or short, nor powerfully built or lean. Freckles dusted his cheeks, and his brown hair was windswept. Had he been anyone else, I would have called him ordinary, but the word simply refused to fit.

I shook my head and tried to listen to the conversation, but the words just flowed past me. I took a deep breath to focus, then realized my heart hadn't slowed down since I climbed into the trees. In fact, if anything, it was pounding harder than before.

I wiped the back of my hand against my forehead to remove the sweat beading up. My muscles twinged, and I was beginning to feel distinctly odd, like I was coming down with fever. Even my bones ached.

Not wanting the men to pick up my scent, I moved to the downwind side. I watched them, still mostly focused on the young man. I wished Dad would ask him for his name, but considering I couldn't remember the conversation over the last ten minutes, he might have already asked.

It was hard to see his eyes. Were they blue or brown? I leaned forward, squinting. A branch I was hanging onto for balance, cracked and gave way, sending me careening to the ground.

The sound had all eyes darting over to me—his eyes were brown!—as if time had been frozen, and I hung motionlessly, captivated by his eyes, which were widening.

Then time caught up and my headlong plummet to the ground continued—yet I couldn't look away to try and grab the branches whipping past me!

He raced forward, shifting mid-step as his nails dug into the leaf litter and sent clumps flying into the air behind him. At the last second, he twisted sideways so I landed on his side. The impact sent the air whooshing out of my lungs. His speed sent him crashing into the underbrush as I rebounded into the nearby shrubs. Scoring a perfect 0/10 for my worst descent ever.

I groaned and tried to sit up. Wolf fur and ribs might have been softer than twigs and dirt, but it still hurt. A wave of heat swept through me, sending me into the leaf litter as my arms gave out. My ears rang as I struggled to draw a full breath after such a fall.

"Avery, can you hear me?" Mom's worried voice was distant, although I could feel her hand on my shoulder. In the background, Dad's rumbling snarls kept our visitors from approaching.

I groaned again and tried to sit up, but my arms weren't working properly. I shook my head, trying to clear it. My eyes blinked blearily, revealing grey paws by my face. I leaned back from them, and they pushed into the dirt. I blinked again, noticing the angle of the leg.

They were my paws.

I lifted one, then set it down. I had paws. That meant...

I struggled to sit up and looked over my shoulder to see dappled grey fur leading to a furry tail that slowly began to wag from side to side. I had finally shifted. I felt like dancing, but I'd probably fall over until I got used to running around on four feet.

Dad's snarls increased, and I looked over. His fur was completely on end as he snarled at a brown wolf who gazed on in concern, barely staying out of reach of the protective Enforcer.

"Will, let him through. They're mates," Mom said, also noticing the one-sided standoff.

When Dad didn't move, Mom frowned and leaned over to yank his tail. The snarl disappeared into an indignant snort and a disbelieving look over his shoulder. The brown wolf quickly snuck around my Dad and whimpered in concern. My Dad's ears were pinned back, but he let the wolf approach.

I was utterly captivated by the wolf in front of me, who was bobbing his head up and down as he approached with a single ear trained cautiously back on my parents.

I staggered to my feet, finding my balance easier than I had expected. Had I been human, I would have reached out my hands to ruffle up his fur and see how soft it was. I had no idea how to properly greet him in wolf form. Remembering how my family usually greeted one another, I walked forward and nuzzled his neck.

Sparks ran along my skin—fur?—from the contact, and he nuzzled me back as well, his tail wagging. Faint voices whispered in the back of my mind—the pack mindlink—but, of course, I had no way of talking to the handsome wolf in front of me since he wasn't in our pack.

I really had to know this guy's name!

*"How do I shift back?"* I asked Mom.

*"The first few times are the hardest. Remember what it's like to be human and push your mind toward that. Recall how you balance on two feet, the feeling of the wind on your skin, and stuff like that."*

Being human was all I knew until a few minutes ago. I remembered how my hands were able to grasp branches as I ran through the forest highway—how I wanted to run those same hands through this guy's fur. I wanted my human mouth so I could ask for his name—

I didn't even finish that thought before heat flashed through me, and I was suddenly taller. Seeing me shift, the brown wolf also shifted. The heat haze obscured him for a split second.

Yep. His eyes were definitely brown.

And I couldn't stop staring into them.

"I'm Colton. What's your name?" His voice was like honey, smooth and golden.

"Avery."

His answering smile outshone the sun.

"How did she shift?" Tracey whispered to someone.

"The mate bond," Mom replied just as quietly.

I managed to tear my eyes away from Colton, but slipped my hand into his to maintain some sort of contact. "Is that why I couldn't look away from him earlier?"

She leaned against Dad and nodded slowly. "I could sense it building as you watched him, but the bond itself didn't truly awaken until your eyes met."

"Something happened when she landed on me," Colton commented. "I felt it reverberate through me, and it wasn't just the physical impact."

Mom furrowed her eyebrows, deep in thought. "The eye contact seemed to awaken the bond, but it didn't really solidify until then." She shrugged. "Some mates need to come into contact for the bond to fully form. My guess is that this was one of those cases."

My hand tightened around Colton's. "Well, in that case, *I'm* happy he caught me."

"As am I," he replied.

I sent him a shy glance, which he answered with a soft smile. It felt like my heart was melting.

I wanted to bounce around in excitement—I'd found my mate, I could finally shift, and I could hear the packlink! But bouncing around would involve letting go of Colton's hand, and that just wasn't happening right now.

I gazed into his eyes happily.
Yep. I wasn't letting go of him anytime soon.

# About the Author

Hidden in a remote town in northern Canada, Crystal Scherer often spends her free time writing during the snowy winter. She started writing various fantasy and zombie stories on Wattpad in 2016, gathering over 30 million reads within the first 7 years.

Her passion for reading and learning sometimes inspires some unusual stories, and despite her cats' best attempts to walk on her keyboard, her books are free of swear words.

Her favorite hobbies include things like gardening, volunteering at the local church, and trying to figure out which snowbank her car is buried under this time. Her life is pretty boring and uneventful, unlike many of her characters.

www.CrystalScherer.com

For New Book Notifications, please follow my Amazon Author Profile or subscribe to the newsletter on my website.

If you enjoyed this story, I would be grateful if you could leave a review on the platform you purchased it from.

www.ingramcontent.com/pod-product-compliance
Lightning Source LLC
Chambersburg PA
CBHW050025180626
46810CB00002B/579